The Killer of Cancer Rising

By
Torena O'Rorke

Strategic Book Publishing and Rights Co.

This is a work of fiction. Names, characters, places, and incidents either are a product of the author's imagination or are used fictitiously, and any resemblance to actual persons, living or dead, business establishments, events, or locales is entirely coincidental.

Copyright © 2015 Torena O'Rorke. All rights reserved.

No part of this book may be reproduced or transmitted in any form or by any means, graphic, electronic, or mechanical, including photocopying, recording, taping, or by any information storage retrieval system, without the permission, in writing, of the publisher. For more information, send a letter to our Houston, TX address, Attention Subsidiary Rights Department, or email: support@sbpra.net.

Strategic Book Publishing and Rights Co.
12620 FM 1960, Suite A4-507
Houston, TX 77065

www.sbpra.com

ISBN: 978-1-62857-127-1

Design: Dedicated Book Services, (www.netdbs.com)

For information about special discounts for bulk purchases, please contact Strategic Book Publishing and Rights Co. Special Sales, at bookorder@sbpra.net.

CHAPTER 1
December 2006

The humming of a cell phone awoke Christian Vargas, jarring her from another terrifying dream. This time the perpetrator was chasing her with a strange-looking hammer. Gulping air, she fought to emerge from the murky world of trauma-driven sleep. Jerking upright, her head still swimming in the zone between dreams and consciousness, she threw back the covers. Sweat poured in rivulets down her back. Her thin, damp T-shirt clung to her heaving breasts like a second skin. The twenty-nine-year-old probation officer had taken a sleeping pill the night before in hopes of avoiding the inevitable nocturnal battle. It was anniversary time. Her late husband, Tony, had been dead for two years on Friday. The feisty Irish-American didn't expect to get through the week without a nightmare or two. Tangled sheets had kidnapped her legs. Kicking them back, she tried to avoid waking her lover. She fumbled for the phone, issuing a hoarse whisper. "Hello."

"Hey Vargas, this is Simpson Jolly from detention. Some girl called for you a few minutes ago, says she knows you. Something about her friend Whitney is gonna die. She said this Whitney's out in Benton City with another punk named Cole. We got cut off before I could get the address."

A new anxiety clawed at her mind. Tonight's nightmare had been a warning. She exhaled deeply. "Did you get the caller's phone number?"

"Heck, no. Like I said, we got cut off." The guard sounded half asleep. Nightshift always did. She slipped out of bed and tiptoed into the walk-in closet.

"Check the system's caller I.D."

"Huh, it doesn't show up, but the girl said she was in Utah. She said she got this phone number from some other girl named Stephanie." The guard mumbled something to himself. Christian tried to think.

"I don't know a Whitney. Did the caller give you Cole's full name?"

"Nope."

"Call dispatch, have them trace the call. Then call me back. And next time, don't wake me up unless you have more information."

"Huh, well, yeah. More information is probably better."

The probation officer stifled the urge to rip the novice a new one. There was nothing more frustrating than an under-zealous trainee.

"Again, call dispatch immediately. I'll have my cell."

She closed the phone and glanced back at the nightstand clock. It was four-thirty, but gauging from the lack of light from her transom windows, the night hadn't budged much. Pulling her sweats from the closet, she shivered from the morning chill. A fairyland sparkle of frost would offer some ambient light in the barren Eastern Washington landscape. The slender woman reached down, giving her dog, Bear, his morning hug. His tail thumped on the wood floor; his tongue on her cheek a wet reminder of his love. Smiling at her pet, she wondered if she should negotiate the puddles of ice with running shoes or her hiking boots. Her Christmas tree sparkled in the corner of her living room as she wandered out of her bedroom in search of her boots. It was nearly the holidays and for the first time in two years, she and Bear wouldn't be alone. The dog sat quietly behind her, awaiting her next cue. "Come on, big guy. We're taking our walk early this morning."

* * *

The bedroom where the boys sat was dank and littered with garbage. Several small piles of dog feces were scattered in the corners. The old Welsh terrier had refused to go outside for most of the winter. The dog was asleep on the younger boy's bed, snoring loudly and on occasion, passing pungent gas. The vulgar lyrics of Marilyn Manson drowned the creature's vociferous sounds and forced the teenagers to shout in order to hear one another. It was two o'clock in the morning on the Friday before Christmas Eve.

Outside, freezing rain pounded the earth. Thick sheets of ice had formed primitive ice-skating rinks on the street and yard. The abandoned vehicles scattered around the two acres of property looked like igloos after a snowstorm the night before.

The two boys sat on the floor with the Ouija board between them, their grimy fingers lightly placed on the plastic compass called a planchette. True believers, they had become Saints a few months earlier after they'd been introduced to the religion by their older friend, Jared. They'd been intrigued by his stories about a man of great power and knowledge. During his months away, Jared had studied under his master of the dark arts. Taken by their friend's new religion, Cole and Thomas had joined his cult, which met in the high desert on the full moon of every month. There, the month before, they'd been given their sacred names. Cole was now known as Moloch and Thomas had been christened Miasma. These were special names requiring a special form of initiation. Moloch and Miasma knew that it was a perilous game they were playing, but the high stakes made it worthwhile. The cult's leader, otherwise known simply as Cancer, had promised to pay them five hundred dollars for their efforts.

Once they'd set up the board, the boys had offered a couple of crude prayers to Satan for help. Then they waited. Moloch picked his nose for a while. The drugs made him fidgety and he wasn't a patient boy to begin with. Within minutes he had given himself a bloody nose. He casually wiped a smear of blood on the old carpet, its discoloration now further enhanced. Miasma, on the other hand, had the ability to wait it out. The silver piercings in his lower lip, known as snake eyes, glistened in the dim light. Once in a while his tongue flicked out of his mouth like a serpent's, moving the rings to and fro. After several minutes of waiting for the small triangular apparatus atop the Ouija board to move, they began to lose interest.

The younger boy's mother worked night shift at the local Wal-Mart. Cole's older sister was at her boyfriend's house and so it was just the three of them. The girl had already passed out from drinking nearly a pint of vodka. The boys were highly agitated from a lethal mixture of Smirnoff's and methamphetamine, but they'd been discreet with the latter. Though it hadn't cost them much, a wired Whitney could be a pain in the ass, so they'd waited until she was unconscious before indulging themselves.

The older one put his nose to the tattered chessboard that they used as a snorting table. "Man, this is like the best crystal ever," Miasma hollered as his eyes rolled back in his head from the pain of inhalation.

Just fifteen years of age, the older one was tall and well-built. Despite his youth, he'd grown a tuft of facial hair that appeared below his bottom lip. His large round head was shaven and a fresh tattoo in the shape of a tear could be seen below his right eye. He sported several other tattoos including a Latin phrase, *Lex Talonis*, which stretched across his muscular back in an ornate, gothic-styled script. Miasma would have been handsome if not for the wild look in his eyes and the disgusting meth mouth that was further injured by the fact that he never bothered to brush his teeth.

"This is the real stuff. Joe says they call it 'la glass' cuz its so f-in' pure. No junk in it at all. I got lucky cuz he owed me a big favor."

"What's that?" Miasma countered, his eyes narrowing menacingly. He liked to brag that he was the boss of his friend. Any time Moloch went on a drug run with his older sister's boyfriend, Joe Sliver, Miasma became enraged. Instant anger from the drug rush took him over the edge and he threw a shoe at the stereo system. The music stopped abruptly.

"Hey, why'd you do that?" Moloch asked, twisting his child-like features into a frown.

"How do you expect Satan to reach us when we can't even hear each other?" Miasma's long-lashed eyes widened. "Oh God, will you look at that." Though they had temporarily forgotten the Ouija board, it apparently hadn't forgotten them. The planchette was slowly moving from the D when it had originally rested to the letter A. The boys sat in stunned silence as the marker then moved to H and stopped for a full thirty seconds. Moving slightly away to the M, the plastic piece then moved back over the letter and hovered momentarily. Then, as though yanked by a string, the marker swung over to the E and back onto the R. The boys were speechless, awaiting the planchette's next move. After a long two minutes of waiting, Moloch hissed, "DAHMER."

The older boy's normally olive complexion turned a sickly green. His mouth opened as if to reply, but he seemed to be temporarily frozen. Trembling with fear, Moloch jumped up and started pacing, muttering vulgarities under his breath. "DAHMER. What does that mean?" he croaked.

Miasma lifted his head and turned to Moloch. "Jeffrey Dahmer, you idiot. Remember? He's the killer who ate his victims." With eyes aglow with an unearthly light, he pointed to Whitney. "You go first. No pain, no gain."

The younger one felt a harrowing rise in his belly. He gazed at the beautiful girl. Her head was tilted back at a strange angle. Her long hair swept across the dingy pillow like a golden fan, its natural curls nearly perfect in their corkscrew shape. Though her eyes were closed, Cole could envision their gaiety. The softest of smile lines crossed the top corners of her pale cheeks and her rosy mouth was a cupid's bow, ready to be kissed by a handsome prince. He trembled, wishing that Miasma would somehow disappear and that he wouldn't have to do this. The older boy pushed him hard.

"Go on, ya pussy."

Cole felt as though the world had slowed, like he was swimming under water while God was watching; a grim line across his great bearded face. He had gone to Sunday School with Whitney. They'd played in his fort when he lived up the road in his Uncle's old house. Cole remembered her sweet singing voice and the glorious way that she would lift her chin to the Lord as she sang the simple hymns. Her smell, like summer grass and girl sweat, still clung to her skin as he moved closer. His entire body was sticky with sweat. Leaning over, he took her tiny wrist in his hands and opened her palm. She had written something there. Squinting, he looked down. The words, 'I will love my baby' were scored in her fancy handwriting. Tears stung his eyes as he hesitated. Miasma started to chuckle and rubbed his hands together as he hissed, "Come on! Suck it up, punk. Then it's my turn."

* * *

Whitney shifted slightly, disturbed by the musty smell of the filthy pillow. Its scent reminded her of the dirty kid, Charlie, from her elementary school. There was always a dirty kid in every grade. Cole had been one of those, and so what! Whitney had become his friend anyway. She watched the boys from bed, keeping her eyelids low as to avoid detection. She didn't care for Cole's friend, but there was nowhere else for her to hide. She had exhausted her resources. She was scared, for her baby more than herself, but she was making plans. Her boyfriend's aunt lived in Montana. If she could just reach him, the teen knew that she could convince him to buy a bus ticket for her to Ennis. His Aunt Cathy had been very kind to Whitney during her last visit. The mother of three had seen the bruises inflicted by Whitney's father and had made a CPS report, though apparently that had gone nowhere.

Her dad was rich and powerful. He could stop a runaway train with a wink if he wanted to. Besides, by the time the authorities had gotten around to visiting her house, she'd been sent to the relatives in Salt Lake City. Her older sister had undoubtedly covered for her parents. "Whitney? She doesn't even live here," she could imagine her brown-nosing sister saying to the police.

To worsen things, Whitney felt as though her mother had always hated her. Maternal nurturing had given way to an underground animosity, born from envy, Whitney was sure. She was a beautiful child. At least that was what everyone in the family had told her. Her father had doted on her in improper ways until the neighbor, a gentile from Seattle, had reported her suspicions to Whitney's mother. From that day on, her mother had treated her differently. Then, once her brother had been sent away, all bets were off.

That was why she'd started to pal around with Cole. He was an ugly outcast, treated like trash by the boys and girls alike. She was pretty and smart. Subsequently, she was vehemently hated by many of the girls in their seventh grade class. A natural duo, they made up games of make-believe to soften the cruel world in which they lived. Eventually they'd started their own Buffy the Vampire Slayer society. She would don the identity of Buffy. There were so many vampires in her life, for real.

She had heard the boys talking about her and watched as they'd played with the Ouija board. They were oblivious to her, believing that she was passed out from too much vodka. She had faked it. The peer pressure got to her, so when they weren't looking, she'd poured out the clear, pungent liquid, replacing it with tap water. She hadn't told anyone yet about the baby. She wasn't sure about the father, but even if her child was a result of the rape, she didn't care. She wanted this baby. No one could take that away from her. When it came to the baby, Whitney Clist had no regrets.

* * *

North of Pasco, Washington, Patty Clist stared out her enormous kitchen window. The sun was high in the sky, conjuring warmth and resiliency, but once she stepped out of the door, ravishing cold crackled and snapped at her skin like canvas sails whipping in the wind. Her bones ached from the years of housework and too many pregnancies. She had never been a particularly strong woman, in any sense of the word. Her frailties were abhorrent to her husband. When they'd built the house, she had balked at the size, knowing that she would not be allowed to hire help. Her husband had insisted on the six-thousand square foot home and her health had paid a price.

Yet if she were honest, the house wasn't the only reason that exhaustion was her best friend. Her son's incarceration and her younger daughter's forced departure were the heavy weights on her heart. Tears filled her eyes as she thought about little Whitney. She was like a precious doll, ebullient with light. Her platinum blonde hair and innocent blue eyes had always been a mother's source of great pride. Later, when they learned about the girl's intelligence and her magical aptitude for music, she thought her heart might burst with joy. Yet pride was to be her greatest sin and rightly, she had been punished for it. The father of her sweet little girl had found temptation and so she had to be sent away.

If only she could erase time. If only she had paid more attention to her commitment, and to her husband's needs. God only knew how much she despised his nightly advances and vulgar urges of the flesh. He said that fornication was his right. He was God's conduit and that she must obey his wishes. It was a bitter pill to swallow.

After that night, when her precious daughter had returned for a visit home only to disappear within days, her life seemed devoid of meaning. Yet Patty had made flyers, had asked that her child's photograph be placed on a milk carton, like the other missing children on TV. Flyers were distributed throughout the state as well as in Utah, according to the officials in the City of the Great Temple. Several times they had received tips, but Whitney had seemingly vanished like a sand castle in the rising tide.

The front door slammed. She heard the slow, methodical steps of her second son. He had been a quick child, always moving through the house like a little tornado. However, ever since her favorite of her brood had spent time 'in the pen' as he liked to call it, he had learned to move with deliberation. Brandon strolled into the kitchen and promptly gave his mother a peck on the cheek.

"Hey Mom, how's it going? It smells terrific in here!" He gazed into the bowl of cookie dough and took out a huge hunk, stuffing it into his open mouth. "I never thought I'd love the raw stuff so much. You're a great cook, Ma."

She smiled with pleasure as he opened the refrigerator and rifled through its contents. The milk carton was on his lips before she could scold him. She reminded herself that he deserved the liberty. The poor child was still afraid of the dark when the police came to arrest him that mean afternoon in late November. God was not home that day, she'd decided. Brandon took another gulp and put the carton back on the shelf. With great flourish, he collapsed into an oak chair and burped. "A guy at work thinks he saw Whitney," he said quietly.

The woman's knees began to quiver. Explosive hope roiled through her, crushing the air from her lungs. She had to grab the countertop to stop from falling.

* * *

In a back room of the Clist's enormous home, the middle-aged man held the heavy book in his hands, trembling with inner conflict. The ancient text had belonged to his father, a man of great virtue-hard-working, pious and always loving. The Book of Mormon, from his church, the Church of Jesus Christ of the Latter Day Saints, was flawless, though it had been one of the originals published in 1833. He had forbidden anyone in the family to touch it. He only did with gloved hands. Otherwise it was kept in a vault, wrapped in a special cloth to protect its fragile pages.

In truth, Clist wasn't a particularly devout soldier of the Lord. As a child, living in rural America, confined to a remote community that had lacked in resources, he had imagined a different life of magic wagons that could fly. When his father had died, so did his dreams. He had joined the church's youth group, had sung timidly in the choir and served as an altar boy. Their town of three hundred was full of religious fanatics, some with multiple wives and troops of children. He had been a handsome boy and had his younger brother to care for. He did what it took to survive. Mumbling a short prayer, Clist closed his eyes and opened the book. It fell open to the same page nearly every time. The verse about Satan glowed with luminescence as he began to read.

CHAPTER 2

Christian and Doug slipped into the cavernous room behind a gaggle of women. She had never before been in a Mormon stake house, the religion's name for a typical neighborhood church. But she had agreed to come. Doug was her friend and his mother had died. Ah, sacrifice. She wished she was on the ski slopes instead. They followed a large band of moronic-looking children to the back of the auditorium. Though Doug was dressed in disguise, he was concerned that someone in the room might recognize him.

The place was vast with towering white walls and little décor. Rows of hard plastic chairs faced an altar in front. On the raised platform sat over a dozen dour-faced men and two women, who blended into their surroundings like pieces of utilitarian office furniture. Christian gazed around at the crowd. The Mormon women dressed modestly and nearly all had long hair and clothes that looked like they came from a Talbot's catalog. The men were dressed in dark, traditional suits, appropriate for the occasion. The few children in the audience had glazed looks on their faces.

The room's cacophony fell to a hush as the family marched in. There were nearly forty of them, of all ages and sizes. Mormons were known for their large families. According to belief, the more children one had, the higher they were placed on the LDS food chain. The probation officer had once been told that when Mormon patriarchs died, they were promised a planet of their own where their voluminous offspring could live in paradise forever. She agreed that living on another planet could only be fun if you had the right people to hang out with. On the other hand, by the look of these folks, she would rather have lived alone.

Doug nudged her. "Trendy folks we got in the Mormon ranks. There must be a handsome, brainwashed idiot around here for you somewhere." His sarcasm was returned with a swift jab of her elbow. He was infuriatingly irreverent, particularly when dressed in disguise. In the next instant, the room fell to a hush as the coffin was carried in by four men who were cookie cutter images of her friend, only heavier and lacking his contagious vitality. They varied widely in age. Doug was the middle son, thirty-two and gay.

"This is unusual. Normally they don't bring the deceased into the stake house. I guess they've made a few changes since I was here."

"I thought you were ex-communicated," she whispered back, glancing around for prying ears.

"Yeah, that's the lingo. Why do you think I'm wearing this get-up?"

Christian stifled a giggle. Doug was wearing a black wig, a stick-on, Hitler-styled mustache and a pair of over-sized, tortoise-shell glasses, transforming his normally hip, urban appearance. As a hairdresser, he owned one of the most popular salons in town and was famous for his outrageous clothing that included long gauzy shirts, multicolored boots and crystal-studded jeans. Today his flamboyant style of dress was completely toned down. He wore a stiff black suit that could have come from his father's closet, but here, he blended in like a penguin at a mating ritual.

The first speaker was Mrs. Stanford's eldest daughter, Sylvia. She was articulate and wry. A local attorney and pro-tem judge, she was known for her no-nonsense approach toward defendants, though she primarily presided over divorce hearings. The second speaker was the deceased's youngest daughter. Stoic and pitifully homely, Tamara Stanford pontificated as well as any priest. She recounted Alice Stanford's virtues like mothers brag about their babies and reminded the audience that if not for the help of the great Saints of the Mormon Church and of course, their savior Jesus Christ, her mother might have ended up white trash or worse. Next was a small quartet who sang a very long hymn in exhausted-sounding voices. Then another speaker stepped forward. In this case, it was the deceased woman's Bishop who, in a rumbling monotone, extolled Sister Stanford and her relationship with the Savior.

Christian watched in mute astonishment as the attendees slowly began to slide into a sort of hypnotic state. Men were sleeping on their wives' shoulders while the women seemed to stare into space as though studying dust mites. Even the children, who would normally have become unruly by now, seemed drugged by the flat delivery of appreciation and honor.

After another hymn, the Bishop announced that the coffin would now be open for viewing. She watched as the elder lifted the lid with great pomp and circumstance. As he gazed down, with an already beholden expression on his face, he suddenly froze. His mouth fell open and his eyes darted around in confusion, settling on the deceased husband's face in the front row. Sylvia stood up in response to the Bishop's disturbing reaction and bent down to look into the casket. She released a terrifying scream. Another daughter stood up and immediately did the same. In the next instant, chaos reigned. As Mr. Stanford rose to see what was causing the commotion, Tamara reached out and slammed down the lid of the coffin in haste. Behind her a little boy, who appeared to be about six years old, had come up to the box and had placed his hands on the edge of the frame. He instantly began to howl as his fingers were crushed by his mother's hasty attempt to hide the vision inside. In the next few moments, the entire crowd began to stand and move about, uncertain as to what to do in the state of obvious crisis. Doug grabbed his friend by the arm.

"Please, get up there, pull out your badge, whatever it takes. Tell me what the hell is in that coffin!"

* * *

"It was unbelievable," Christian shook her head as she glanced at the list of morning emails the following Monday.

"Doug had said that he hadn't anticipated that the casket would have been opened. Apparently neither did the killer."

"What happened after you saw the girl?" Daniel asked anxiously, his soft brown hair falling over one eye. He brushed it back hastily and thumped the desk to alert his office partner to his excitement.

"Obviously the girl was stacked on top of the old lady, so I showed the bishop my badge and explained that I'm a juvenile probation officer. I said we had to prevent further contamination of a possible crime scene and asked that he immediately direct his people out of the stake house. Then I called dispatch to report what had happened."

"What do you think happened?"

"They began a search once they arrived. According to the bishop, the coffin had been delivered the day before. The bishop told the police that when they'd dropped off the coffin, the only person at the stake house was the janitor."

"So now what? Did they identify the girl?" Her savvy partner never took no for an answer.

With a sigh, Christian finally looked up from her computer, her porcelain skin reddening with irritation. "All I can tell you is that someone killed the girl and hoped she'd be buried without incident."

"What else?" Par for the course, Daniel had guessed there was more to the story than what she was telling him.

Christian took a deep breath. "The girl was so pretty and so young. I would guess fifteen or sixteen. Her forehead had this strange puncture wound, which is apparently what killed her."

"Had she been sexually assaulted?"

She glared at him, her dark blue eyes flashing with discontent. "Now how would I know that? Her presentation was perfect except for the puncture on her forehead. It was a perfectly round entry wound, like someone had pounded a large nail into her brain. But other than that, she was woundless. Her hair looked as if it had been combed and there didn't appear to be blood on her clothing. Later one of the family members identified the girl as Whitney Clist. She was also Mormon and from the blocks."

"Good information. I'm calling Captain Jack. He was at the scene, right?" Daniel had already started to dial the phone.

"Why?" Sometimes her partner could be such a pain.

"Because I know you. You're now in it, whether our boss likes it or not. Maybe I want a little of the action. The least we can do is to check her identity against JTS."

"Why are you going to do that?"

"So we can find out if she's in our system. If she is, we could identify friends and possible suspects. Have you checked the runaway roster lately?"

Christian stared out the window without responding. Then she remembered the thought that had been hovering at the back of her mind since discovering the dead girl.

"I got a weird call a few weeks ago from detention. He said a girl named Whitney was in danger. I didn't know who that was, but now it makes sense." She shivered, wondering why she always seemed to know when bad things were going to happen.

"What kind of information did they give you?"

"That knucklehead, Officer Jolly, called me in the middle of the night, but didn't have any more information."

"Did anyone at the funeral talk about the girl once they recognized her?"

Christian shook her head. "There were so many people and such chaos, so no, I didn't hear anything personal about her." The frantic sound of Daniel's fingers on the keyboard was reminiscent of a Chihuahua racing across a linoleum floor.

"Bingo!" He raised his hands in victory. "No Whitney Clist in JTS, but there's a Brandon Clist. I remember him. He's a sex offender who was sent up." He shot her a smug smile. Ignoring him, she turned back to her computer as Daniel dialed his phone. "Hey Jack, it's me." As her partner chatted amicably to his former high school buddy and current

Pasco Police Captain Jack Devin, Christian continued to dig through the mass of emails that had collected over Christmas break. She'd taken the previous week off and had spent the holidays with her boyfriend, Matt, in the Oregon coastal village of Seaside to visit some friends. As she read through the litany of first appearance messages, an image flashed across her mind's interior screen. Since seeing the victim, she'd ruminated on the weapon used to kill the girl. Though there was a single puncture approximately a quarter of an inch in diameter, there was also a perfectly round bruise that circled the wound. The probation officer had recalled the last time she'd hung a picture in her hallway. She'd hit the wall so hard with the hammer that she'd left a small indentation from the hammer's head in the sheetrock. The poor victim's forehead appeared to have suffered the same fate. Now she focused on the image again and wondered about it. In her mind's eye, she saw a unique tool, which she'd seen on the wall in a famous oyster bar in the beachside village. Used in oyster spat production, the oddly-shaped hammer was clearly an operable weapon.

Daniel let out a booming laugh, causing her to jump. Her partner continued to laugh, wiping his eyes with one hand while holding his belly in the other. "Okay, enough already," he replied. "Yeah, I'll catch you later."

"What was that all about?"

"Just another dumb blonde joke." His eyes dropped guiltily to the paperwork on his desk.

"And you know better than to repeat it, right?" It was a dirty blonde joke, she thought, wondering how a police captain could get away with such unprofessional behavior.

"Oh, come on, partner. Don't be such a prude. He actually had some interesting information, but you'll have to beg for it now."

"Whatever. It's not my case anyway, so why should I care?"

"The girl had been reported by her parents as a runaway. Also, she was possibly still alive when she was tossed in the box. Furthermore, her brother Brandon, along with a kid called Comely, are the primary suspects."

"Oh, dear god!" Christian felt sick.

"Yeah. Now do you remember the story about him?"

Nodding, she swallowed hard. She'd learned some information about the Clist family from Doug after they'd left the crime scene. Whitney Clist was from a very conservative Mormon family. Her father was a Bishop in the church and her mother was a school board member who advocated for prayer in schools, an appealing concept in the local populace. Now she got up and went to Daniel's desk. "Let me see."

Bending close to her partner, she read. Two years prior, her older brother, Brandon, was arrested at the home of a well-to-do Mormon family on three counts of Child Rape 1. Several months after the boy had been released to juvenile prison, there were two missing person reports that had been posted by the authorities. Whitney Clist and another girl, Stephanie Patterson, also a member of the LDS church, were listed as last seen at the Kennewick Wal-Mart on October 16, 2006.

Christian shivered again. Life always reminded her of her history. It was probably her fault for choosing a profession where crime was the grist for the mill. She closed her eyes and gave a little prayer for the girl. When she opened her eyes, the photograph of Bear, her dog, gave her cause to smile. Her screensaver showed the big, hairy Hines 57 in a sheriff's costume. A gag gift from Daniel, the costume's front piece had a badge, a bright red bolero and bolo tie with stuffed arms that hung down, giving the illusion of the top half of a person. The large cowboy hat and Lone Ranger mask completed the humorous picture. Her friend's joke wasn't far from the truth. Earning fame in his own right, Bear was a local search and rescue dog.

"So what else did Jack tell you?" Christian drew her gaze to her partner's concerned eyes.

Daniel returned her stare with a secret, yearning look. She moved back to her desk, unnerved by their sudden intimacy.

With a shrug, he continued, "They've arrested a couple of juveniles. Apparently Whitney had been staying with the one by the name Comely. According to the coroner's office, though the vic didn't appear to be raped, she definitely wasn't a virgin."

"How can they tell that? I mean hymens can tear…"

He held up his hand. "Spare me the girlie gyno lesson, will ya? She was pregnant. A couple of months along."

The female probation officer's heart felt like it had been placed in a vise. "What else?"

"In her skirt pocket they found a small seashell and some sand, like she'd just picked it up off the beach. And there a knife wound on her wrist and a note in her pocket that read, 'Lex Talonis' whatever that means."

Christian's fingers flew over the keyboard. "I've got it. It's Latin and it comes up under religions. It means 'Law of the Talon', in other words, 'an eye for an eye…'"

"'and a tooth for a tooth.'"

Daniel leaned back, grinned widely, adding, "As far as I know, she had all of her teeth."

"Shut up. This isn't funny. The phrase is also the name of a sect who practices Satanism." Copping an attitude, she tossed a chunk of Hershey Bar-colored hair over her shoulder.

He issued a low whistle. "Listen, maybe we shouldn't jump to conclusions. This is really interesting…" and she began to read.

"Satanists are a group of worshippers, just like Christians or Muslims. And like those religions, they come in many varieties. Most Satanists believe in Lex Talonis, or the Law of the Talon. This is essentially the Old Testament belief in an eye for an eye. Satanists believe that Lucifer was a noble hero, for he was the bringer of knowledge."

She looked over at him, "Garden of Eden."

He snapped his fingers, "Got it, and the snake that broke the good news. Keep going."

"Modern day Satanism is not Christianity in reverse and most Satanists do not worship the devil, so to speak.

Satanists believe in personal responsibility and therefore expect punishment to be swift and immediate. They believe that today's penal system is too relaxed and that people must be prepared to face the consequences... Daniel, this sounds like your philosophy."

Glancing over, she looked at her friend. His mouth was hanging open in surprise. Slowly he nodded. "That is unreal. I had no idea that was what they were all about. That does sound like something that I would say. What else? Go on!"

"*Satanists have five axioms of which to live by. 1) Autonomy of the individual, 2) Striving for perfection of self, 3) Gifts to the deserving 4) Lex Talonis and 5) That Satan represents the admirable qualities of mankind such as self-sufficiency, individuality, free will, pride, power and knowledge.*"

"This is scary."

"Why?"

"Because, if you were to ask most of us in this building if we agreed with those five principles, not mentioning Satan of course, we would probably all agree that those are the principles, minus Lex Talonis, we try to teach our kids on probation."

* * *

Six hours later, Christian was sitting in the courtroom, waiting for her only case to be called. She'd worn proper court attire that day and was glad for it. The knee-length pencil skirt was made of soft brown suede and the fitted silk blouse was indigo blue with brown buttons, which accented her eyes. Still, though she felt pretty sitting on the bench, the weekend's discovery had tainted her attitude.

Her client, Joe Sliver, had been brought over from Benton County jail. At nineteen, he was still on Christian's caseload. She loathed working with the young adults, who after receiving stiff sentences in the form of extended juvenile probation time, were always difficult to track and even harder to rehabilitate. The probation officers' adage was always the same, 'if you can't fixed them by the time they turn eighteen, it was probably too late'.

Normally the offenders from the adult system were the first to be processed during first appearances. Sure enough, immediately after the courtroom introductions, the prosecutor called Joe's name. Christian perked up.

"Joe Sliver, your date of birth is April 5th, 1987. Is that correct?"

The youth gave the judge a sneer and nodded.

"Please speak clearly into the microphone, Mr. Sliver."

"Yeah," Joe drawled. He was an unattractive young man- severely skinny with a face covered in pockmarks and long, shaggy hair. Many months ago, when he had first met with the probation officer, she'd seen a silverfish wiggling through his greasy locks. Lice were bad enough, but silverfish were nigh impossible to get rid of in jail.

The judge nodded to the prosecutor, continuing, "You are here on a first appearance on a probation violation for failure to remain in contact with your probation officer and failure to pay fines and fees. Prosecutor?" The older man looked down his nose, tired and yet fierce. Judge Stanzik was a no-nonsense guy who'd fought in Vietnam and had received a purple heart among other medals of honor. He had literally been in the trenches and didn't have a lot of compassion for hardcore offenders, of which Joe Sliver was one.

"Sir, we would like to submit the report by Christian Vargas, Mr. Sliver's probation officer." The deputy prosecutor, Sidney Camden, was a bubbly young woman, fresh out of Seattle University's Law School and determined to make a name for herself. Christian liked her confidence and willingness to negotiate the tough cases.

"Your honor, may we please?" cried the defense attorney suddenly. Bennett Mason, better known as Eddie Haskell in attorneys' circles for his suspender-snapping, jaunty attitude, was clearly in a hurry to get out of there. "My client explained to me that he had tried to reach his probation officer on several occasions and she never returned his calls. He has been working out of town a lot. We would like to see him released so that he can get back to his trucking job."

Christian sighed softly, taking the prosecutor's cue. Standing to face the judge, she stated, "Your honor, if I may. You will see from my probation violation report that I have not met with Mr. Sliver in over three months. As far as I know, he has never called me, nor has he been in contact in any fashion. He has a pending drug trafficking charge and was picked up over the weekend on my warrant. Therefore he is being held in Benton County jail at this time. When I go to see him, I will have the officer administer a urinalysis. I expect it to be dirty. His last UA was dirty for cocaine, amphetamines and marijuana. Frankly, I'm also curious about his trucking job. Records show that his new charges occurred in Benton County during the month of December, so I'm curious as to how much *travel* he's really doing." Her sarcasm was not lost on the judge.

His bison-like head swung toward the prosecutor. With a conversation via eye contact, the judge slammed down his gavel. "Very well. We will abide by Ms. Vargas's recommendation of fifteen days jail, with six days conversion for uncompleted community service hours." At that, Joe Sliver shot her a look that could kill.

* * *

Several meetings and a house call later, Christian finally left the office around five-thirty. By the time that she arrived home, it was nearly seven o'clock. Her hip hop dance class had left her soaking in sweat. The house was empty, and so straight to the shower she went. Singing her favorite Sheryl Crow tune, she hardly heard Matt and Bear clamor into the bathroom.

"Hey girl, welcome home," Matt hollered over the sound of the water as Bear's heavy tail pounded on the shower door. "I started dinner. I hope Pad Thai chicken is to your liking."

Ever since Matt had moved in, nearly a year prior, Christian's life had changed for the better. After her first husband had died of a sudden heart attack at the mere age of thirty, the young woman had accepted the fact that she'd probably live on her own with Bear for the rest of her life. A private person, she didn't feel the need for company as long as she had her dog and her mysteries. Then Matt had come along and turned her world upside down. Now a high school teacher by profession, he was everything that she wasn't- Black to her White, laidback to her high energy, practical to her creative and down-to-earth to her impulsivity. They worked well together, not to mention that he was a fabulous lover and gourmet cook. As far as she was concerned, they had the perfect arrangement. She cleaned, he cooked and they both doted on the mutt.

Though she was tempted by the dinner's wonderful aroma, she couldn't assuage her greater desire. Dressed in only an oversized tee-shirt, she walked into the kitchen and put her arms around Matt. Her lover immediately took the hint. As he lifted her to the kitchen counter, pulled up her shirt and began to nuzzle her bare breast, he mumbled, "Yep. Dog's walked, dinna's on and da man's on fire."

CHAPTER 3

"When the house was raided, they found sixteen ounces of 'la glass', the pure stuff, hidden inside an Ouija board box. The biggie was that murdered girl's I.D., though. The cops found it under Cole Comely's bed, along with a bunch of *Buffy, the Vampire Slayer* comics. Ironically, it was the kid's mom who turned him in."

Stella was standing in Christian's doorway on Tuesday morning. Dressed in a fitted powder blue cashmere suit and knee-high black leather boots, the fifty-something probation officer looked like she'd just stepped out of Vogue magazine. Christian shook her head, her thick waves of hair moving generously around her face.

"I bet the drugs belong to Joe Sliver. Cole's older sister, Carlie, dates Joe. She's a piece of work. I think she's pregnant with her third baby and the first two have already been taken to foster care."

"Cole's on your caseload, right?"

Christian nodded. "And the other kid, Thomas, is a repeat offender. I'm guessing our generous Michael Faust will assign the case to you."

"Yes, unfortunately. Thomas was higher than a kite on meth, booze, and who knows what else. They found a few blunts in the bedroom, too. He told detention staff that his name is Miasma, whatever that means." Stella's blonde hair, cut like Victoria Beckham's, fell dramatically over one carefully-made-up eye. The older probation officer took a long swig from her Starbucks cup. "Oh, no. You're looking it up, aren't you?"

Christian shot her friend a confident smile and read from her dictionary. "*Miasma: a vaporous exhalation formerly believed to cause disease; an influence or atmosphere that tends to corrupt."*

"Believe me, based on my experience with that kid's breath, he named himself appropriately. So guess his little buddy's A.K.A.," Stella encouraged. "And no fair looking it up on JTS."

The JTS system was a modern day miracle for the Benton County probation department. The cream of the crop in computer software, JTS held all of the data required for the juvenile justice center staff to do their job. From gang insignias to parent's cell phone numbers, nearly any piece of information on a youth was accessible at the tap of a finger.

Christian gazed up at the water-stained ceiling with a look of deep concentration on her face. "Let's see...I'm going to guess...Moloch...like in *Buffy the Vampire Slayer's* Moloch the Corruptor."

Stella stamped her foot. "Not fair. You did look!"

What the prescient P.O. would never admit was that, in fact, she hadn't. The young woman had been born with the strange ability to pull answers out of thin air. She'd paid a hefty price for the arcane skill, which came infrequently and without warning. Her short history had been wrought with death and loss, but she was a survivor and so appreciated every good thing that came along.

"You're right. I cheated. I was on JTS before you got here."

"I call bullshit. JTS has been down all morning," Daniel crooned as he walked into the office, sidling past Stella to make his way to his desk.

Stella gave her a long, hard stare. "Every time I turn around, you've pulled another answer from God knows where. And don't start with that crazy old lady and her magic."

"Hey, wait a minute." Daniel held up his hand in protest. "That old bag of bones, who I believe is not much older than you, Stella, just happens to be my grandmother."

"That's enough of you for one day." The voluptuous blonde gave him a dark scowl and stomped away.

"Hey, take it easy on Stell." Christian cautioned after her friend was out of sight. "She's got Michael on her back and a caseload from hell at the moment."

"She started it with her comments about my gramma," Daniel quipped. "By the way, have you seen the old bag lately?"

Christian rolled her eyes. A born and bred Catholic, her partner had no tolerance for psychics, astrologers or 'card sharks', as he like to refer to his grandmother, Maria, and her psychic readings. Christian, however, had developed a close relationship with his *abuela*, who was a well-known *La curandera*, or Mexican shaman. The mystical woman had helped the young woman deal with her metaphysical tendencies that she often found imposing and undesirable. Yet the probation officer's haunting visions had helped to solve a local crime or two, so she was learning to deal with them. Though none of her friends really understood her friendship with *La curandera*, Maria was a reassuring influence in the probation officer's life. Still, Christian refused to say anything other than they shared an interest in medicinal herbs. Determined that her proverbial cat would not get out of the bag, Matt was the only person who knew of Christian's unusual powers and that was only because he had a few tricks of his own.

She sighed. Her work family had the annoying propensity of knowing one another's business. "I haven't talked to her in a while." She was instantly saved by the arrival of Michael Faust, the probation department manager, who stormed into the room in a fury.

"Darn it anyway, O'Callahan, how many times do I have to tell you to stop getting in the middle of the police investigations? I got a call this morning from Commissioner Selling. After you hounded your friend, Jack, he went to Selling and said that you had some kid on your caseload that killed that girl. Now why would you tell him something like that?" Purple rage veined the fat man's face as he leaned over Daniel's desk. His bulging belly landed precariously close to a full cup of steaming hot java.

"That's not what I said. I told him that one of her kids is into the whole vampire thing. That's it. I didn't suggest that he was the killer in any way." Daniel did his best to look sheepish.

Their boss stood up slowly and rubbed a hand across his sweating forehead. Strands of hair from his dyed comb-over hung on his right collar like reeds of dried summer grass. "Well, those guys over at the station are all over it. They're ready to send in the crime squad and that will cost the county a pretty penny, let me tell you. Fortunately that kid was picked up yesterday, and they found the dead girl's I.D. in his bedroom, otherwise you'd be in a butt load with me." With that, Michael scratched his wide backside and waddled out.

"Next victim," Daniel muttered under his breath.

"That little kid is not the killer, by the way."

"So he says. The kid's into the whole *Buffy the Vampire Slayer* thing. There's a whole group of kids out there in the Blocks farming community who are into that. And half of them are Mormons."

Daniel looked at Christian as they both barked at the same time, "And it was a Mormon funeral."

* * *

Her visit with Cole Comely was a fragile foray into a child's troubled mind. Cole was a kid without much going for him. Scrawny and homely, his nickname in school had been Ugly Bug. He had peed his pants so many times in first grade that he'd been held back a year. According to his diversion file, the school had cited development difficulties. His I.Q. was low enough that he was placed on an individual educational program, which essentially forced a district to educate a youth, despite behavioral, academic or physical limitations.

He was sitting in the cage in detention, shivering like a wet dog. She introduced herself and gently asked the boy if he would like to have something to eat. Based on his time of arrival, he'd been there since six o'clock the night before and his breakfast still hadn't arrived yet. That meant that he'd sat in his worn Rams sweatshirt and tattered jeans on a cement floor in a veritable cage the size of a large dog kennel for over twelve hours without food.

Finding an extra breakfast tray in the kitchen, she was tempted to scold the staff for their lack of attention to Cole. However, after a brief glance at the intake list, she realized that the two detention officials on duty the night before had processed nine kids. No wonder the little guy had been forgotten.

She brought him a cafeteria tray of rubbery scrambled eggs, a couple of doughy pancakes, a cup of apple sauce, a carton of milk and a sticky mound of oatmeal. The kid muttered something she couldn't hear and followed her out to a private interview room. By his offensive smell, she could tell that he'd defecated in his pants, so she immediately turned him around and went back. The staff supervisor had come in late and stood patiently at the door as Christian hounded him about Cole's condition. Chase Tovich was an easy-going sort of fellow. Thick around the middle with the pinched features of a retired schoolmarm, he handed the boy a clean detention uniform and directed him toward the showers instantly.

While she waited, Christian listened to the morning rumble as the new shift came on duty in master control. The juvenile detention unit, the dismal equivalent to the adult jail, could accommodate forty boys and twenty girls. Most of the time, it was full. There were the typical articles of incarceration scattered around the main entry area. Dark green rubber sleeping mats were stacked next to cubbies of gray sweatshirts, grayer sweatpants and various sizes of plastic sandals on the north wall of the interior space. Above two laundry bins of ancient underwear, one marked "boys", the other "girls", hung several sets of shackles and handcuffs. An electronic security barrier was mounted a foot from the entry point for police and arrestees. Gray metal lockers, which held personal effects, lined the opposite wall where an ominous-looking restraint chair appeared, an electric chair without the wires.

The place had frightened her the first time that she'd seen it. The sensitive young woman could only imagine what it did to a thirteen-year-old out past curfew. In the few years that she'd worked for the juvenile system, she'd come to realize the inadequacy of a system which locks up kids for ridiculous reasons, only to give them an opportunity to adapt to an environment which, though dedicated to reforming them, gave them the exposure and toughness to partake in the criminal world.

Cole was out of the shower quickly. Despite his speedy clean-up, his breakfast had grown cold. While the boy dressed, Christian slipped back to the kitchen to grab another tray of hot food. By the time that she'd returned, the boy was waiting in the interview room. His scraggly hair was wet and slicked down on his forehead in some semblance of style. The kid smelled better, but was unfortunately as emotionally remote as he had been before.

"Hi, Cole. Do you remember me? I'm Christian." She offered an ambitious smile.

"Why am I here?" he asked, sniffing a little. His eyes gleamed with sudden tears, but he was able to control himself.

"As you know, your friend, Whitney Clist, was found dead a few days ago. When your mom called in to report that you had paraphernalia in your room, they found some things in your room that belonged to Whitney. They hope that maybe you can help tell us what happened to her."

Cole shook his head. "I don't know nothin'."

"I'm sure you're confused and upset. I know she was a good friend of yours. I just want to help you." Christian tenderly touched his hand. "Hey kiddo, you need to eat. How about you take a few bites of food before we talk." Cole began to wolf down the food in front of him. In less than five minutes, he'd finished his breakfast. He gave a little burp and closed his eyes. A deep shiver shook his skinny frame as he began to cry.

"She was so pretty and she was always really nice to me. I didn't mean to cut her so hard. We were just supposed to do the tattoo. I wasn't supposed to kill her, just keep her there until my friend could come and get her. Did I kill her?" Hiccupping loudly, he rubbed his runny nose, moving the mucus further across his pixie face.

Christian leaned forward. "You cut her?"

"It was just a game. We all did it. We are like... you know...from the dark side. We put our secret phrase on her."

Christian watched his face for signs of deception. He fidgeted with his Spork, tapping it on the table. He didn't look capable of squashing a fly, she mused, reminding herself to keep an open mind. "Nobody dies of a few simple cuts. Whitney died of a head wound. Do you know anything about that?"

Cole looked away, biting his own lip until a small spot of blood appeared. He licked it and gave a small smile. "We had fun the last time she came to visit. We played X Box all night."

The youth was obviously disorientated from lack of sleep and the events of the night before. She also knew that she wasn't supposed to do too much questioning prior to his assigned attorney's first visit. Standing, she took Cole's breakfast tray and motioned to him to follow her. "Cole, the detectives and your attorney are going to come here today and ask you a lot more questions."

His little hands clenched as he hissed, "I didn't want them to take her. They did it for Cancer. He wanted her back." She listened as his emotions exploded. He slammed his little fist against the wall. "He's the one."

"Who's Cancer?"

Before the child could answer, his court appointed attorney rolled around the corner. Bobby Saxton was a narcissist who spent more time facing a mirror than he did reading briefs. The arrogant man knew he was gorgeous and flaunted it.

"Ms. Vargas?" He looked her up and down with obvious appreciation. "I believe you are done here with my client. Young man, follow me." Cole Comely stood up. She guessed he was not even five foot in height and less than eighty pounds wet. Dutifully, he followed them out of the room.

"After the meeting, please get Cole to his room so he can rest before court," she ordered, ignoring the attorney's look of surprise.

CHAPTER 4

Wednesday morning's visit to the jail to see Joe Sliver was not exactly what she'd expected. In hindsight, the adjective 'fruitful' came to mind. Joe was in the new section of the Benton County Justice Center which had the capacity to house up to 560 inmates. Most were petty criminals-thieves, druggies or drunks and domestic violence offenders. A portion of them were transported in from other jurisdictions which had exceeded their own capacity, thereby helping to plump the county coffers. Christian knew that many of the inmates were people whom she might see every day-the checker at the Seven 11, the busboy at a local restaurant or even a local celebrity or two. Yet here, in the cold, gray environment, bleached of any sign of humanity, the prisoners all seemed identical to one another. In their faded orange and white striped jumpsuits and uncombed hair, they had become laboratory rats.

There was a separate pod for the kids under twenty-one and so she found Joe in section J where he sat among a group of five or six other young men, watching *The Days of Our Lives*. Their glazed eyes conveyed the same blank message of boredom, though occasionally a man's expression would stand out from the others. Christian had learned long ago to avoid their lascivious stares. The sexual deviants found pleasure at the sight of any women and made it clear that if they could strip her clothes and rape her on the spot, they gladly would do so.

Joe stood up and sauntered over to her, giving a little bow. He was cleaner than he'd been in the courtroom. He had actually gotten a haircut and his skin, normal pallid and acne-ridden, was a little clearer. He had grown a small goatee, which actually improved his appearance and covered the scars from earlier acne outbreaks.

She looked at him hard for a moment, recognizing her need to take control. When his eyes finally dropped from her gaze, she motioned to the side interview room. "In there," she pointed and waited for him to make the first move. She didn't want him behind her, despite the presence of a guard.

She shut the door behind her as Joe flopped down on a metal chair and ran his hand through his hair. "Nice hair, Joe. What made you cut it off?" she asked casually, putting her file on the table and pulling a pen from her purse.

"There was talk about a murder of a girl I know. Somebody said I'm a freakin' suspect! Then those Shriner guys came a-volunteering to cut hair and the like. I thought if I was going to get yanked in for questioning, I might as well look like the clean-cut type."

"I'm impressed. So what have you been doing with yourself lately other than avoiding me?" Her expression remained benign.

"I have a new business. I take electronic parts to Portland. I got a truck and everything." His eyes glittered as he stabbed the table with his index finger. "And it's legit, Christian. No contraband, got it?"

"You're not peddling dope?"

"Nope. Like I said, I got a real business now. Me and my girl are gonna to get married soon." Joe glared at her as though insulted.

"So why is it you look like you're still on crack?"

Joe's face reddened with anger. "Give me a pee test if you're so sure of yourself," he growled.

"Don't worry, I plan on it. So let's talk about Whitney Clist's murder. What makes you think that you're a suspect?" Christian was in no mood to placate the kid. If anything, she had it in for him. The last time he was busted, he was caught with an underage girl. She felt no love loss when it came to Joe Sliver.

He shrugged. His skinny shoulders moved like levers under his dingy uniform. "I know the family. I grew up with the Clists. I saw Whitney a few days before she was killed.

She came to me for help. I guess my girl's little punk brother told the police that I was with her."

"Cole was finger-pointing at a few others, too. Do you have an alibi?" Christian could smell the fear in the young man.

"Yeah, man. The day she was murdered, I was on my way to Portland to drop a load."

Christian nodded slowly. "Tell me about Whitney. Why did she want your help?"

Joe grimaced, forcing his upper lip to rise. His teeth were surprisingly white and straight in his bony face. He was lucky that he didn't have meth mouth yet, she thought absently.

"All I know is that she was sent down to a town in Utah, somewhere south of Salt Lake to get away from her freaky dad and pervert brother. But something happened down there, so she ran. I was friends with Whitney's older sister and later with Whit. I took care of things when an older boy at church started bugging her, so she looked at me as kind of a protector, I guess. Anyway, Whitney called me, all worked up, so I went to Comely's to see her. She wanted me to find a place for her to hide. She said there were some men would eventually come for her and kill her."

"Why didn't you tell her to go home?"

"I didn't want her to go back there. Like I said, her parents are freaks. And then there was her brother, who also had it out for her."

"So what about Brandon Clist? Why did he have it out for her?"

"That little asshole is a piece of work. He was sent up, ya know, for messin' around with little kids." Joe's face soured, his narrow cheeks puckering dangerously around their sharp bones. "I might have made some mistakes in my life, but I'm not into that sicko stuff."

Christian shook her head. No wonder the girl hadn't returned home. "Joe, is there anything you can tell about the people who were after her?"

"I just know that she was sent down to live with some relatives. It's one of those Mormon places where the men all have a bunch of wives. Whit said that the men of the clan force themselves on the young women who live there. And the girls aren't allowed to leave without the leader's permission. When I talked to her, she was scared as hell. She said that the leader down there was someone we both knew well, but she wouldn't tell me his name. I guess the big cheese found out that she came back here, cuz she said she thinks she was being followed when she got into town."

"Is there anyone else whom she might have talked to about this?"

Joe closed his eyes to think. "She had a friend named Stephanie who had dated Brandon at one time. Stephanie had a bad life and she was looking for a way out. Last I heard, Stephanie had followed Whitney to Utah, but Serena, Stephanie's older sister, still lives around here somewhere."

Christian offered the young man a smile. "Thanks, Joe. You've been really helpful."

"Are you a detective now or somethin'?"

"I guess you might say something like that." She rose from the table and opened the door. "That's it for today."

"What about the UA?" Joe leaned close to her as he stepped through the door. His breath smelled like death as he whispered. "I'll tell you now, it's dirty, but only for weed."

Christian stepped out the door. "Thanks for your honesty. I think we'll skip it this time." She thanked the guard and left immediately. Passing through two electronically-controlled doors, she padded silently down the long, dark corridor, her mind swirling with disturbing mixture of curiosity, disgust, anger and hope. The grey cinderblock walls did nothing to improve her mood.

When she arrived back to the office, she looked up Serena Patterson on I-Leads, the county's criminal tracking system. Serena Patterson was three years older than Stephanie, which made her an adult by a year. The nineteen-year-old appeared in the system for a number of petty crimes. Her address listed was a known gang house in East Kennewick.

The weather was temperate for January. All of December's snow and ice had melted away, leaving golden skies and blustery winds. At sixty degrees, the sun was a cheerful ball in a robin's egg blue sky.

She bypassed the highway, instead taking the road called Canal Drive, noted for the muddy brown irrigation canal that wove a serpentine path through the east side of town. Kennewick had originally been a community fed by 19th century midwestern farmers looking for open space and cheap land. Welch's, a primary employer, had a large juice plant near the railroad line, but it had closed recently due to a lack of supply. Now wine grapes were all the rage. And, over time, Kennewick's city council had approved commercial property status to much of the juice grape growers and dryland wheat farmers. One by one, the land had been rezoned or sold to developers. Street names like Vineyard, Fruitland and Gum were some of the only reminders that Kennewick was once a lovely little breadbasket along the mighty Columbia. She turned off Canal Drive and headed past the old Grange Hall. Traffic was busy on Kennewick Avenue.

Soon the urban landscape began to change. The streets narrowed and the homes became shabbier. By the time that she'd arrived at the dilapidated house near the railroad bridge, she remembered why the address sounded so familiar. A couple of years prior, there had been a gang shooting at the residence. Parking a block away to divert attention from the county car, she warily climbed out and looked around. The path up to the battered house was covered with weeds. Burrs and cheat grass stuck to her cream-colored, crepe pants as she tried to avoid stepping on dog poop and wads of gum. Cursing under her breath, she wished she'd worn more appropriate clothing for the ghetto visit. There was no answer when she knocked on the door. With caution, she opened it and peered into the darkness. It reeked of rotting garbage and cigarette smoke. "Hello," she called, trying to keep her voice casual. "Is anyone at home?"

After a minute or two, she stepped back and walked around the perimeter, hoping to see someone through the filthy windows. When she had no luck, she continued around the small building to the back where an old garage sat, surrounded by a dilapidated car, a number of broken-down appliances and a rusty oil drum, which looked like it was used for barbecuing.

There was little grass, but an ancient white picket fence, like a row of broken teeth, was the original enclosure surrounding a large fir tree and a few struggling rosebushes. The discouraging look of the place told the story of a home which had seen brighter days. A distinct percussion beat reverberated in the air as she approached the garage. A set of fingerprints could be seen on the grimy window near the door. She knocked and the sound of music faded away. Unconsciously, she slipped her hand to her gun as the door squeaked open about an inch.

"Who is it?" a woman's voice cracked.

"Christian Vargas. I'm looking for Serena Patterson."

"What for?"

"I need to talk to her about her younger sister, Stephanie."

Some shuffling movement could be heard as the door swung open. The room was a complete mess. On one side was a Chevy Impala, taken to pieces. Its rusty engine sat on a card table leaning precariously as though it might collapse. Next to the opposite wall was a twin mattress on the floor. A pile of clothes was on the concrete next to the bed, along with several McDonald's wrappers, Big Gulp cups and ashtrays overflowing with butts. The smell was atrocious- gasoline mixed with stale smoke and something else evil. It took a minute for her eyes to adjust to the dim light.

"Are you Serena?" Christian asked gently. The bright light from the open doorway revealed a reclining figure. Her face was a purple mask, her right eye swollen completely shut.

Fingerprints marked her neck with ugly pink circles. Her shoulder-length dyed hair was the flat black of old tar. The half-smoked cigarette hung from her mouth, creating a veil of smoke around her inclined head.

"Yeah." The simple answer was laced with despair.

"What happened to you, Serena?" The probation officer dropped to her haunches to get a closer look at the young woman. Silence took its sweet time, but eventually she murmured an answer.

"Primanada." Christian quickly searched her brain for the meaning of the word...something about feudal kings having sexual rites over serf virgin brides before their wedding night. Her awkward bafflement prompted a deep sigh from the girl. "I got jumped into the gang last night. Gang-raped. They call it 'the rites of primanada'."

"Do you want to be in a gang?"

"Hell, no. My old man don't give me a choice."

"Okay, well I'm taking you to the hospital and then to the domestic violence shelter. Do you have any children?"

"Not yet, but after last night I could have a few in there, I suppose." She shrugged with indifference. Carefully Christian pulled the girl upright and began to walk her out of the shed. As they rounded the side of the house, two men stepped out of the back door. The larger one held a machete.

"Where you think you're goin' with her?" he growled. Wearing only a pair of shorts, the disgusting ogre was tattooed from head to toe. His beer belly, as big and hard as a Pilate's ball, hung down precariously, hiding any sign of a crotch. His five o'clock shadow looked like a coffee grounds on a Halloween hobo and his greasy dark hair was long and knotted. The other man, wasting away from a life of drug use, looked over the fat man's shoulder with menace in his eyes.

Christian let go of the girl momentarily and stood erect. "Get away from her. I'm getting her some medical attention."

The fat man stepped forward, swinging the machete back and forth, a lethal weed eater, ready to chop anything in its path. "The hell you are." He grinned and took another step. Fear crept up the back of Christian's legs, restraining her like iron shackles. She couldn't have run if she tried.

Serena began to whimper. "He'll kill us."

In the next second, Christian remembered her weapon. Slipping her hand into her pocket, she held the gun up at the men. "I'm getting her out of here. If you mess with me, I'll blow your heads off."

The fat guy's eyes grew wide as the other one slinked back into the house. His stubby hands rose up in defense. "Whoa, mama, probation officers ain't supposed to carry guns. I ain't gonna do nothin'. Take that little bitch. I don't give a shit." Indeed she was not supposed to be carrying a gun, but she did it anyway for her own safety.

"Get back," she ordered, grabbing Serena around the waist. "You tell anyone we were here, I'll have you strung up for rape and battery assault so fast, you'll sit the rest of your days, what's left of them anyway, in a cell."

Serena was silent as Christian helped her into the car and drove her to the hospital. Gratefully, the Kennewick General Hospital emergency room was nearly empty when they got there. The intake staff took one look at the battered young woman and hustled them immediately into a private room. While they waited for a doctor, Serena finally said, "I want to get those guys. Tell the doctor to do one of those kits, you know, when women get raped."

"Sure, honey. I'll let them know." She started to stand, but the young woman's grip was like a steel trap.

"No. Don't leave me. I want you to stay with me. I'm scared."

The rest of the day became a grueling exercise in privacy destruction. The rape kit, a criminal investigation tool, required that a woman be degraded for the good of justice. Her nails were scraped and cut, her genitals prodded for samples, her pubic hair snipped, and her anus inspected. The Kennewick police were called to take a full report. The longer it took, the more frightened the girl became. When the domestic violence shelter staff person arrived, Serena's mood began to improve slightly. She was done with 'her man', she told them, though at the height of crisis, that's what they all said. Then a good thing happened. Serena gave them a phone number. In a few minutes, they'd reached her father in Georgia. Christian talked to him, explaining the horrors of his daughter's life. The government engineer had not had contact with his daughter in over a year. Before their conversation was over, the girl was crying and an airplane ticket to Savannah had been purchased.

On her way back to the office later that day, she thought about Serena. They'd had little conversation about Stephanie. The only thing that Serena could say was that her little sister had gone to a town south of Salt Lake City with Whitney Clist and had started prostituting down there. Yet as Christian prepared to say good-bye to Serena at the shelter, the young woman had grabbed her arms and between whispered thanks, begged her to find her little sister. Entrusting the probation officer with a letter to deliver should she find the girl, Serena requested that Stephanie proceed to their father's home in Savannah as soon as possible.

* * *

The next morning, around nine, Christian woke up. After a shower, she grabbed a cup of coffee and headed to the living room to do the daily crossword. After a few easy clues, she came across the description of the word, miasma. It was enough to get her thinking again about the case and Whitney Clist's death.

The death of a family member was the most devastating event in a person's life. Christian knew from experience. Leaning back, she scanned the arched ceiling above her. Luminous paper mache stars swung softly to and fro in the ceiling fan's slight breeze. Less than a year ago, there'd been seventeen stars in memory of the loved ones whom she'd lost. Her eye moved to two stars at the far left of the celestial cluster. The stars were different in size, created to reflect the age of the person at their death. Her sister had drowned during the ill-fated sailing accident that had also killed Christian's parents. Cassidy was turning eight years old on that blustery day. That horrible day would forever burn in Christian's memory. A tear trailed down her cheek as she sent a wish to her sister's star.

Her dog, sensing her rising emotion, made a low whining sound in his throat and climbed gingerly onto the couch next to her. Though he weighed over one hundred pounds, the Great Dane-St. Bernard mix had managed to curl himself up as small as possible, hoping to avoid scolding, and softly laid his head on her lap. Then, with his liquid brown eyes full of obedient love, he issued a heavy sigh. In the next minute, her cell phone rang.

"Hello?"

"Hey, Christian, it's Harry. I got your message. Not working today?"

"No. This is my four-ten week."

"Lucky you. I heard you're connected with the Clist murder, so I'm calling to fill you in, on the QT, of course. The girl died inside the coffin. However there was little blood left in her legs, which leads me to believe they tucked the lovelies up against her chest to transport her. In the trunk of a car, no doubt. A very small car, or maybe in a box in a larger vehicle."

Harry was a very talented crime lab techie who talked like he was jabbing a punching bag. The Hound, as he was affectionately called, was a good friend of hers. It was his badge-wearing pals who called him "The Hound", in direct reference to his bad boy ways. 'Like a dog after his bitches,' Daniel liked to say. Though the supervisor's promiscuous reputation preceded him, Christian was one of the uninitiated and preferred to keep it that way. "I guess I was wondering about the wound on her forehead. Is that what killed her?"

"The medical examiner hasn't come in yet this morning, but the toxicology report came back last night. From what I can see, her THC levels were fairly low, not much use and the rest of the levels were negative. The blood work also indicates that she was about two months pregnant and severely anemic. However, it looks like the blunt force trauma caused severe hemorrhaging, which leads me to believe that it was ultimately the cause of death."

"What about the weapon? Can you identify that?"

Harry gave a soft grunt. "If only I could. She was not tortured, if that makes you feel any better. No, this girl was punched once, hard, by maybe a nail gun, only the tip of the nail was smooth. There was no point to it and…"

"And there was an indentation in her forehead, like impact from the head of the hammer, right?"

There was a soft chuckle of satisfaction. "You don't miss a beat. What else did you see in that thirty second observation?"

"I don't know if I should get in the middle of this."

"You already are and you're good."

"I just recalled this tool hanging on the wall at Doc's Tavern down in Seaside, Oregon."

"Don't tell me you're getting kinky on me now. Doc's 'big tool' where?"

"Seaside, Harry. Get your head out of the gutter. I was down there for New Years. There's this pub with oyster-harvesting memorabilia on the walls."

"I got it. And oysters are aphrodisiacs, right?"

Christian blushed.

"Sorry, sweets. Okay, so you saw a weird oyster cultivation tool and you think it looks like what might have killed this little girl. Can you get me one of those things?"

Smiling, she replied. "Yes, Harry. I can try."

"One more thing. The vic's cut mark, on her right wrist, was at least three days old, according to the enologist's report. She had two new tats- a two inch crab on her right ankle and the initials, L.T., on her left bicep. Based on her birth date, I assume the first one has to do with her sun sign. Do you have a clue about the L.T.?"

Christian contemplated the initials. "At one time, she dated a kid with the alias Lobos. How old are the tats?"

"A few weeks at the most. The skin was still healing."

"Thanks, Harry." An icy realization had settled in Christian's bones as she added, "Has anyone thought that perhaps the L.T. stands for Lex Talonis?"

Harry was silent for a long moment. "Give my brain a minute here." A long, low whistle could be heard. "Christian, do you remember that case a few years back when a prostitution ring with underage girls was busted outside of Othello? The guy who did time has the same last name as our vic here. Gary Melvin Clist's moniker was 'Lex Talonis.' He was sentenced to six years for three counts of child abuse, pornography, a bunch of stuff, but he might have been paroled by now."

"I'll see what I can find out."

"Are you going to solve this one, Chrissie?" His voice had a teasing quality.

"I'm going to try. The little kid, Cole, didn't do this, Harry. We both know it."

"What can I do?"

"I think we need to know more about her pregnancy. Have you done any DNA matching on the fetus?"

"I'm looking." Christian could hear Harry tapping on his computer. "Here we go. A comparison was done on the fetus against the DNA of a Lupe Aguilar. No match."

"That's Lobos, her boyfriend at one time."

"That doesn't rule him out for murder. In fact, a jealousy motive is all the more possible if she was sleeping with someone else." Harry's voice dropped to a conspiratorial whisper. "Hey, got to go. The boss just walked in."

"Bye and thanks, Harry." Christian disconnected, pushing the cell for speed dial. She got Daniel's answering machine.

"Hey, it's me. Do me a favor when you have time. Check out a guy, Gary Clist, once an inmate at McNeil. See what he's up to." She gave a satisfied sigh. Now they were getting somewhere.

She recalled that the staff at the funeral home had followed orders to deliver the coffin from a phone call that had come from a prepaid cell phone. Their best guess was that the offenders had snuck into the building while the janitor was cleaning the night before the funeral to put her body in the coffin. Yet due to the weather and the multitude of cars at the scene, uncovering evidence was truly like trying to find a needle in a haystack, Christian mused, as the doorbell rang.

Despite Doug's flair for outrageous work attire, this morning he was dressed in a typical Eddie Bauer hiking outfit. The dark green neoprene jacket accented his sparkling green eyes while his long dark hair was pulled back into a ponytail. His sexual orientation, normally highlighted by his flamboyant style, was not so recognizable now.

"Hey sweet thing, how's my favorite girl this morning?" he asked, planting a firm kiss on his friend's cheek.

"I'm good. How are you holding up?" Christian asked as she grabbed her backpack and keys. They stepped through the side door to her garage. Bear attempted to wedge his way between them in his excitement to get into the car.

Soon they pulled into the Badger Mountain parking lot. "Hey, I need to check my messages. Here's ball for Bear. I'll meet you in a few minutes," Christian said.

"Sure thing." Doug sauntered off with the dog in tow. As she began to check her phone, she noticed a blue Ford truck rolled by behind her. Daniel had left a short message stating that a Gary Clist had been paroled from McNeil Prison two years earlier. She wondered if the perpetrator had come back to his old haunts as she leaned against her new SUV. The sunroof was open, but she couldn't be bothered to close it. It was a lovely day after all.

Doug was waiting with Bear at the trailhead. "Hey, want to hear a strange one? As you know, Whitney Clist was a distant cousin of mine. My dad's sister, Aunt Joan, was her mom's closest cousin when she was growing up. Joan's husband was from a wealthy farming family. They had farms and ranches all over the Northwest."

They advanced onto the narrow path ahead while Doug threw Bear's ball into the ravine below. The three-legged dog barreled through the sagebrush in search of it as they climbed the steep terrain. "There's more to it. Joan didn't divorce her first husband. He ran off to join one of those Mormon polygamy groups and she refused to go with him. The church excommunicated him and basically annulled the marriage for her."

"I thought Mormon women were generally submissive."

Doug laughed uproariously. "You don't know Joan. She's one big-assed bitch. Sorry for the reference, but she was the enormously obese woman at the funeral. Anyway, one of her cousins is deep into the whole *Big Love* lifestyle and apparently her horny ole' hubbie thought that he was missing out."

A jab of intuition suddenly hit her gut like a hot poker. "What was her first husband's last name?"

"Joan's? He was from around here, I know that." Doug closed his eyes and pointed to the sky. "Actually it just came to me. His name was John Sliver, but we joked that his name was Long John Silver."

Christian froze in her tracks, causing Doug to bump into her. "Whoa, girl!" he cried. "What's wrong?"

"Do you know if this John has any brothers?"

"Let me think." Doug paused dramatically. "I know that there is James, Jed, Jeremiah, Jared…the youngest is Joseph." He paused for a long moment. "I can't think of the other one's name. Is there another New Testament name that starts with J?"

Christian turned to face her friend, her features marked with concentration. "Judas," she answered flatly. "Look, maybe this is just a coincidence, but I have a youth on my caseload by the name of Joe Sliver. I'm just wondering if there's any relation."

The conversation fell to mutual huffing. The steep hiking trail climbed a vertical of eight hundred feet in a nearly two mile stretch. The winding trail passed desert flora, coyote dens, and several rattlesnake holes. Popular with the locals, the typical weekend brought hundreds of climbers who jockeyed for space along the narrow trail. By the time they'd reached the top of Badger Mountain, every cloud had meandered to the south, leaving the sky perfectly clear. To the north, the White Bluffs seem to have been painted by a landscape artist. Christian drew her breath and lifted her hand to shade her eyes.

"Will you look at that," she said with a soft hush. "The bluffs remind me of Dover's cliffs, from a distance, that is."

Doug peered into the distance. "England, right? Is there anywhere you haven't been?"

She shrugged.

"Imagine my luck," Doug replied, good-humoredly. "Born to an LDS clan who believe that travel consists of a mission trip where you wear hideous black suits, ride bicycles to work and knock on people's doors in a half-hearted attempt to convert them to our great faith. The good thing was, I lived with a very cute boy the entire time and found my true calling. There was one time and one time only that the Mormon's God actually listen to my prayers. My mission trip was to San Francisco. Two years in the gay capital of the world and my destiny was set in stone. I loved the church back then, only for all the wrong reasons."

An hour later, they were back to her car. Christian opened the back end of the hybrid for her dog. Bear, however, refused to get into the vehicle. His growl told her that something was amiss. She looked over at Doug.

"What's wrong?"

"I don't know. Bear won't get in."

Doug opened the back passenger door. "Here Bear.... whoa, what the hell?"

Her friend's face suddenly turned as white as a page of copier paper. "Christian, there's a snake in here. A rattlesnake. Dear god, how did it get in here?"

Christian ran around the car and looked in. There, on the floor behind the driver's seat, was a very large coiled snake. She paused to admire the creature's raw beauty. The snake's skin bore an elegantly patterned design, but the sound of his rattle reminded her of the danger. Bear growled again.

"Take Bear back up there." She pointed to the end of the parking lot. "I'll get rid of this thing."

After her friend and dog had moved safely away, Christian closed her eyes, trying to stop the flood of memory. She had been bitten by a baby rattlesnake at the age of three. Whispering a prayer taught to her by her shaman, she waited until her breathing slowed. Carefully she opened the rear driver door closest to the snake and began to hum an ancient chant. The snake seemed to resist at first, rattling more furiously. Rising up menacingly, the serpent had the girth of a garden hose. Its coloring was remarkably like that of the desert floor. He hissed, bearing his fangs, his head bobbing back and forth, looking for an easy target. She was calm. Maria had taught her to work with the animals and tune into their energies. She understood the snake; its fear and confusion. Soon her lilting song seemed to do the trick. With a little prodding from the end of her tennis racket, he slipped over the side of the door jam and slithered into the bush. Quickly, she jumped in the car and drove to the end of the parking lot where Doug waited with the dog.

"How did you get rid of it?" Doug squeaked, his tan-in-a-bottle complexion now bleached to the color of a raw banana.

"A trick that an old lady friend of mine taught me once. The question is: how did the snake get in the car in the first place?"

"Hell if I know. I was scared shitless. Why would a snake be out this time of year anyway?"

Doug was right. Rattlesnakes didn't make their appearances until spring. In fact, the more she thought about it, it was likely that the creature had been placed there by human hands.

CHAPTER 5

Christian gazed at Matt. He was asleep, but still held her tightly in his embrace. Earlier that year, the handsome African-American had asked her to marry him. Many of their friends had started their families and it seemed that nearly every party that they attended now was a baby shower in disguise.

She ran her hand down his torso and gently stroked him until he was hard. He awoke then and moaned happily. "Am I a lucky man," he whispered as she climbed on top of him. They rocked slowly, enjoying the warm simmer that would eventually grow into a powerful flame. Soon Christian sat up, the covers falling away from her. Her long wavy hair swayed as she increased her rhythm. Learning to please Matt had been easy. She began to move faster now, feeling the ecstasy rise from deep in her belly and tingle throughout her body. Then she lost herself in pleasure.

Soon Matt climbed out of bed. "I'll make the coffee. Then we need to talk."

Minutes later, he handed her a steaming cup. "You need to walk away from the case." His tone was firm.

"Why?"

"Chrissie, every aspect of this case is dangerous. Someone has the balls to put a girl's body into another woman's coffin on the grounds of a church. We're talking sacrilegious sickos."

"Who told you that?"

"Daniel. He said you've been a mess over this, which tells me you are riddled with guilt, thinking to yourself, what if she was alive while I was parking the car? What if I could have saved her?"

"And you wouldn't think that way?" She stood her ground.

"Of course that would cross my mind, but that's as far as it would go. You now believe it's your job to find her killer. That's not the way I think."

"I'm getting dressed." She turned her back, headed for the bedroom. "I'll be ready to leave for the ski slopes in a half an hour. The weather is supposed to be beautiful today."

* * *

The kid was hella scared. He'd begged the detention staff to keep him away from Miasma, but they'd put them in the same room anyway. The older boy had murmured a death threat as they'd passed in the corridor. He'd been locked up in B Pod, but the stupid guards couldn't handle the gang problem, so that afternoon, they'd moved kids around. Now he was stuck with Miasma and that wasn't a good thing. His friend blamed him for his arrest.

Moloch, as he preferred to be called, had managed to steal a pencil off Miss Candy's desk when she wasn't looking. He'd nearly finished the homemade tattoo. The swastika bubbled up with dark red beads, which he promptly squeezed into the paper cup.

Miasma loved to see someone endure pain. It signified courage to him. The little boy shivered with fear, hopeful that by the time Miasma came in from the basketball court, he'd have the respect that would keep him alive.

* * *

Christian's home phone was beeping with a message when she and Matt returned from the White Pass Ski Resort. Quickly checking the number, she saw that it belonged to the Benton County Juvenile Detention Center's master control. "Honey, there's a call on the machine from detention. Can you start dinner so I can find out what's going on?"

"Why don't you leave it until tomorrow?"

"Not a chance." Immediately she dialed the number and began to speak to Tim Shannon, supervision in charge.

"Cole Comely and that Miasma kid got in a fight today after rec time," he explained. "Jolly overheard Thomas say something to Cole about being the murderer and that he was going down. Later when they called the boys out of their cell for dinner, Thomas started screaming. He told Officer Chance that he'd been sleeping, so he didn't see it."

"See what?"

"Cole had snuck a pencil into his room and had stabbed himself with it. He's in the hospital, in ICU. Apparently he hit an artery." Stunned, she sat down hard on the bed, her head in her hands. She must prove the kid's innocence if that was the last thing she did.

* * *

Judge Stanzik had decided to release Cole Comely to Lourdes psychiatric inpatient unit based on the fact that he was at risk of harming himself. His decision let the county off the hook and gave the boy the mental health support that he obviously needed. By the time that Christian reached the treatment center on Monday morning, Cole's mother had arrived.

"He didn't hardly know that girl, ya know? That damn prosecutor made it sound like they were best friends or somethin'. And devil worshippers, my ass! Them two kids know nothin' about that kind of stuff. And Whitney, she was only over at the house once, if I remember right. She was talking about going with her uncle to Utah, to live in some kind of a commune. Then, the last I heard, she'd gone the other way, to the coast to visit another relative."

Christian glanced out the window of the small interview room just outside the children's inpatient unit, wondering if Ms. Comely was a truthful woman. Cole's mother was epitome of what Stella had once coined, 'White Trash Fashionistas' or WTFs. She wore her hair in a true mullet. The stringy bottom half was a faded brown, but the crew cut length top was splattered with gray grow-out. The terrible haircut paled by comparison to the rest of her. Dressed in a too-small polyester top that said, 'USA', her otherwise skinny body had the mid-torso tire of fat otherwise known as a muffin top. It bulged dramatically over the top of her low cut, skin-tight Wranglers. Her teeth were also part of the WTF motif. Most of them were a dark brown in color though her left eye tooth was gone completely and several on the bottom looked ready to fall out the following day.

Unlike her mother, Cole's sister was a stunning girl with flaming red curls and a body out of *Playboy* magazine. Yet she was a product of her environment. Using her sexy body and good looks to her social demise, she was prostituting by the age of fifteen. The year before, when she was seventeen, Carlie Comely and Joe Sliver had gone into a dealer's house, held him at knife point, stole his stash of cocaine and proceeded to get caught when they drove off in his car. Carlie spent three months at a juvenile prison while Joe got six months in county.

"Mrs. Comely, I'm so sorry about all of this. I will try to help Cole in any way I can without jeopardizing the investigation. Tell me more about Whitney. You said she came to the house?"

"Yeah, last month some time. The kids were talkin' about one of those Mormon farms where the men have a bunch of wives. She said her parents treated her bad. She was a runaway, ya know?"

"Mrs. Comely, tell me more about Joe Sliver."

"Carlie's boyfriend? Ah, he ain't so bad, ya know? They got a good thing goin' now. Joe does deliveries and has his own truck even."

Christian was about to ask another question when Cole was brought in by a staff person. He was a fingerprint of his mother-the same, small forlorn face and stringy hair.

"Hi, Cole." She greeted the boy tenderly. "I'm so glad you are here. This is a safe place. They can help you."

The boy dropped his head and nodded. A large bandage covered his lower left arm where he'd plunged the pencil. "Do I have to go back to detention?" he squeaked, his voice still prepubescent.

Christian's tone was soothing. "I'm going to do everything in my power to make sure that the judge allows you to go home."

"I did cut her, but like I already told you, it was only a game. "

"When did you see her last?"

"She come over after she got back from Utah, just before Christmas. She was really scared. Like I already told you, she said that some guys was coming after her."

"If you could tell me a little more, I think I could get the cops off your back once and for all."

Cole grabbed his mother's hand for comfort. "Joe wanted to help her. He didn't want her to get hurt, but I didn't think the great master was like that. See, we all know the great master. We got a secret tribe with him. Once he likes you enough, you get to go live at his ranch."

"So I'm guessing that Whitney was living at this master's ranch. Do you know what happened to Whitney down there?"

"She told me that the girls had to have sex with all these guys. I ain't saying I wanted to go down there for the sex and all, but..." He looked down, aware that his mother was watching him. "I know that Stephanie, our friend from school, went down there with Brandon Clist once, too, but I don't know if they are still down there or not."

"Who is the Great Master?"

The kid's dull eyes searched the wall for an answer. "Cancer? He's the guy who runs the Lex Talonis church. He's the king of the clan."

CHAPTER 6

The six men sat in a circle around the smoky fire. There was little cover on the lonely plateau, but they were far enough away from civilization to prevent detection. As though in angry disapproval, the dried sagebrush snapped fiercely as it burned, releasing a pungent odor into the cool air. High above, the flashing light of a plane or perhaps a satellite in its orbit moved lazily across the black night sky. Amongst the brilliant cast of stars, Venus twinkled seductively. The moon, like a faded happy face symbol, was their ritual's only witness.

The clan was dressed in long black gowns with chains around their waists. Swastikas had been drawn with charcoal on the middle of their foreheads and the letters SLT were sewn onto their robes with silver thread. Beneath their simple gowns, they were as different as a garden of wild flowers, but adorned in their costumes, they were as one, a handful of ebony pebbles in a vast ocean of sand.

Nearer to the fire, four teenagers knelt on the ground in front of their elders. The fire lit up their childlike features, which were marked by fear and trepidation. The adolescents wore only black biking shorts, which caused the lower part of their bodies to appear invisible while accentuating the pale skin of their bony shoulders. Their faces, like Van Gogh's images of *The Potato Eaters*, were the mocking parody of a late night horror movie.

The ceremony began with a Gregorian-sounding chant. Its echo was pure and rich, intensifying their religious frenzy. Voices rose and fell in harmonic scales, the tenor and the bass voices seemingly more pronounced as a result of their contrasting range. The youngest boy had the sweetest tone of all and gave his voice over to his new God as the song grew more complex in rhythm and force.

Finally, one by one, the men grew silence, though the very air seemed to quiver, as though longing for more of their vocal caress. The leader mumbled incoherent verses from the medieval Asetic Bible, asking for Satan's guidance. The man next to him, heavy-set and sweating, pulled nervously on the nipples of the scrawny boy in front of him, making the child squirm. Nearby sat the half gallon bucket of blood; its metallic odor simultaneously sour and cloyingly sweet. The second in command, whose head was like an oversized melon on his slight frame, rose from his stump and lifted the vat to his lips, drinking thirstily from its contents before passing it to the next man. One by one, the devotees drank, until the last man emptied the contents, smacking his lips with pleasure.

The scantily-dressed cluster was not allowed to drink from the warmed container. It wasn't yet time. They had not yet been initiated, though tonight would be their moment. Slowly the six older men stood up, and the first boy, christened Miasma, took his cue. He had passed his test by collecting the blood from a pregnant woman, and in doing so, prepared himself for the initiation rites. Slipping off his spandex shorts, he bent over the stumps, his cream white buttocks gleaming like mounds of butter in the flickering light. The men proceeded with their rites, though the boy's cries were not to be of concern. The desert would sequester their secret, as it had for centuries before.

One by one the boys were initiated in the same way. The groaning and slapping lasted for nearly ten minutes. Then a final howl sounded as the leader signaled his completion. The others quickly followed suit. Afterwards, the group covered their heads with the silver-trimmed hoods, whispering thanks for the evening's rites of passage. Lifting the boys up, they gently carried them to the motor home where they were tucked into the makeshift beds. Driving away a few minutes later, the men complemented one another on the success of the evening, forgetting the bloodstained container in the wake of their delirium.

* * *

Sophia's soft, round features pinched in concern as she watched the pretty young woman leave the building. Dropping the Venetian blind, the psychologist swiveled around in her chair and looked down at the file on her desk labeled 'Christian Vargas'. The probation officer had been her client since the year before when a terrible double murder had rocked their pastoral community. Distracted by her unyielding determination to solve the crime, Christian had suddenly stopped coming to therapy until the perpetrator had been arrested, tried and found guilty. Several months had passed before she'd returned to Sophia for help.

Christian was a complex case. Her life was the stuff of stage tragedy. By the age of three, she'd lost her parents and only sibling. As a result, Sophia had diagnosed her condition as a post-traumatic stress disorder, the perennial favorite of therapists, with a secondary condition of acute counter phobia. The probation officer was drawn to terror in order to assuage the pain of her own.

During the course of therapy, Christian had recounted her work history as well. As a college student, she'd volunteered in the cancer ward at the Seattle Children's Hospital. Her first job out of college was working for the King County Sexual Assault Response team, specifically on aggravated rape cases. Then she adopted a dog and trained it for search and rescue. Now her work involved working with violent, albeit juvenile, offenders.

Then there was the officer's spiritual conviction that her father's ghost was her guide in life. The young woman talked about the appearance of her father like she'd sat down for coffee with him. In most cases, the well-trained therapist would have added another code from the DSM IV- the Diagnostic and Statistical Manual of Mental Health, the veritable bible of psychiatry: highly delusional with occasional hallucinations. Yet this was a woman who was otherwise in her right mind.

Sophia pondered the situation. Most recently Christian had wanted to focus on her romantic relationship and her fears of commitment. Yet by the end of their first hour together, she talked more about her work partner, Daniel, than her lover, Matt. When Sophia had probed this discrepancy, her patient had adamantly refused to acknowledge that she had feelings for the former. They were simply office mates, she'd replied, though her tone had been prickly and armored.

Now Christian had become obsessed with solving another crime. Their conversation today had centered on her belief that the victim had been part of a satanic cult. Her research had been admirable, but once again, Sophia felt that any progress on her patient's personal life had been stymied.

There were only a few cases in a therapist's life work who were worthy of intense study. Most people came in to complain about their lives. In the process, a few developed some insight into their dysfunctional behaviors or misaligned beliefs. Generally the majority of clients blurred into oblivion over time, but Christian Vargas was different. She was both open and insightful and yet, mysteriously impenetrable. For selfish reasons, Sophia didn't want to lose this one.

* * *

He'd been waiting for over an hour. His bladder felt like it was ready to burst and his skin itched from not showering for a few days. Hiding out in his brother's car was taking its toll. Stretching languorously, he released a boisterous fart. Finally the bitch in question exited the psychologist's office. She appeared preoccupied and didn't give a glance in his direction. Though he couldn't yet see her face, he watched as she pulled on her helmet, her shiny, chocolate-colored hair trailing down her slender back. She was tasty-looking little piece of meat, no doubt about it. Too bad he couldn't bang her first, he thought, feeling his horny parcel begin to hum. Stroking himself absently, he thought maybe he could do her after he killed her, providing there wasn't anyone around.

He'd thought about offing her for a while. There were so many ways to do it without getting caught. She really had stuck her nose in too deep. He'd heard about her so-called heroic investigation after the Maltos murders. As fate would have it, she was the probation officer to Cole Comely. The kid was so stupid; he'd undoubtedly already told her everything.

Indeed, the bitch had to be stopped. Unfortunately his clever snake trick had failed. His next idea was risky, but he had no choice. Everything was going along fine until she'd started asking questions. His cousin had warned him that she was going to have the cops start looking for him now.

She fired up her Ducadi motorcycle, and slowly glided out of the parking lot. Eager to follow her, the young man hastily pulled the car away from the curb. He'd figured out how to do it. She would be an easy enough target. Motorcyclists generally were. He would follow her from a distance until they reached Columbia Drive. A sharp cliff bordered one side of road while a row of upscale homes lined the other. It would be an unfortunate place for a motorcycle to slide off the old Richland highway.

He glanced at his watch as they traveled west. The man grunted with delight as he watched her maneuver the bike around a sharp curve, gear up and take the motorcycle to a higher speed. She was a graceful and experienced rider, he thought, his groin growing hot as he admired her taut curves and fine ass. Biker chicks had always been one of his favorite types. They were normally down and dirty and ready for rough sex. He wondered if this copper was the same. The kid said that she didn't wear a wedding ring and had never talked about a husband. That was good news, though she might have some kind of a live-in boyfriend. Hell, she might be a lesbian for all they knew. Yummy! There was nothing more titillating than using force on a resistant lesbian.

The sky was darkening to a deep purple, like an old bruise, he thought, as he moved closer to the bike. She was aware of his presence. He was close enough to see her darting glances in her rearview mirrors. This broad is starting to panic, he realized, pressing down on the pedal so that the truck was just inches from her hind end. Now it became an exhilarating game of death tag. She roared ahead and he followed in pursuit. Licking his lips, he began to imagine her naked. He got so close he could see curve of her waist and swell of her thighs. Rubbing his hand over his crotch, he moved to the lane next to her and gave her a sinister grin. "Got you," he mouthed, watching her expression turn to terror.

They came around a bend and suddenly the sun was in his face. He was having a hard time seeing her without his sunglasses. "Fuck," he muttered as she careened around a couple of cars and got ahead of him. He tried to keep up, but traffic had jammed up around some local road construction. He growled in anger as he found himself behind a large semi-truck. Punching the steering wheel in frustration, he cursed loudly as he came to a dead stop. By the time he got around the snorting mechanical mammoth a few minutes later, his target was long gone.

* * *

In the dream, she was back at Mrs. Stanford's funeral. The stake house's main room was different than it had been that day. An indigo-trimmed canopy arched dramatically over the audience, like the Sistine Chapel of medieval horrors. Pornographic frescoes of nymphs and angels, engaging in violent sexual acts, were painted in large, lifelike imagery. At the front of the room, against a wall painted the color of lapis lazuli, people were milling around the coffin. Christian was standing before it, handing out a program which described Whitney's murder in graphic detail. Near the front door, Mrs. Stanford hovered like a worried mother, directing people to get into line to see the dead girl.

In the next moment, she lifted Whitney out of the mahogany box and, with the victim in her arms, had slowly floated up to the ceiling, joining the painted scenery as though she was a flattened paper doll. But the girl was too heavy. She would not adhere to the plaster. Letting go of the child, she watched from above as the corpse tumbled down and broke into a hundred bloody pieces like a glass statue dropped on a marble floor.

The vision ended and she awoke. Shaking with terror, she tried to breath, but it felt as though as an invisible rope was cinched around her neck. Now fully awake, she gasped, swallowing air like a drowning victim as an icy chill enveloped her. Burrowing back under the thick down comforter, Christian wished that Matt was beside her.

He was at the regional basketball championships. At the last minute, she'd opted not to go, knowing that time was of the essence. She was determined to find Stephanie Patterson.

The girl was in danger, of that she was certain. The authorities were no closer to finding Whitney's killer. Cole Comely was a long shot. Though the boy had obviously become involved in a dangerous and complex society, he had never seen the man he called Cancer, nor did he know where to find him. The authorities were searching every data bank in the country from the local I-LEADs Benton County police tracking system to FBI files. Neither the Lex Talonis church nor the name Cancer appeared anywhere according to her contacts in the department. Therefore Cole Comely's admission did her no good. Whitney's ex-boyfriend, Lobos, was on the radar and Cole's friend, Thomas, was of interest, but there were no other suspects and the case had started to grow cold.

After hours surfing the internet for answers, she'd come up with nothing. Cole's *MySpace*, however, had displayed some pictures of a group of hooded men dressed in strange costumes. He claimed it was a Halloween photo, but Christian knew different. A few hours after she'd seen it, the boy's *MySpace* account had vanished entirely.

If only she could get a location for the Lex Talonis Church, she'd be able to pursue this. Stalemated, she needed a break in the case. As her eyes adjusted to the dim light, she noticed a shimmering reflection in the northeastern corner of the room. The image began to stretch and change shape as she stared intently, the hair on her arms rising to attention. Tingling air swept past her face as her father's ghost presented itself. This was the third time she'd seen the poltergeist. Each time, his appearance became more obvious. Each time, his appearance had significance, as though he was sending her a message. She knew to pay attention. She counted to ten and said softly, "Daddy?"

Now the air in the room warmed slightly. She tried to remain still, waiting his next move, but the shimmering light faded and disappeared into the darkness. Bear came into the room from the hallway, whining low in his throat.

"It's him again, Bear. Quiet now." It was painful to see her father. Yet she also experienced a sense of peace. It was as though he were speaking to her without words, reminding her to have purpose and make a difference in the world. It was his way. He had been a fireman after all.

The clock read four. Bear wouldn't stop his pacing. Growling, he ran to the front door, scratching desperately to get out. She slipped from bed, grabbing her oversized terrycloth robe from the back of the door on the way. She put it on and shoved her feet into a pair of boots by the front door. Bear whined, his hair on his back still standing at attention. By his agitated behavior, she sensed there was someone in the yard.

Once outside, she and the dog wandered around for a few minutes. Stepping onto the back porch, Christian sat down in the rocker, childishly hopeful that somehow the heat from her father's form might have magically penetrate the thick canvas cushion to give her the sustenance that she craved. Yet only coldness seeped through as she brushed the top of Bear's head with her foot. Rhythmically she rubbed the dog's head and rocked, humming softly until the sun rose in a crimson dawn.

* * *

"I talked to Scott last night. He said to send his regards," Christian mumbled, doing her best to get a first appearance report done before noon. Her new assignment, brought into detention the night before, was coming down off a lethal combination of Ecstasy, Vicadin and Ritalin with some marijuana and vodka thrown in. The composition of a First Appearance report required detailed research in order to back her recommendations. After several calls to school counselors and staff, a mental health therapist and Child Protection Services, she hoped that she had a handle on things.

"So how is your older cousin-adoptive big brother these days?" Daniel asked as they worked, his head buried in his own exceptionally high caseload.

"He just finished his legal part of the Jewish Society Center bombing case. He was the civil attorney and helped to collect a pretty penny for his clients, let me tell you."

"Good for him. Did you tell him about our new case?"

"*Our* new case? Since when did you become so interested?" Christian teased.

"To keep an eye on you, that's why. The gang task force meeting is in fifteen minutes." He reached over to grab some keys to one of the dilapidated county cars. "Come with me and we can talk about it."

Nodding, Christian closed her files and stood up, stretching her legs. "I'm there." Once in the car, he launched into a diatribe.

"According to Jack's interview with the Clists, Brandon is on his mission trip, which excludes him from suspicion. As a result, Cole, Thomas and Lobos are the only suspects at the moment."

"That is ridiculous!" Christian crossed her arms angrily. "I don't believe for a minute that Cole killed her, but the satanic stuff could be the key. Cole gave me access to his *MySpace* account. I saw a few disturbing photographs, but nothing more about the guy he calls Cancer. However, on the site, Miasma had written something about their full moon initial rites. He also referred to 'The Sign of the Nail', which is significant, don't you think? Whitney's forehead looked like someone had punched her with a nail. So I followed that lead by Googling 'Sign of the Nail'. It took me about two hours of searching, but finally I came up with a ranch in southern Utah that uses that name. The "Sign of the Nail" ranch raises cattle. How coincidental! I called around to slaughterhouses in Utah and came up with one just south of Salt Lake City that buys from the ranch. The young man I spoke to was scared, I could tell, but I let him know that the authorities would be snooping around if he didn't give me some information now. He didn't have an address, only a P.O. Box. He thinks the ranch is one of those Fundamentalist LDS places."

"Which means?"

"There is a branch of the Latter Day Saints that maintains that polygamy was Joseph Smith's original intention for Mormons. They still practice it in a few places, primarily in parts of southern Utah, Arizona, Texas and, believe it or not, Canada."

"So you think you can just waltz in some freaky Mormon compound and tell them to give you Stephanie Patterson, oh, and confess to a murder while you're at it."

Christian rolled her eyes. He was impossible. "I'm going to Utah, whether you like it or not. You will not tell anyone what I'm up, too. This is it. I feel it." She didn't mention that after her father had visited, the words *Go to Utah* appeared on her mirror after a steamy shower. That was his ghostly way-to leave messages there.

Daniel pulled into the Pasco Police Department parking lot and stopped the car with a jerk. "Are you crazy?"

"Absolutely. Crazy to solve this case and protect another young woman. I have some vacation time coming and I'm going to use it to go down there. Someone needs to find out who killed this girl. I'm talking to her parents again tomorrow about Stephanie."

"But you don't even have her on your caseload."

"I do as of this morning. Stoppard kindly transferred her file to me. She's on warrant status and he's overloaded, so I offered to track it."

Daniel shook his head. "You're like a bulldog, but I'll be your bitch as long as you'll drag me along."

"I think the weapon was a spatting hammer."

"A spitting hammer?" Daniel's face was marked with confusion.

"Spatting."

"Isn't spat past tense for spit?" Her partner was winding her up and she knew it. She ignored him.

As they walked toward the building, she added, "Joe Sliver said that Whitney was really scared. She indicated that she needed help. He told me that she'd wanted him to hide her."

"And you believe *him*?"

"Yes. Pasco P.D. did a video check on the gas stations in the Portland area that Joe said he frequents. He was spotted at two different stations on the day that Whitney was killed. In all of the video shots, it was just him and his girlfriend, Cole Comely's sister. If he'd killed her, he was still stuck in Portland due to that terrible snowstorm that shut down the Gorge highway by the time Whitney ended up in the coffin."

"So what's next?"

"Utah like I said."

"Are you inviting me to go along?"

The female P.O. felt her face grow hot. Now she'd done it. "I didn't say that."

"You're not going alone!"

"I thought Doug might go with me."

Daniel threw his head back in laughter. He shook his head, trying to catch his breath. "You've got to be kidding me. You're going to a Mormon compound with an ex-Mormon poof? You're even crazier than I thought!"

"Okay, then. Come with me."

"What about Matt?"

"Don't flatter yourself. Matt is a perfectly reasonable guy. He will back me on this if I ask him to. He's not, I repeat, *not* jealous of our relationship. He's got basketball championships, so he can't go."

Daniel raised his eyebrows, offering a sly grin. As soon as she spoke the words, she knew that Matt's feelings weren't the real problem. In truth, there was a different danger with which she'd be forced to contend.

As they sat through the gang task force meeting, her mind wandered to the probabilities: the probability that someone from Utah had come all the way to Washington to kill a young runaway; the probability that the same person would have access to an oyster spatting hammer; the probability that she could go to Utah in the same car with Daniel and survive the sexual tension; the probability that Matt would accept such a lunatic-inspired plan.

* * *

"Just don't tell Matt I'm going," Daniel suggested. The meeting was over and they were on their way back to the office.

Christian closed her eyes and counted to ten. God, he could be so irritating. "Look, I'm not going to lie to Matt under any circumstances. Michael's going to be the problem." Daniel gunned the car passed an old blue truck that suddenly swerved dangerous close to them.

"Well, maybe our golfaholic boss can pick up a little slack for a change. His three day-a-week golf schedule doesn't start for a few more weeks." His sarcasm oozed.

"Okay. You can come, but not unless Doug can go. That way Matt will feel better about the whole thing."

"Yep. I agree. Much easier that way." He drove into the parking lot and shut off the car. Slowly he turned, his dark eyes blazing with something between desire and success. "So he really is jealous of me?"

Christian groaned. "I didn't say that, but how would you have felt if your ex-wife had taken off with another man for a week?"

A happy smile crossed his handsome face. She'd just handed him the winning ticket. "Me? What would I feel? Relief. Complete and utter relief."

CHAPTER 7

The kid was hooked. There was no way he could have ever guessed that his experience with his master would be so strange and wonderful. The Lex Talonis lifestyle was not just for little boys and movie stars and it was definitely not just for Goths. If anything, the Goths who he knew had no idea about the stuff that he learned over the last few months.

Power. That's what he'd always wanted in his life and the Lex Talonis Church promised to provide it. From drugs, rituals, and a brotherhood like his dad used to talk about...before his Dad went all religious on him. He had already been assigned his role. He was a chosen one. According to the law, he was to create chaos for his tribe in times of trouble, so as to distract the enemy.

According to his Master, when the time was right, he would be allowed to join him full-time at the headquarters. For now, however, he was being tested. He'd passed the first level of initiation by dealing with Whitney. He'd found it harder than he'd expected. His emotions got in the way for awhile, but then he remembered that she had always been a problem for him.

Then there was the elixir of life. Drinking blood was normally associated with vampires, but in the Lex Talonis church, they were drinking the blood in order to commune with Satan. Cancer explained that the blood was drawn from children or young women who were still pure and innocent. Then it was contained in a special, secret refrigerator on the ranch that was blessed by the Great Master and several of the elders on a daily basis. Stacks of Bibles and the Book of Mormon surrounded the stored blood. Each day, various children of the clan would be brought into the holy chambers for blood-letting. Then, one night a month, the men of the clan would partake in a ceremony, culminating in the drinking the liquid. If he were honest, it had taken him awhile to get accustom to the taste. As a kid, he had terrible hangnails. When the small wounds would bleed, he would suck his own blood, but to drink someone else's blood took courage. Cancer had also said that drinking the blood would keep him strong and healthy.

The sanguinarian is someone who feels that he or she needs to consume blood to maintain their health, he read slowly, attempting to sound out the long word. Wikipedia is a great tool, he marveled, his fingers flying over the keyboard like a pianist playing a symphony as he looked up the next reference. *Renfield's Syndrome: a psychological condition in which a person who drinks blood is classified as suffering from a delusional symptom of schizophrenia.* Now what was that? He wondered, unable to say the word much less understand the last word. There was a knock on his door as his father called him out for dinner. With a heavy sign, he closed down the Dell for the night.

Moloch's assignment had been a lot easier than the one that Cancer had most recently given him. He was proud of that fact. It proved he was better than that little punk, Cole. He was to knock off the probation officer. All that Moloch had to do now was sneak back out to their initiation circle and collect the abandoned bucket with the leftover blood in it. That is if that little jerk ever got out of the loony bin.

* * *

"I just don't get it." Matt had his back turned to her. Broad-shouldered and muscle-cut, he had the perfectly-shaped rump that so many women adored on African American men. She forced herself to look away. In order to state her case, she needed to avoid such tempting distractions.

Digging through his drawer for workout gear, he continued, "Based on the evidence, she died after being placed in the coffin, right? That means someone put her in there before the first guy showed up to unlock the stake house doors the next day, which was January 2."

Christian nodded thoughtfully. "Cole and his buddy said that Whitney had only stopped by Comely's house the night before she was murdered. She told them she was going to her boyfriend's aunt's house in Montana. There was a terrible snowstorm that weekend, remember? The highways were closed. Not possible."

"That's what I'm saying. She was here when she was murdered." He pulled a tee-shirt marked with the Gonzaga ZAGS logo over his head and faced her to continue. "So why are you so set on going to Utah?"

"Because that's where I'll find Stephanie Patterson. I'm convinced she's back at the ranch and knows who was after Whitney."

Matt's normally cheerful face had turned grim. "I love you, but I'm not going to endorse a wild goose chase and furthermore, I can't stand the thought of Daniel going along. He wants in your pants so bad, it's not even funny." Though his voice was casual, her lover knew that Daniel's desire for her was a touchy topic.

Curled up in bed on a cold Saturday morning, she watched him as he yanked on a pair of boxers. As he pulled on his sweatpants and bent down to put on his shoes and socks, she finally spoke. "I've had this dream…actually several dreams. In every one of them, I'm trapped in a large, somewhat dilapidated house with a bunch of girls. It's in the desert, because when I look out the window, I see enormous rocks. Then there's my Papa. He keeps popping up and giving me little signs of encouragement." Christian squeezed her eyes tightly closed, trying to block out the grotesque scene that had repeated itself night after night for over a week. "I need to go down there. There is something evil going on. I feel it and I'm going to stop it."

"You went to Whitney's funeral yesterday, didn't you?" His voice was more tender than accusing. She stared down at the satin coverlet, trying to avoid his eyes.

"Chrissie, how many times have we talked about this?" Matt came to the bed and sat down. Glancing at his watch, he murmured, "Damn, I'm going to be late. Look, if you really believe there is a tie to this whole thing in Utah, then at least go see Maria. In my mind, she's like your psychic back-up. I trust her. If she says, 'go', I'll..." Matt hesitated, obviously torn by the need to protect his woman. "I'll support it because I know I don't have any other choice." He bent down and kissed her on the nose. "Still, I think it's like throwing snake eyes."

She tilted her head in confusion. "Throwing what?"

"Snake eyes. It's a gambling term. Throwing a pair of dice and landing double aces. In other words, I think your idea is a big gamble." He shrugged disarmingly. "Basketball practice should be over by noon. Do you want me to pick up anything at the store on my way home?"

Reaching up, she stroked his smooth cheek. "No. I've got everything I need. Have fun with the kids...and thanks. I'll call Maria right now." And she still had to talk to Doug about the trip.

From what little more Christian had been able to find out, Whitney had returned to the Tri-Cities a week before Christmas and had stayed with various friends for a few days before moving on to the Comely home. Daniel's friend, Jack, had told him that the girl had called her mother once during that time, but that Patty Clist had been hysterical during the post-mortem interview and had to be sedated.

Now, nearly six weeks later, the case was at the standstill. Cole was no longer a leading suspect, but the connection to Lobos appeared to be a dead end as well. Lobos mother had sworn in an affidavit that her only son had gone to Mexico the previous summer, but didn't have an address for him. Border control had been notified. In many cases, Latino kids who grew up in the United States eventually returned home. If he did decide to come back, his birth certificate would be flagged.

The day before, Harry had given her a glimpse of Whitney's diary after her mother had turned it in as evidence. The last entry had been made a month before Whitney had been sent to Utah. It was an adolescent's journey through high class hell. She wrote that she was always trying to please her mother, and yet she inferred that she hated her. She wrote about Brandon and how afraid she was of him. She worried that when he got out of jail, he would hurt her. There had been something sinister about her comments about her father as well, Christian thought as she sat at her desk, shoving a turkey sandwich in mouth before she made the call to Maria.

Thinking back on the victim's funeral, she made a quick note to herself. She'd attended Whitney's funeral with the hopes of talking to Stephanie, despite the high probability that the girl was no longer in town. Unfortunately, she hadn't seen her in the crowd.

Since then, she'd crossed Cole and Joe off her own working list and on a whim, had added Whitney's father. He continued to claim that they hadn't seen their daughter since she'd gone missing in October, but the probation officer had a gut feeling that wasn't exactly true. Gerry Clist had appeared on television to appeal to the public for its assistance in solving the crime. There was something about his anguished zeal and overly-scripted dialogue that rang wrong for her. It was as though he'd rehearsed the plea like an actor on a stage, not like a father tormented by the murder of his beautiful young daughter.

Yet her inner voice said that the answers lay in austere and isolated badlands of Utah. Out of respect for Matt, she would put everything on hold until she'd spoke to Maria. She called the woman immediately. At the sound of her voice, Christian could hear the joyful smile on her mentor's ancient map of a face. Noone in the Daniel's family actually knew the old woman's age. She had crossed the Rio Grande with her parents in the early 1900s, but she had no birth certificate. A fanatical gardener, Maria grew award-winning roses as well as a variety of herbs, which she gathered and prepared for medicinal purposes. Daniel often joked that her herb potions must all have a little marijuana in them and otherwise only had a placebo effect, stating, "Any concoction that she's ever given me just makes me feel good, but hell if it cures anything."

La curandera invited her young friend to her home immediately upon hearing her voice. With an evening of friends and wine-tasting already planned, the amateur chef was glad that she'd prepared hors d'oeuvres the night before. Climbing into the shower, Christian revisited a conversation that she'd had with Whitney's mother at the funeral. The woman had recalled the P.O. from an intake meeting a few years before. It was the first step in her son's sexual offense conviction, which sent him away for a couple of years. When Christian saw the grieving mother, she had offered her condolences. As they stepped into the lady's room, Mrs. Clist nearly collapsed in her arms.

In a jumbled regurgitation of sorrow and despair, the woman had said something that Christian would never forget. "My husband wasn't even here when the police called me. He was on his way to our cabin on the Oregon coast to meet up with his younger brother, Gary. Because of the storms, I couldn't reach him for over a day."

Despite Matt's concern over her compulsion for attending funerals, this wasn't the first time that her instincts had paid off. In the next sentence, the frail mother had handed over an unexpected gift. Through gushing sobs and disconnected thoughts, Mrs. Clist had invited Christian to her home, telling her that she wanted the younger woman's help in finding her daughter's killer.

Deep down, Christian knew that the girl's appearance in the coffin was not a fluke. Mrs. Stanford had been sick for a while and was expected to die. Furthermore, she believed that the killer had derived some psychological advantage from placing the girl in the coffin. Her research on the motives of murder and the typical preoccupations of a killer led her to believe that the perpetrator had derived some emotional benefit from killing as well. Was it the convenient timing of the old lady's death that drove the perp to kill when he did? Yet the absence of sexual violence draped an ambiguous fog on the theories of motivation. Sixty to seventy percent of the time, murders were a result of a gunshot wound. Blunt force murder was fairly rare. The idea that someone had accidentally killed the girl during an argument seemed plausible until the hiding of her body was considered.

The person must have planned it. Then there was the possibility that the murderer had actually gone to Mrs. Stanford's funeral that day. If they had gone for the pleasure to continuing their fantasy, they hadn't expected that the casket was going to be opened. Such knowledge would have placed the fiend at too much risk.

Driving out to her friend's home was like a Map Quest video game. The first time that she'd visited the shaman had been over a year ago. Ironically, it had been Christian's birthday when Daniel had insisted that she join him for a night of homemade tamales at the gathering of his *familia*.

As she veered off the highway and began to climb the sun-baked desert hills to another small farming community, the word 'austere' came to mind. Like a clip from an old Western film, the scenery was raw and uninviting, conjuring images of death from dehydration. Sagebrush and low scrub gave the land a faint palette of greens. Beige, tan and peanut butter-colored rubble choked the otherwise sandy surface that was better suited to reptiles and scorpions than vegetation. A pale blue horizon yawned beneath the open sky as the sun hung low in washed-out winter gold. Clouds that would never offer a drop of water banked the rising cliffs to the north. This was drought country, saved only by irrigation canals and deeply-dug wells. Dark blue shadows had settled into the shark-tooth crevices of rock which were now turning ochre in the fading afternoon light. Occasionally a lone cluster of cottonwoods appeared as she wound her way through a gully toward a town that was once little more than migrant housing and potato sheds. In fact, the farming communities of north Franklin County evolved from need, not desire. Simple outposts, they offered a hard life, without the luxury of a shopping mall or even a movie theater.

Slowly she wound up a narrow track of road until she reached an expanse of flat land. The landscape now showed signs of life. Barns and grain silos dotted the horizon as endless rows of dried corn stalks and furrowed fields appeared. Finally, when she was sure that she was lost again, a tiny mailbox appeared, decorated with a wooden cut-out of angel. In front of her was a small cinderblock house, next to which was a small building that leaned precariously to one side, driven by the fierce winds. The front walk to Marie's reading room was a path of white gravel. Along the border were shriveled rosebushes, made bare by the cold winter.

To her neighbors, the Latino woman's prayer room was a wonder in a place of comfort's denial. The old woman lived alone on two acres north of Pasco, though in days gone by, she'd raised a brood of ten, cultivating more than just flowers. Her hard-working husband had died an immigrant field hand, illegal and therefore without residual income to speak of. The resourceful crone made ends meet by selling her herbs, babysitting for her neighbors and offering the highly-sought services of a Mexican healer. One didn't actually pay for her medicinal skills and spiritual advice, however, at least not without offending her. Yet Daniel had directed his partner to leave a twenty dollar bill under the large statue of the Madonna whenever she visited *la curandera*. That was Maria's form of 'under the table' income.

The shriveled woman appeared at the door of the shed as Christian walked up the rickety steps of its primitive porch. Daniel's grandmother was tiny, perhaps less than five feet in height, with long white hair, which she wore in a high bun on her head. She dressed in traditional Mexican attire. On her feet she wore soft leather huaraches and her dress was embroidered with swirling flowers of every color. Her face melted into a million smile lines as she hurried toward her young friend and reached up for a hug.

"Welcome the pretty lady with eyes like the sea," she gushed in her thick accent. "My dear, how you been doing? Gracias for the beautiful wreath you sent for *La Navidad*. I love it and keep it always."

"I'm so happy you liked it, Maria! How are you?" Christian cried, reaching down to give the woman a warm embrace. There was a deep connection between these two women, one that didn't particularly make sense to either. As Maria often said, "When the good Lord brings you a gift, receive it graciously." She was a devout Catholic and prayed before every reading.

"I'm very good, young lady. I have missed you. Are you happy now?"

"I'm very happy. But there is a new case that I'm involved with and I need some of your wisdom. The dreams have started again."

Nodding, the woman took Christian's hand. Pulling her into the magical room, she hastily shut the door. Lit with numerous candles, it was as the younger woman remembered. With a deep groan, Maria moved a chair towards the small table upon which sat a set of crudely drawn cards, religious votive candles and a statue of Mary. "Here, sit."

Christian took the chair opposite of the shaman. The room had floor-to-ceiling shelves of paper Mache and clay figurines. The antiquarian's death doll collection numbered in the hundreds. There were dressed-up, sophisticated skeletons nearly a foot tall and homely little peasant skeletons less than three inches in height. There were comical men dressed in serapes and co-joined couples and babies and even dashing teenage skeletons. *La curandera* had explained that the Mexican culture celebrated the Day of the Dead with feasting, song and gifts to the dead. It was to give hope and encouragement to those loved ones who had passed from this world.

Christian closed her eyes and offered a prayer to Whitney's family as Maria began to pray loudly in Spanish. A few familiar words came through, but mostly the younger woman was unable to translate her mentor's entreaties.

Suddenly the surrounding candles swayed dramatically as though a giant hand had swatted their fragile flames. The hair on her arms rose and her skin tingled as though she had touched an electric current. Like after a lightning strike, the sharp tang of ozone saturated her lungs. Maria wagged her head to and fro; her eyes still closed, and mumbled strange words to herself. Slowly the tarot cards began to shift on their own accord. As though someone had bumped the table, three cards slipped forward and fell into Christian's lap. At that moment, the crone's eyes shot open and she gave a loud cry as her client picked up the cards. In her hand was a collection of major arcanas: the devil, the high priestess and the wheel of fortune. Maria made a tsk, tsk sound and said, "Oh, my child. This is a dangerous time. This one here," she said, pointing to the devil card, "is a dark one, like a cancer rising from the smallest part, growing larger and larger and taking over the innocent body. It is a dark one, but not as you might believe. This is not of the shadow people; there is no evil from the other world. This is evil that is of our world. This evil is far away, in a place of sand and stone. Take care to avoid the *culebra*. The snake is dangerous and has no fear." Shivering slightly, she pulled her knitted shawl around her shoulders before she continued.

"The high priestess, she is you, Miss Christian. She is strong and powerful and has great wisdom of the heart. Do not fear. If you go about your business as the priestess, you shall overcome the evil." Maria closed her eyes again, her head nodding as though she were speaking to someone. Her face expressed little signs of agreement. Uttering soft 'uh huhs', and '*si, si*', she rocked to and fro and finally released a deep sigh.

At the periphery of her vision, Christian saw the room expand and contract as though it was alive and breathing. Her skin felt warm, but her body was cool. In her ears, she heard a distant buzzing sound, like the night song of crickets. She looked around, waiting as her friend completed her inner dialogue. Then her eyes rested on a particular figurine which sat on the shelf directing to the right of her. The artist's depiction was clearly that of a young girl. The skeletal creation had some words printed on the front of her colorful, peasant-styled blouse. She leaned closer, watching in suspense as the words seemed to grow larger and jump out from the form. Her recognition was instantaneous as she read: *Lex Talonis*.

She opened her mouth to speak, to tell Maria of the coincidence, but the older woman was not to be interrupted. She signaled to Christian, raising her hand. "He says that the wheel of fortune is the key. You must follow your…" Maria pointed to her lower belly. "The gut. The wheel is right side up. That means success. Take your vision quest and go to the land of sand and stone."

As Christian drove away a few minutes later, she looked down at the small baggie of leathery brown strips that Maria had taken from a closet in the reading room. The narrow cabinet had housed several strange-looking items. Most were baggies that dangled from hooks, each filled with healing potions. The shaman had pointed to the dark lumps with great enthusiasm. In addition to herbs, the bags held dried animal organs. From skunks' livers to coyote ears, from freeze-dried frogs to skinned rattlesnakes, the woman professed to have any remedy for any ailment.

Maria had cured her the first time they met. After feeling poorly for several weeks, Christian had gone to her new friend when the doctor couldn't diagnose her weariness through blood tests and scans. The old shaman had simply taken an egg from her own coop, rolled it all over her patient's body and then had broken the egg into a clean glass. Rather than appear as a raw egg normally would, the egg was a filthy brown mess. Therein lay the remedy. According to Maria, the younger woman was just covered in dirty energy. It had been shortly after she'd been attacked by a gang member. And in fact, she'd felt better immediately.

Now she'd been told to eat dried reptile meat. Marie knew that her friend had survived a rattlesnake bite at the mere age of three. That, along with her belief in animal totems, had convinced her that Christian was best protected by consuming a portion of rattler every once in awhile. Hocus pocus or otherwise, the shaman's fledgling would do as she was told.

* * *

"So she gave you what?" Stella gasped in horror, her goblet of Syrah tipping precariously towards her lap. With a lovely turquoise Caroline Herrera dress at risk, Christian took her friend's hand to steady the glass.

"Calm down. It's a Mexican folk remedy. People eat weirder things," Christian assured her.

"No! No they don't. I mean, I'm not counting those freaks that eat chocolate-covered ants, okay? Really. Why do you buy into this voodoo?"

Daniel had crept in late and slipped onto the couch next to Stella. "I'm with you, Stell. I call it Mexican gourmet. Nothing like a rattlesnake covered in steak sauce."

"Gross! And you were the one who encouraged her to go to your crazy grandmother."

Christian held her hand up in alarm. "Stop this right now. If I knew you were going to react like this, I wouldn't have told you."

Stella shrugged and stood up. "I think I'll go talk to a normal person. Matt's brother is looking real good right now."

After she left, Daniel grabbed his office partner's hand. "Don't get up just yet. I have something for you. Only you.... and don't worry, it's not fried cricket, or poached frog."

Christian glanced around the room to make sure everyone was comfortable. The majority of the guests were milling around the kitchen island and the wine-tasting Valentine-themed party was definitely in full swing. The hosts had instructed their friends to each bring a bottle of Shiraz, also known as petit syrah, from either the Columbia, Yakima or Walla Walla appellations. The local popularity of wine was not lost on this twenty-something crowd.

"Okay. It looks like everyone is good to go. So what is it?" Christian eyed the brown paper bag in Daniel's hand.

"I bought this especially for you, in honor of our trip to Utah. It won a bunch of honors at this year's big wine competition. And the name plus 'magic' is perfect for what you do." With great flourish, he pulled a bottle of Powers Cabernet from the bag.

"Wow. This is supposed to be a wonderful vintage. I hope you don't mind if I share it another time." She fought the urge to give him a hug.

"Sure. Save it for your birthday, or whatever," he replied casually. "Hopefully you'll include me." His warm smile radiated success. Christian felt her skin tingle with embarrassment. Despite her obvious unavailability, Daniel continued to woo her. Yet his methods were confusingly benign. It was difficult to know how to respond. His feelings for her were clear and she couldn't honestly say that she had none to give in return. She hesitated, unsure of her next move.

"Look who's here!" Matt called out from across the room. "Just in time. We're just about ready to start the tasting." Doug and his boyfriend, Tye, were greeted by the group as they joined them at the bar.

Christian reached over and squeezed Daniel's well-muscled arm. The tingling sensation now began to pulse in her lower body, but she blamed it on the wine. "Thanks again. Let's join them now." With that, she hastily stood and moved to the bar.

It wasn't long before the group learned of Maria's prescription for Christian. When Stella begged to see it, Daniel played on it. Though he'd often been embarrassed by his grandmother's archaic remedies, he found it extremely funny to share his partner's fascination with friends.

"Yep. It's rattler. I can tell just from looking at the baggie. Come on, partner, show them your courage." The group joined in with words of encouragement. Christian glared at Stella and Daniel.

Noticing her discomfort, Matt announced the second flight of wine, which came from a boutique vineyard near

Richland. The conversation moved on. Sitting next to Doug, Christian whispered, "I can't get my mind off the Clist murder and then I start thinking about your mom again. I feel so badly that this happened to you and your family, Doug."

He sighed heavily. "Can we talk privately?"

"Sure. I prefer white wine anyway."

They left the clamor of the inebriated crowd and slipped into the small study where Christian did most of her investigative work. A large bulletin board cluttered with newspaper clippings and random computer print-outs covered one wall. A marked-up whiteboard filled the wall opposite.

"So these polygamists, where do they mostly live?" He asked, staring at the marked-up map.

"As you can see, they're spread out around the state of Utah in isolated pockets. Warren Jeffs, the famous polygamist, and his clan were in Colorado City."

"Do you have an address for your uncle's ranch?"

"No, why?"

"Because you're going with me to Utah to find Stephanie Patterson."

"I am?"

"Yeah. I told Daniel that you were coming with us. I can't get Matt to agree unless you do. Besides, I need your help in order to execute my plan."

Doug let out a soft chuckle. "I guess I owe you one. I can drop my mom's personal Book of Mormon at the temple in Salt Lake while we're at it. My dad asked that one of us do that soon."

"Great." Relief came to her like the sun after a storm. He was in.

"You need to talk to the Clists again before we go anywhere. If I know you, you'll get that mom to spill her guts pronto."

Perched on the edge of her rocker, directly in front of the bay window, Christian couldn't help noticing a truck parked a couple of houses down in front of the house. She watched as the driver lit up a cigarette, but didn't get out of the idling vehicle or drive away.

"Looks like we have company." She pointed out at the street. Doug turned to gaze out of the window. The blinds were tilted at an angle, giving them better cover.

"I've seen that truck outside your house the last time we went hiking, Chrissie. I thought it belonged to a neighbor of yours."

Christian shook her head. "Nope. You know, I think I saw that truck about a month ago. I was on my bike, coming home from work. The driver wouldn't get off my tail." She peered out. "Can you see the license plate?"

Doug squinted and pressed his face closer to the window. As he did, the truck's headlights came on, shining directly into the room. "Get down," Doug ordered.

The engine roared to life as the truck came toward them. Christian screamed as the sound of gunshots pierced the air, shattering the glass and knocking her to the ground.

The house was silent for a couple of seconds.

Then Matt burst into the room followed by Daniel. "What the hell happened?" he cried. The room was full of people suddenly, all screams and shouts. She mumbled for Doug. Matt lifted her into his arms, telling her that Doug was fine, but she couldn't respond. Her arm hurt like hell.

Daniel hollered that he had called 911. Somebody yelled for bandages and antiseptic; someone else ran outside. Christian couldn't get her bearings. Her ears felt full of water and her arm hurt. The sickly, metallic scent of blood filled her nostrils just before she passed out.

* * *

Christian awoke the next morning in a fog. She vaguely remembered the ambulance arriving. The EMTs cleaned her up, but didn't take her into the hospital at her insistence. She had only been wounded by flying glass. At some point everyone left the house, but by then, Matt had given her a pain killer and she was drifting off to sleep. She heard Daniel talking to the police and then she was out.

Matt walked into the bedroom with breakfast on a tray. "Hey, sleepyhead, good morning."

She pushed herself up against the pillows. Her head was pounding. "Hi. What time is it?"

"Nearly noon. How are you feeling?"

Her arm throbbed, too, but she was otherwise okay. "Too much wine?" she whimpered.

Matt smiled tenderly. "We have around the clock security for the next few days. They said they don't think the guy will come back. They collected a couple of shell casings. Daniel arranged to have the window fixed this afternoon."

"Is Doug alright?"

"He's fine and unfortunately more determined than ever to go with you to Utah. I'm hoping you are in your right mind and will cancel. This is serious, now, Christian. These people know where you live."

Just then the phone rang. Still shaky, she grabbed it off the bedside table. "Hi, this is Christian."

Jerry Shaw barked his name and said, "Your kid, Cole Comely, was brought back into detention. He was caught out in the hills with a bunch of kids after curfew. The cops found a container with dried blood, an old fire pit and several sets of foot prints. Cole apparently told them that they were forced to participate in some kind of a weird ritual. He looks higher than a kite to me. Already wet his pants and is crying for his mommy. Just thought you'd want to know."

"Thanks." She turned off the phone and stared into space. The news had jolted her awake. Matt was right. The case was more complex than she'd originally believed. Things were becoming more dangerous.

"What now?" he asked.

Christian turned to face him. "This is getting weird. I need to talk to the Clists as soon as possible.

"Before you go to Utah?"

She gave him an imploring gaze. "So you're okay with me going?"

"No."

She sat there, reluctance threatening her resolve. Matt waited for a long moment. Finally, when she refused to speak, he stood up and stomped out of the room. Over his shoulder, he growled, "I'm really not okay with it. In fact, just know that I might not be here when you get back."

CHAPTER 8

The clock read seven-thirty. He cursed himself for waking up so late. The sound of traffic reminded him that he was no longer in the badlands or at the beach. Reaching for his glasses, the man opened his wallet to count the cash. The hooker had left him short, but she'd been worth it. He always surprised the streetwalkers with his good looks and boyish charm. They never expected his style in the bedroom. As he examined the last of his money, a photo fell out from the middle of the fold. It fluttered to the floor and he cursed again. He picked it up, his muscular arm, strengthened into a sinewy log of flesh by the work on the property, glowed like honey-covered sandstone. Clearly his arms were capable of crushing a woman, or better yet, a disagreeable man. He'd proven that more than once.

Gazing at the photograph, he recalled his victim's last words before he used the unusual tool to do his final calling. He had been remorseless and still was, though he missed the little babe. Yet Whitney had gotten out of control. After threatening to turn him in, she had sealed her own fate.

He remembered their last moment, running his index finger over Whitney's exquisite face. He hadn't really noticed her beauty until later on in her childhood. And she'd always been good in the sack, even when she was barely in middle school. Sighing with pleasurable memories, he closed his eyes and recounted their defining moments together. She'd resisted for more times than he could count, but eventually he had won, though force was often the means to an end. So what! He'd been taught by an evil life to do evil things, and had learned his craft exceptionally well.

Why had he lost control of Whitney? Now he hurled his wallet across the room. It hit the wall with a thud. He had lost the only woman that he'd ever really loved. Yet killing her had been his only option. After his mother had lost her mind, he'd learned the signs. Whitney had been unraveling for some time. There was no telling what she might have done to destroy him and all the work he'd done in order to build a life.

* * *

Lisa Monahue was waiting in their office when Christian arrived to work. Articulate and engaging, the mental health therapist who managed all of the mental health issues in juvenile detention was not yet thirty years old, but was more capable than most therapists twice her age.

"I thought you should know, when I was talking to Cole Comely's social worker, Mark Lopresti, this morning, he made a comment that caught my attention. Cole said that he thinks that this great master he keeps talking about is related to Whitney. Lopresti believes that Cole knows more than he's telling us, but that the kid is too terrified to say what that is. He's suggesting that the investigators give Cole a lie detector to see what else might come up."

An intolerable chill settled deep as Christian closed her eyes. "That poor little guy. He is in way over his head."

"I agree, but I just wanted to you to know. Also, I called Jack Devin, but he's not in, so I asked for Detective Graham. He's been assigned to the case, along with John Divinity. Anyway, they're on their way to that Miasma kid's house now to pull him in for one, too. Hopefully something else will come up. They want to see what's on Thomas's computer as well. Cole has also said that most of his contact with this great master guy is over the computer. He hinted that this Cancer communicates through a website called Lex Talonis. I did a search on the web for anyone associated with that phrase, but didn't come up with the site. Lex Talonis is actually a religious term, old scripture."

Christian gave a heavy sigh. "Yeah, I know."

"Yet Cole and Thomas are professing to be practicing Satanists who were once Mormons. What a strange connection." She pushed her stylish glasses up her delicate Asian nose.

"Yeah, so now we need to find someone who is a member of both. So what do you suggest?"

"If I were you, I'd be looking at all of the current and old social files of all Mormon kids who've ever been on probation, starting with one in particular."

"Which one?"

"Her twisted brother, Brandon."

A few minutes later, Christian went to the agency vault. The vault was not a large room. Approximately ten feet by ten feet, it held over twenty years of juvenile criminal files, dependency cases and diversion records. The files ranged from a few pages to several inches thick, depending on the youth and their activities. Though the goal of the juvenile probation department was to reduce recidivism, sometimes, the karmic wheel was already turning for a life of crime. The causes were numerous. Recent studies indicated long-term trauma, coined ACEs or 'adverse childhood experiences', were the primary reasons for the increase in juvenile crime. Other studies fostered the idea that poverty and lack of resources fueled the criminal coals. Stoked by the desire for plenty, youth engaged in crime as a way out of their hovels of existence. Still other psychologists believed it was a genetic drive for power and a limited intellect that fed the hunger of anti-social behavior. Christian believed it was a little of everything with a spiritual component thrown in for good measure.

Flipping the Clist file, she began to read the diagnostic report. A thorough document presented to the court for sentencing of a juvenile to a state institution, a diagnostic report told the social history, academic and psychological studies, familial issues and any other impairments or environmental factors that could contribute to a crime. Reading feverishly, she retrieved information about the juvenile's early upbringing, including his birth and subsequent toddler years, his siblings' birth order, his extended family member interactions, the church involvement and his academic and athletic prowess. There were two incidents in elementary school, which were notable. One told of Brandon at age six on the playground. He had persuaded a younger child, a little girl from the morning kindergarten class, to hide with him in the grove of trees known at Amon Elementary as 'the nature area'. A 'duty' had found them. Both of the children's pants were off and Brandon was 'humping' her. According to the school records, the little girl was hysterical afterwards and the boy was sent home for the rest of the week for a 'cooling off' period.

The report indicated that Clist had struggled with bed-wetting as a child, otherwise known as enuresis, and was prone to fire-starting. At the age of ten, he'd started a fire in the field next door to his parent's home and had nearly burned the house down by the time the fire department had put out the blaze. She shivered as she thought about the profiling of serial killers. He lacked one distinct behavior, animal torture, but then again, perhaps he had never been caught.

In the next minute, the court buzzer sounded, indicating that the afternoon docket was about to begin. Frantically, she pushed the file back onto the shelf. Her first appearance was third on the list, unless of course, the defense attorneys played their game of docket bingo.

* * *

"Would you stop the tapping?" Stella complained in a harsh whisper to Christian the following morning. The younger probation officer couldn't sit still, especially after reading Brandon's file. She felt certain now that he was involved in his sister's death. As they waited in a full courtroom for the judge to enter, Christian glanced at the crowd. The moderately sized room, decked out in pale harvest gold paint with finely hewed maple benches and a raised circular ceiling in the middle, was filled to capacity. Over sixty occupants as well as the several staff sat chatting quietly. A long bench along the south wall held fifteen young prisoners, all appearing as though they'd just woken up from a long winter's nap.

Miasma, whose legal name was Thomas Witherspoon, sat on the bench with a benign if not somewhat ridiculous look on his face. He appeared completely nonplussed by his arrest. The detectives had found him at home. His father, a former Vietnam vet, was obliging when the officers knocked on his door. When they asked to see Thomas's room, the man led them down a filthy hallway and into a space that was more closet than bedroom. In the corner, fairly well hidden, was a large bong pipe. Detective Divinity just happened to trip on a pile of clothing which in turn, causing the pipe to tip over and crash to the linoleum. As a result, they were able to arrest Thomas on a possession of drug paraphernalia charge.

The prosecutor from Franklin County called his case next and Thomas shuffled over to the defense table from the wooden bench, lined with several kids who had been brought in the night before. He winced as though his shackles had been put on too tightly.

The judge asked if he knew his charges. Thomas didn't reply, but instead shrugged and looked at his defense attorney in confusion. His attorney, Calden French, was fresh out of law school and with limited experience, started in, giving a soliloquy on the injustice nature of the arrest. Most of the time, kids with misdemeanor charges weren't arrested and brought to detention.

However, in this case, the prosecutor had personally called the judge, requesting that Thomas be held on a $1,000 bail due to the fact that he may also be implicated in the Whitney Clist murder. In the meantime, Thomas's father was willing to assist the prosecutor's office, turning over the family computer. However, according to the county computer geek, nothing of consequence was found. The laptop had been purchased only the week before.

Christian's agitation was contagious. Stella was right. She needed to relax. She could hardly wait to talk to Thomas and was sorely disappointed when she heard that the kid's father had asked about obtaining bail. Distraught, she turned over her list of questions for the boy to the prosecutor, hoping that a polygraph would be administered, though the kid's defense attorney would undoubtedly fight it.

Finally Christian's client was called up. She was quick on her feet, and polite, which was enough to convince Judge Stanzik to let her compulsive thief, Vanessa Maxwell, also a mother of two toddlers, out of jail.

By the time she'd returned to her office, Daniel was back from his meeting. He was typing a probation violation report as she began to explain the latest information from Brandon Clist's file.

"Listen, Daniel!" Her voice was tight with frustration. "Brandon molested a bunch of girls, possibly including Whitney before he was found guilty of sex crimes, so why wouldn't he do it again? Supposedly he is on a mission for the church. I don't believe it and I'll tell you why. Doug said that the church would not send sex offenders into the field. It's like hiring a recovering alcoholic to be a bartender. Talk about easy access to kids. Convince some lonely single mother that she needs the father church, woo your way into her spiritually-impoverished heart, and eventually into her trusting child's bed. No, Brandon is not on a mission. His parents are attempting to keep parole off their backs. They told Joe Stuart over at parole that the kid was sent to Indonesia to spread the good word. I call bullshit. They are lying through their holier-than-thou teeth."

Daniel heaved a sigh of surrender. "Okay. I can see that I'm not going to get any work done until we clear this up. When was the last time we played good cop, bad cop anyway? What time is the appointment?"

"I told Mrs. Clist that I'd be over around four today." Christian tossed her head passionately, her azure eyes ablaze with determination.

"Alright, I'll go with you. By the way, I've already left a message for Joe Sliver. I'm one step ahead of you, Ms. Vargas."

"What for?"

Daniel rolled his eyes dramatically. "I think we might be able to get the prosecutor to close out his probation if he does me a favor. Also, he might know where to find that little graffiti freak, Lobos. And I thought you wanted my help!"

* * *

"The container didn't have much residue, but what was there matched Whitney's blood. I don't know how much there was to begin with, but in checking the medical examiner's report for a second time, she appeared to be more dehydrated than an ordinary corpse. I thought it might have been due to her pregnancy or her health in general, but now I'm wondering if the blood loss was a factor in her death. The loss was substantial, based on her levels, but the wound didn't appear to be the reason. Now I wonder if she didn't lose all of that blood another way. I didn't mention it to you before, but she had a lot of scars. It's pretty typical of a sexual abuse survivor. By the way, how's the kid?'

"Harry, he's a mess. They put him in isolation this time. He tried to kill himself the last time he was in here, so when they brought him in to prepare for the polygraph, he was put in one of the cages near master control. He's scared and miserable. I asked Lisa Monahue to spend some extra time with him, just to calm him down."

The crime lab techie mumbled something, which sounded as though he'd put his hand over the phone. Then he let out a whoop. "There's something else I need to mention. The fetus DNA is a match."

"What do you mean?" Christian held the phone close to her head as Michael sauntered into her office and threw a pile of new cases on her desk. Grinning with fake encouragement, she gave him a thumbs-up. With a wink of satisfaction, he trudged out.

"I'll give you the kindergarten version. Based on the way this thing reads, the fetus had the same grandmother as the vic, indicating that one of her brothers is more than likely the father. Fortunately for us, one of Whitney's brothers is on file. I took your suggestion and had the lab check the fetus's DNA against Brandon's DNA. It's the only thing that makes scientific sense."

"And?" Her anticipation grew like an athlete's energy on steroids.

"At least according to the first DNA comparison, some of the characteristics of the fetus's DNA are similar to Clist's. However the sample has possible contamination, so...."

"So say it wasn't contaminated, or we can get another sample. Explain to me how this DNA thing works."

Christian, as always, wanted more. "DNA is a strange and magical science. Saliva, blood, semen, even hair follicles tell us about the person's unique characteristics, unless of course the person is an identical twin. Then it gets tricky. But say in this case, this is not the case. The issue still stands, however. Perhaps we can prove beyond a doubt that Whitney's unborn baby was fathered by her twisted brother. Still, that doesn't place him at the scene, nor do we have a murder weapon with his fingerprints and her blood. Note that I didn't say, individual DNA exclusively. They could have both held the weapon, but without her blood, it is useless to us."

"Even her blood could be useless. I mean, without the weapon, we're nowhere, right?"

"Well done, Watson. There is always a fight for who can prove what. Usually the smartest lawyer wins. Ever thought of becoming one?"

"And have to strut my stuff? Forget it." Christian could hardly do court testimony without getting sweaty. "What about motive? He might have wanted to kill her if he thought she was a threat. He's still on parole with the State of Washington."

Harry chuckled. "Ah, but the state of Washington does not extradite juveniles and rarely adults on juvenile matters. If she ran into her brother, say, while on the run, and he raped her."

"Okay, so your theory, if it's correct, is that he raped her, she threatened to report it, he got scared and just lost it."

"Yeah, but only because of this strange DNA outcome. In the meantime, I'm stuck on how Clist got the money to race back and forth from Indonesia to kill his sister!"

"Because he's not in Indonesia. I have called every bishop and Mormon top dog I can find. A few have talked to me. Doug had his brother make some calls, too. There is no record of Brandon going on a mission. His parents either don't know where he is, or they are covering for him." Christian paused, allowing her thought processes to define her instincts. After a long minute of silence, she added, "So assuming that she didn't threaten him with the rape or pregnancy, what would have been his motive, just for theory's sake."

A second long silence followed. Finally Harry asked quietly, "Have you ever heard of catathymic crisis?"

"No, but I can look it up."

"I'm sure you will, but to save you time, please allow me to impart my wisdom. It can occur during a murder when the perp is in a dissociative state and has a freaky, but intimate relationship with his vic."

"Go on." Christian felt the thrill of new knowledge hedging its way into her brain.

"Here, I looked it up: *a sudden release of emotionally-charged psychic conflict and tension resulting in extreme violence in an interpersonal relationship.* Wow! That's a mouthful. You know, I don't get to talk much in this job. It's nice to be able to communicate about…"

"Okay," she interrupted impatiently. "So what you're saying is that Whitney and her brother had this twisted relationship and he got a charge, literally, out of hurting her, sexually or otherwise. Obviously, if this is correct, the last time was truly the last time."

"Yeah, basically. We don't have any other evidence. If that kid killed her, he learned a thing or two in prison about evidence. Do you know much about Brandon Clist?"

"Not a lot, though I did pull his social file and read a bit of it. His psychological assessment was very interesting. His I.Q. score was 145. He was an excellent athlete and very popular with students and teachers. That being said, he didn't win any awards at church."

"Seriously?"

"From everything that I've read and seen, Brandon Clist despised the Mormon Church. There wasn't any record of his attendance to seminary, which is generally a mandatory high school class for LDS kids. I also talked to a friend of mine who teaches at Chiawana High School. He told me that when the youth was in his social studies class, he did several papers on the church. Most of the time, the punk ridiculed it, but one paper in particular extolled the virtues of a former practice of the church."

"Let me guess…polygamy." Harry's voice had taken on disgusted tone.

"You've got it. But I think there's more to it. I think there was a secret war going on between the boy and his father."

"And the territory in question?"

"Whitney." Just then Christian glanced up from her desk. Her boss, Michael was back. "Got to go. I'll call you later."

Michael had his hands on his pudgy hips. A dark scowl had formed on his otherwise placid face. "What is this I hear that you are going down to Utah to find yourself a compound?"

"Who told you that?" Christian winced as the heat of embarrassment burned her cheeks. She was dreadful at hiding her feelings.

"Oh, just some little gossiping birdie around here. I am prohibiting you from any crazy joyrides, do you understand? I know what you're up to."

Annoyed, the probation officer took a deep breath. Use tact, she reminded herself. "Michael, don't worry. I'm just going down to Bryce Canyon to do some hiking and enjoy the scenery. If I come across a commune or compound, whatever, you'll be the first to know."

Faust sputtered and fumed, like a mini-volcano trying to decide if eruption was the choice of the day. "I'll be the first to know? Just promise me you'll take a weapon along. You don't know what or who is down there. I keep thinking about that crazy fool polygamist, what's his name?"

"Warren Jeffs?" Christian was surprised that her boss had found her wavelength.

"Yeah, that guy. I have a second cousin who lives near Colorado City. He thinks that guy is the devil incarnate."

"I assure you that I'll be safe. I'm going with a couple of friends and they wouldn't let a mosquito near me if they could help it."

With Michael out of the way, Matt nearly convinced, and the new evidence that Harry had verified, Christian was on a roll. According to her sources, the detectives on the case were in a spin. They had hoped that Whitney's baby was Cole's and had reduced his motive to a lover's quarrel. That had immediately changed when Harry's lab had expedited the DNA tests and it was clear that Brandon Clist could be the father to the unborn child. Now Cole's motive was scrapped. Furthermore, the word from Lisa was that nothing else had turned up as a result of the polygraph. The kid thought that Cancer and Whitney could be related, but since he'd never met the man, he was only speculating. What they knew was that the two kids were friends, that Whitney had spent time at Cole's home and that sometime during her stay, her blood ended up on the carpet. That wasn't enough for a murder conviction.

Christian had a gut feeling that if Clist was hiding down in Utah, Stephanie may be a hostage by proxy. She'd tried to talk to Cole's attorney about it, but his counsel had interrupted her as she sat near the cage where her client was trying desperately to keep his less-than-appetizing institutional lunch down. "I'll pull you into court for interference," the young buck of a defense attorney had threatened. She'd estimated that he was no more than twenty-six or so himself, fresh out of law school and the world of late night studying and even later night casual sex.

"The last time I checked, supervising my client is not against the law," she'd countered in the haughtiest tone she could muster. Nonetheless, Cole was now off limits and so there was nothing more to do on the case besides interviewing the Clists. Even that was pushing the envelope. Stephanie's mother had never returned her calls. From the word on the street, she was living in a drug house on 3rd Street on the eastside, a section of Pasco that was known for its gangs and drug dealers. Christian wasn't interested in searching the woman out, particularly without police escort.

CHAPTER 9

Lupe 'Lobos' Aguilar was small for his age, but he had been born with an artist's hand and a rather large male part and for that, he was proud. He had been on the run for nearly eight months, and in that time he'd slept with over fifteen women. Some were old enough to be his mother, though in all fairness, his mother was only fourteen when he was born. Still, he had never had another woman like Whitney Clist. She was experienced for her age in a strange sort of way. She knew exactly what he wanted, when he wanted it and how he wanted it. She knew enough about oral sex to put Heidi Whatshername to shame. He didn't have to please her, either. He was not always in control of his enormous power tool and sometimes he would come unexpectedly. Whitney acted as though he'd won a freaking metal when that happened and would simply start all over again. He missed her.

They hadn't gone out long, but not because her brother had threatened him. No way. The letter that she'd shown him was nothing to a gangbanger like him. His homeboys would crush Brandon so fast that he wouldn't know what hit him. In fact, a few phone calls had taken care of it. While in the prison, Mr. Clist had been buggered more than once by the boys in the hood. They needed some action, too, and a lily white, child-molesting jerk-off like Clist deserved it.

Lobos, as he preferred to be called, heard sirens and anxiously pulled the curtains away from the small window to look out. The basement was a good place to hide. He only went out at night and only then if he absolutely had to. His friend, Joe Sliver, had warned him to keep out of sight, especially now that Whitney was dead. Still, he knew some information that the cops might want. He had the license plate number of the guy in the blue truck. When the older man had grabbed Whitney in the restaurant parking lot, Lobos had frozen with fear. She was screaming as the O.G. threw her in the truck and drove away. He'd written the number down, though.

The kid was tired of being cooped up. A gangster could only play so much Halo. The apartments were not far from the church where Whitney had been found. Something in him stirred. She deserved a proper send-off from her best lay. Compulsion overruled his logic as he glanced around the cramped space. A couple of cans of spray paint sat on a high shelf near the electrical panel. Tonight he would paint something worthy of the lovely girl with the golden hair. Then he'd call that probation chick, just like Joe advised. He'd give her the Utah license plate in exchange for a 'get out of detention free' card.

* * *

The house was enormous. It looked like something out of the television program, *The Rich and the Famous*. Mr. Clist was a well-known real estate developer. He hadn't skimped on the house. It was nearly ten thousand square feet and rumored to have an indoor Olympic size pool in the basement. The grounds looked like a mini-version of the gardens of Versailles. Apparently the residents had green thumbs or a lot of help.

Daniel and Christian drove up the long driveway and parked a few feet away from the front doors. The home's palatial entrance was marked with tall Grecian columns. Two larger-than-life bronze lions guarded the entrance, both with video cameras installed in their ferocious-looking heads.

From where the house stood, the entire Tri-Cities lay at their feet. Perched on the highest bluff in Franklin County, the elegant home offered sweeping views of the snow-capped Blue Mountains to the east to the Washington State University campus and the historical Hanford Reach to the west. Across the Columbia River, new construction marked the hillsides of Kennewick. Like patchwork quilts, the burgeoning neighborhoods capitalized on space between vineyards and orchards. Over time, much of the rural land had given in to commercial development of some kind. New home growth was at the highest level in the area's history, particularly with the influx of immigrant populations. Pasco, once a town dominated primarily by African Americans, was now called Little Mexico by some. For several decades, the industrious Latinos had labored in the potato fields, fruit orchards and grape vineyards. Over time, they had proven their worth and in turn, had prospered by sheer determination and cultural pride.

Christian rang the doorbell. Chimes echoed from behind the door like a Sunday Service call. When no one answered immediately, Christian walked away from the front door and down a path that led to an enormous fountain and reflecting pool. Longingly, she gazed at the Columbia River as it snaked lazily across the horizon. She narrowed her vision to where it met the Yakima River at the cluster of inlets known as the Yakima Delta. From where she stood, the rise in land below was barely visible from her modest abode. It wouldn't be long until kayaking season, she reminded herself with an indulgent smile.

Eventually Patty Clist opened the door. A startled expression marked her small features. High, arched eyebrows contributed to the overall impression, but it was the sadness in her eyes that bore the brunt of the image. She was a lonely-looking woman, and had good reason to be, Christian thought as she reached out her hand to clutch the woman's delicate one. Mrs. Clist nodded furtively as the younger woman introduced Daniel. Then she turned and beckoned them inside.

"Would you like some tea?" the woman asked nervously as they circumvented a life-sized bronze statue of Jesus which stood in the middle of the marble-wrapped vestibule. Following her into a living room that was the size of a school gymnasium, Christian replied, "No thanks," as Daniel simultaneously replied, "That would be nice." They sat down on the plush powder blue leather sofa to wait.

As the lady of the house scurried away into the bowels of the mansion, Christian gave her handsome partner a dirty look. "I wasn't interested in having a tea party today."

"This is not about tea, my dear," he retorted briskly, standing up and rubbing his hands together. "This is about you and me taking a good look around. She will be a few minutes, which gives us some spy time. I'll check the study, or library, whatever you call those rooms in rich people's homes. It's off to the right as we came in. Hopefully I can find something that might tell us where Brandon is hiding out. You're my cover. If she comes back, tell her I went looking for a toilet. In the meantime, check out that wall of photographs." He pointed behind her to a wall that was nearly thirty feet long. On it were clustered what appeared to be family photographs and other personal memorabilia.

With a sly wink, he slipped away.

The gigantic room was stiflingly hot, despite the height of the ceiling. Christian pulled off her jacket and dropped it on the sofa. Then she wandered over to the wall as her partner had suggested. The first thing that she noticed was the number of children in the professional photographs. She counted at least nine offspring. In most of them, the children were identically arranged. The first-born boy appeared to have Down's syndrome. He was always standing or sitting next to his mother. Next to him was a girl who was evidently the second born. Unlike her blonde mother and sisters, she was dark-haired and rather homely. Clearly she had her father's features. Mr. Clist had a David Letterman-like chin, which the poor girl had obviously inherited. Near to the mother's cluster were three babies, who eventually became toddlers and then youngsters as the photos progressed through time. Of the three, two were twin red-headed, freckled-faced boys. The youngest boy was no more than five at the time the last picture was taken. On the opposite side of each group sitting was the patriarch's cluster.

Next to their stern-looking father were Brandon, Whitney and two younger girls. From the looks of it, the children were born approximately every two years. In each photo, Brandon was the most captivating. Handsome, with a sparkle in his eye, he stood out from the rest.

Whitney was the prettiest of the girls. Tall, willowy and fine-featured like her mother, she had apparently been the apple of her father's eye. Inevitably, in every image, he was touching her in some way, whether holding her as a baby to his hand on her knee in the last picture where she had become a beautiful young woman. It was a perplexing observation and perhaps not one to miss.

Amongst the family photographs were several awards and recognition plaques. Brandon was the Clist clan's athlete. From an early age, he was the best T-ball player, the most valuable soccer goalie, the football coach's most improved. There were several pictures of the boy and his father after the hunt. A huge, dead elk lay at the small boy's feet in one photograph. His wide-toothed grin said more to bloodlust than to childhood pride. Like a poster boy for Hitler's perfect Aryan race, his appearance was remarkable. As early on as Brandon's kindergarten class picture, one could see the signs of the handsome man in his square jaw, high cheekbones and pale blue eyes. However, unlike the other children, his name did not appear amongst the church recognitions. Many of the other children were listed as LDS choir members, youth group leaders and ward volunteers.

The most evident of all was the lack of any awards for Whitney. Yet when Christian recalled the girl's juvenile case notes, the girl had garnered a long list of accomplishments. She had been a Natural Helper at Lewis and Clark High School, a Homecoming Princess, a player on the junior varsity volleyball team and an ASB officer during her freshman year. Why had the family refused to acknowledge her? Christian wondered if they had removed her plaques due to her death in short order, though the wall didn't appear as though pictures had been moved or replaced.

Then a frightening possibility dawned on her. After her disclosure about her brother's sexual abuse to the police, was it possible that Whitney had become the family pariah? Had the girl's relocation to Utah been a means of banishment rather than an act of protection? Disgusted in more ways than she could count, Christian looked around helplessly, feeling sick to her stomach. Like so many dysfunctional families, this one had an elephant in the living room and, considering the enormity of the space, perhaps there was a herd of them.

She nearly jumped out of her skin at the man's greeting. From another hallway that she hadn't noticed, an older man had appeared. Dressed in a pair of designer jeans and a crew-neck polo, Mr. Clist was nearly unrecognizable in comparison to his television appearance. He was very youthful with a masculine glow that couldn't escape the average woman's awareness. "Hello, young lady. May ask what you are doing in my home?" Though his tone challenged, his droll smile indicated something else entirely.

Her mouth felt full of sand as she spit out a ragged introduction.

"I'm Christian Vargas, I was at Whitney's funeral where I briefly met you." Where was Daniel? She panicked, trying to interpret the father's fathomless calm, knowing that her partner was probably rifling through the man's private belongings somewhere else in this magnificent abode.

"Ah, yes, I remember you now." He didn't take his eyes of the probation officer, though in that moment, his wife entered the room with a silver tray.

"Oh, I didn't know you were home," Mrs. Clist stuttered, nearly dropping the tray in her nervous surprise at seeing her husband.

"I was just leaving. I had to pick up some paperwork before I head over to the stake house. Nice to see you again, Ms. Vargas. Please, if you are here on police business, don't upset my wife. She is rather fragile." With that, he turned without acknowledging his better half, disappearing from whence he came.

The homemaker carefully set the tray on the coffee table. On it were several cups, a teapot, a plate of cookies and other accoutrements. Christian swallowed hard, praying that Daniel had also heard Mr. Clist's interruption. As she started to explain his absence, her partner stepped easily back into the room.

"Just had to get my notebook," he said with a beaming smile. Glancing briefly at Christian, he gave the slightest nod. She was bewildered as to how he had forgotten it earlier.

"I hope this is suitable. I don't make tea very often. You know, we don't consume caffeine. It is against the church rules. But I always keep a little tea on hand, in case we have guests such as you." She poured the tea and offered cream and sugar. Christian wasn't a fan, and so took her offer seriously, dumping several teaspoons of sugar in the dark brew, along with a hefty portion of cream. As they settled down, Mrs. Clist surreptitiously glanced toward the hallway where her husband had emerged. Her nerves seemed frayed, but eventually she appeared to relax.

Taking that as a cue, Daniel began. "Mrs. Clist, we know this is a terrible time for you, but as you can imagine, we are deeply concerned with the whereabouts of your daughter's friend, Stephanie Patterson. She went missing the same time as Whitney and has not been seen since. Stephanie is on our caseload and has been placed on warrant status. Unfortunately our warrants are not active across state lines. In other words, we have no jurisdiction outside of Washington State. We were told that she followed Whitney to Utah sometime last fall. If you could give us some assistance as to where the girls were, perhaps we can find Stephanie. We are not only seriously worried about her welfare, but also believe that she may have some pertinent information regarding your daughter's untimely death."

A deafening silence ensued. The overwrought woman appeared as though she were going to cry. Her eyes became cloudy and her chin dropped precariously toward her chest.

After several moments, she took a deep breath, lifting her head. "What I am about to say must be kept anonymous. If my husband finds out that I have told you this, he will…" she paused and gave a slight shudder. "… he will be gravely disappointed in me. He's convinced that Whitney was mixed up with drugs and that someone of *that* world killed her. I'm not saying that I disagree with him. I knew that my daughter and her friend were seen back here by one of my son's friends around Christmas time. I tried to call the Sliver boy, Joe, who was a friend of Whitney's and always someone she trusted." Her body slumped forward and she began to cry in earnest. Christian leaned toward her and gently placed a hand on the woman's shoulder. "I told my husband we shouldn't send her to our family."

"I'm so sorry. We didn't intend to bring up these terrible memories."

Mascara darkened her cheeks as she replied, "No, it's something I'm getting used to. Still, I don't want Whitney's death to be forgotten. I want the killer found. I want him to pay for this."

Daniel didn't miss a beat. "We were wondering about one more thing, Mrs. Clist." Christian shook her head as though to stop his questioning, but he just ignored her.

"I read in the paper that your son is on a mission in Indonesia. Funnily enough, I have a close friend in the church who later told me that couldn't be possible, due to the nature of his juvenile criminal history. I'm aware that Brandon is an adult now and you aren't expected to keep tabs on him, however, if you are aware of his whereabouts, it would help clear up any doubts as to his involvement."

Mrs. Clist's features twisted, becoming an ironic reflection of Brandon's angry photograph taken when he was first brought into custody. "We don't know where he is. He has not been in contact with us since his release from juvenile prison. That ruined our son. He was never the same after being sent up."

"So he's not on a mission, nor in Indonesia?" Daniel pressed on.

"We don't know. He talked about going over there, to Thailand, Indonesia...I don't know. We think he sold his truck to pay for an airline ticket, but we can't be sure. My husband mentioned that he had wanted to go on a mission, but that the courts had ruined his chances for that a long time ago."

Then, as stoic as a foot soldier, the woman steadied herself and glanced at her watch. "Now if you will excuse me, I need to pick up the boys. They are done with soccer practice in a few minutes." She rose, somewhat awkwardly and they did the same.

Once they'd turned down Taylor Flats and headed onto the highway, Daniel reached into his pocket and using his nails to avoid fingerprints, pulled out an envelope. "I know; I'm bad! But I didn't have time to write down the address. Besides, I left the letter behind. When and if we get a search warrant, I know exactly where I hid it, too."

Christian grabbed a pair of leather gloves from her purse and slipped them on. Gingerly, she smoothed out the crumbled piece of paper and looked at the upper right corner. There, in a scribbled script, was an address: 10023 NW PR 2, Cannonville, Utah.

"PR stands for private road," he interjected, his beaming grin nearly blinding with pride.

* * *

Brandon Clist watched the two probation officers leave his home from the upstairs bedroom window. He couldn't believe that the female was the one who Comely had pointed out that day when he was leaving court. The twenty-something woman was beautiful, he thought, rubbing his crotch softly. Even though he was considerably younger, Brandon looked like an older man than his twenty years. Juvenile prison had done that to him. Besides, he had always had a fantasy to be with an older woman. Maybe he could convince her to go out on a date before he killed her. He had scored some roofies just for that sort of thing.

Brandon was too smart to show himself at his parents' home, which is why he'd not gone downstairs. The young man was certain he'd seen the male probation asshole before, so he didn't want to face a shakedown in front of his mother. Those bastards are as bad as cops, he thought, remembering that he hadn't touched based with his parole officer in a few weeks. Still, he'd told the guy he was working a lot at his family's ranch north of town. Officer Pledge had checked up on him twice and each time he'd been there, though the last time, he'd been sent to his first mission overseas. That was why he'd refused to accompany Mel to the beach house the month prior. He knew that his sister was going down, but she'd deserved it as far as he was concerned. She'd turned him in and had threatened to turn in Mel, so she'd lost her place on the planet. Oh well. He just wished that his mother wasn't so sad over the whole thing.

Brandon reclined on his bed and began to pleasure himself. Stroking with increasing speed, he laughed aloud to think how the Mormon's creed had been crammed down his throat and backfired. When they told him that he couldn't have sex until marriage, he'd found another reason to rebel against the vise grip codes of the LDS. Having sex with under-aged girls became his game just after he'd turned thirteen. His first conquest was a ten year old, though one who'd clearly started to develop. After that, he knew how to make little adolescents squirm at the sight of him and it had been easy, but not often enough. His solution was to move on to the kids, both boys and girls, that he'd babysitted when he was in his middle teens. That was when one of them squealed to Whitney and she'd called the cops. He grunted, frustrated by his memory of that day. There would be no getting off this afternoon.

* * *

The phone was ringing as she entered their office a few minutes later. Glancing down, she noticed it was Dave Wilson, a friend from college who'd gone on to become a bigwig in the Oregon State Department of Corrections. She'd called him a few days before, asking that he do a little research for her. Dave had learned that according the country records for Seaside, there was a beachfront cottage owned by a G. M. Clist and G.T. Clist. They had owned the cabin since 1996. For two years, it was listed as a rental property, but after 1999, it was pulled off that market. Property taxes were current. Dave had done her a big favor when he'd gone to the property to see if he could find out anything about the owners. A neighbor was working in his yard when Dave had arrived and had eagerly shared the fact that a young man had been living in the home for several months during late 2006. He said that he'd talked to one of the Clist brothers, who owned the property, about the new resident, and the man had vouched that the youth was his son. No, there hadn't been any suspicious activity, however one weekend near Christmas, the house had been full of visitors, though the neighbor had been hosting a holiday reunion and hadn't paid much attention to the comings and goings there.

Throwing down her bag, she grabbed the phone. "Hey Dave, how are you?"

"Great considering it hasn't stopped raining in two weeks! How's the investigation going?" Her friend's warm tenor voice coursed with curiosity.

"It's strange. I can't seem to convince anyone that the girl's brother might have had something to do with the murder. But my hunches are often the subject of ridicule around here."

"Don't be so hard on yourself. I talked to the gal who works at the local gas station just down the road from the Clist cottage last night. She said a young man had been living at the house back in early November and had come in to buy supplies. She admitted to selling him beer, though he was underage. She also said an older man came in with him a few times. She figured the guy might have been his older brother, they looked so much alike. Then one day, the younger guy came in with a girl. The clerk said that she was very upset and looked like she'd been crying. She asked if the store sold HPTs." There was a pause.

"Home pregnancy tests?"

"I guess. The customers were pretty pissed off with one another, arguing as they left."

"Did she see the vehicle that they were driving?"

"Apparently there was a man waiting in a blue truck. They took off and she never saw any of them again."

"Do they have a security camera in the store?"

Dave let out a hoot of laughter. "Honey, this is the beach, the Oregon beach. Try Carmel for cameras. You're lucky to get a farting old Labrador sitting on the front porch when it comes to security around here."

She laughed and thanked him, promising that she and Matt would come back for a visit in a few months. They'd had a great time with him and his wife during their last trip.

CHAPTER 10

She stood on the patio, gazing out at the large flowerbed that bordered the west side of her yard. Gritty and battered from a vicious dust storm the night before, a cluster of forlorn-looking rose bushes leaned eastward, buffeted by a brisk breeze. They would need a pruning before too long. Severed branches, stubbly tumbleweeds and other debris from the high winds littered the yard. Though a dull sun had risen, a haze of dust filled the sky, striping the hills beyond with a fuzzy golden glow.

A dense shroud of exhaustion enveloped her. With each breath, she felt suffocated by an invisible foreboding. The night had been endless and sleep, a forgotten calling. Glancing in the big picture window behind her, she saw the pale reflection of a woman in dire need of rest and relaxation. Puffy eyes gazed back at her. Her tangled hair begged for a good conditioning, but instead, on the kitchen counter, a box of alternative hair color awaited the wavy mane. Sighing, she stretched her arms over head and inhaled deeply, hoping to gain some clarity.

Christian had to admit, Matt's argument was nothing if not sensible. They had fought for most of the evening prior over her choice to go to Utah. He thought she was crazy to go, especially without a decent back-up plan in place. He scolded her for her obstinate attitude, begging her to consider the consequences should she fail. In the end, she had slept in the spare bedroom, but his persuasive cajoling had left its mark. She knew, without a doubt, that she had to talk to the county's prosecuting attorney before taking the chance of going out on her own. At least a thorough explanation of her findings might motivate his department to take action through appropriate channels.

According to Matt, she was a drama junkie. He'd accused her of acting out of her realm of expertise, thereby placing the entire investigation at risk. He hadn't back down, citing a litany of possible risks, including her own death should she find herself confronting a murderer. She had waved him off, stomping angrily out of the room when he finally accused her of being selfishly single-minded.

In truth, she hated his uncanny ability to see beyond her impulsivity. And it hurt that he was right about her motives. She did get a sort of adrenaline-stoked high from the drive to rescue. Matt had explained patiently, after she'd melted into tears, that he was speaking out of love and concern. At some point, she'd agreed that he was right in calling her out on her reckless nature. Yet she also felt as though his rational and cautious temperament squashed a part of her spirit, much like Tony's critical nature had done for so many years. She had never admitted to anyone that a few months after her husband's death, a soothing sense of freedom began to thrive within her. Despite her devastating loss, the young woman was no longer hesitant to take action for fear that she be told 'the proper way to do things'. Tony had been a browbeater, though only a few close friends knew of his tendency to repress those whom he loved the most. Now despite his good intentions and gentler approach, Matt's own form of repression had started to take its toll. She often wondered if staying single wasn't the best life path for her.

Her theories and subsequent investigation had by no means provided solid answers. According to Harry, the prosecutor's office had basically squashed Whitney's pregnancy as a motive for murder. Furthermore, the DNA evidence was not being seriously considered, due to the fact that the reliability of the science was still somewhat questionable. Though the tests pointed to the possibility of Brandon's paternity, there was no proof that he'd been in Washington when the murder occurred. Meanwhile, his whereabouts remained unknown. However, she had the address found at the Clist residence, which might lead them to the juvenile offender. The means aside, even Matt had agreed that Harry's theory on Brandon's motive to kill his sister seemed to have some merit.

Meanwhile, a friend who managed the local cemetery had called the mortuary and made some inquiries on Christian's behalf. According to Homer Thale, the LDS elder who owned and managed Thale Mortuary Services, his son and another employee had reported seeing a couple of young men in a blue pick-up parked outside the stake house when they delivered Mrs. Stanford's body the afternoon prior to her funeral. Mark Thale had thought he'd recognized one of the men in the truck from high school, but couldn't be sure. Unfortunately he had failed to report that part of his recollection to the police.

The prosecutor's administrative assistant was a childhood friend of Tony's. Though probation officers normally only interacted with deputy prosecutors, Christian had convinced Tony's schoolmate that she needed to see Osmund J. Rellim as soon as possible. Linda Mars was accommodating, stating that ten-thirty later that morning would be fine.

Christian had brought her working file from home that day, but on the chance that she might anger the prosecutor, decided to leave it behind in her office. There was a line-up at the courthouse when she arrived. The wait to get through the security doors was over ten minutes. As a result, she was late for her meeting with Osmund. He was on the phone when Linda ushered her into his large mauve and brown office overlooking the parking lot.

Hanging up the phone, the prosecutor stood up and extended his hand. Tall and lean, he had a boyish face covered in freckles. The only signs of age were pronounced crow's feet at the corners of his eyes and a slightly receding hairline. "Oz Rellim. What can I do for you," he paused, glancing down at his Daytimer, "Ms. Vargas."

Rellim was known for his hardliner approach to offenders, especially juvenile offenders. He was famous for pushing declines, which was a legal method to insure that juveniles could be tried as adults based on their history and propensity to re-offend. He was a death penalty advocate and had sent more than a dozen men to death row during his twelve years in office. Nevertheless, Mr. Rellim was also known as a party boy and political climber. In a community where conservative mores and good ole' boy fun were considered badges of honor, Rellim had no problem in being re-elected time and time again.

Christian leaned toward him, her hand meeting his. His palm was dry and his handshake firm. An awkward moment prevailed. *Get a grip*, she scolded herself silently. He smiled with approval, his warm brown eyes trailing down her body. Fortunately she'd dressed on a hunch that she'd be meeting the illustrious attorney, known in the juvenile court as, "The great and powerful Oz". It was a tongue-in-cheek reference, having more to do with Rellim's prolific dating life than the number of felons that he'd put behind bars. Though she'd never met him face to face, she'd seen the man innumerable times. There was no doubt that he exuded a sexual aura. She was glad that she'd worn the pearl gray flannel slacks and the indigo blue cashmere sweater. It was a premonition that had paid off, judging by the look of pleasure on Oz's face.

His hand lingered in hers momentarily. She offered a non-committal smile. "It's a pleasure to finally meet you."

Nodding to a chair, he said, "Forgive my manners. Please, sit down." She slipped into the leather Hopewell chair in front of his enormous mahogany desk. He studied her for a moment, closing his tapered fingers and resting his chin on their manicured tips. "Please, share what's on your mind," he encouraged lightly.

Her mind became blustery with indecision as she tried to frame her explanation in way that sounded rational, yet without insinuating department insult. "As you might be aware…" she stopped, frozen as to how to proceed.

Oz Rellim chuckled, clearly entertained by her discomfort. "I don't bite. Just come out with it."

Swallowing hard, she allowed herself a moment. "Mr. Rellim, I've been following the Whitney Clist murder very carefully and I've come across some evidence that appears to have been overlooked by our team of detectives. I don't mean to insult anyone, but..."

Rellim snapped his fingers. "Now I know where I've seen you before other than juvenile court. You were at the Clist crime scene. I've wanted to thank you for your quick thinking. You did an excellent job at keeping the crime scene as clean as possible, taking the names of everyone there and of course, contacting Harry. Now you say that you have some leads. I'm impressed. Let's hear them."

With careful deliberation, Christian began to explain her interview with Mrs. Clist, hinting that the mother might know the whereabouts of her wayward son. At the risk of incriminating herself, she shared her connection to Cole Comely, Joe Sliver, and Whitney's friend, Stephanie. She suggested that since Whitney was pregnant at the time of her murder, perhaps her brother had a motive after all. She inferred that the detectives had not been clear enough with the mortuary employees and suggested that since most young women go to Planned Parenthood for services of a female nature, that the agency may have valuable information.

The prosecutor nodded keenly, his expression one of subtle approval. Occasionally, he jotted down some notes while encouraging her to detail her psychological impressions and motivation theories. Finally, when she had completely exhausted her compendium of considerations, he lifted his hand. "That's quite lot of information. I'm pleased, but I can't help wondering why you are spending so much time on this case. Obviously you have an emotional connection to the girl, or at best a concern for our community at large. However, I can assure you that our office and the sheriff's department will do everything that's required to nail the killer. We have not ruled out the possibility that Cole Comely is involved, and frankly, there are a couple of other suspects who are being investigated as we speak. I'm aware of Mr. Clist's history with this department, but the last report that we received from his parole officer and the JRA staff is that the young man is completely rehabilitated. As a result, he is not a suspect."

"But what about Whitney's pregnancy?" There was a shrill tone to Christian's voice that gave way to embarrassment. She looked down at her hands, attempting to infer equanimity.

"I spoke to Harry. He can't be certain that the DNA test is accurate. Apparently the girl was not very far along. We can't put a lot of stock on that type of testing in early stages of pregnancy. Her DNA and her brother's DNA have similar characteristics, to be sure, because they share the same mother. Unfortunately, and this is not to be repeated, it appears that whoever processed the kid's DNA test back in 2000 made the mistake of mishandling the saliva strip, invalidating the test, at least in a court of law. In other words, the defense would screen that piece of evidence out immediately. That is confidential information and should not leave this room. The bottom line is this: we would have to do further testing to verify that Brandon is truly the father and without him here, we can't do that."

She expected him to dismiss her, but instead, his intelligent eyes met hers as he continued, "Murder in the first degree requires the proof of four distinct elements: willful, deliberate, malicious and premeditated intent. These four must co-exist in order to find a person guilty. We don't know if the murderer intended to kill Whitney Clist. As you know, she suffered a trauma to the head. The person who caused this trauma may or may not have intended on killing her. Accidental death is a consideration. The law presumes malice derives from the use of a deadly weapon and the defendant, should we identify one, has the burden of repelling such presumption. We are careful in this office. Pardon the pun, but I've been burned on this issue more than once. Do you remember the fire on South Garrison Street? It happened a few years back." For the first time, Christian saw humility in the man as he swept his hand over his head in a gesture of contrition.

"I failed that victim. I failed her family. I was determined that the perp had acted with malice, but you see, fire is not necessarily a deadly weapon. The defense was able to convince the jury that the man's drug addiction, not his malice, not his jealousy, rage and psychopathic tendencies, was the reason that house went up in flames. Sara Ellig died a horrible, torturous death, but Jonathan Sutfest appealed, based on that criteria. He was released last month. He served less than five years for manslaughter." The man stood and walked over to the large picture window, looking designer-cool in his Italian silk suit. Christian vaguely wondered how he afforded such clothing. Yet despite Rellim's calm exterior, tension emanated from his slender physique.

Beads of moisture had gathered along the lower edges of the glass and the office temperature was less than pleasant. Christian shivered unexpectedly. The atmosphere seemed to thicken with emotion as Rellim turned back to her, subdued by his admissions. So she wasn't the only one in a cold sweat over this case, she realized.

Outside, the wind had started up and a brewing storm rose on the horizon like a sinister swarm of flies. Rellim took a deep breath. "So you see, I'm careful. I have no witnesses, no murder weapon and some hearsay evidence. And honestly, Christian, for all of your work, and obedience to a greater good, that's all that you have as well."

"Sir, there's one more thing. There's a juvenile named Lupe Aguilar. His gang name is Lobos. Anyway, he and Whitney dated for awhile. According to my partner, he told Joe Sliver that he was with Whitney on January first, at a local fast food restaurant. I believe she was going to tell him about her pregnancy, maybe ask him for help. Anyway, this Lobos kid left me a message right before I got here this morning. He said that they were standing in the Wendy's parking lot when a blue truck drove up. The driver was an older guy, in his mid-twenties or early thirties. Lupe said that as soon as he jumped out of the truck, Whitney began to run. The guy caught up with her and threw her in the truck, and drove away. Aguilar got the license plate number. It had Utah plates. JEF381. I thought maybe we could track down the vehicle and find out who owns it."

Rellim blinked at her, apparently in shock. "Now that's helpful. I will call Detective Divinity immediately. We'll find out who owns this vehicle. I'll let you know."

He smiled gently, his face etched with shared compassion. In that instant, she understood why this man had lasted nearly a decade in office. He was human, but could admit his mistakes. He took the law seriously, but moreover, Rellim had a deep, intolerant distain for the wicked. The drive for power aside, Oz Rellim had vision and integrity. If she was going to solve this case, she would have some proving to do.

CHAPTER 11

The following morning, Christian rose early to walk Bear. The day was bright and brisk with the chance of snow showers later in the afternoon. The dog knew that she was leaving by the fact that she'd left her suitcase and a number of traveling items by the front door the night before. He was a nervous wreck as a result. Though Matt had been living with them for nearly a year, the dog was a 'loyal royal', as her lover liked to say and preferred the slender brunette over a man any day. She cooed and cuddled the creature like he was a child and shushed him as she shut the door to his whining.

Matt was talking to Doug through his driver's window as she emerged from the house. She kissed her boyfriend longingly and promised to call often. Waving good-bye as Doug pulled out of the driveway in his beige Pathfinder, she felt like something was broken between them, but she couldn't say why. She cared about Matt, but had begun to wonder about relationships and whether she'd ever truly known love with a man. Her therapist, Sophia, had often said that unresolved issues with fathers led to distrust in adult relationships. Her father was dead. It wasn't his fault, or hers. Yet deep down, Christian knew that she had put her father on a pedestal. He was her hero of mythical proportions and no one, not her high school boyfriend, Chad, her college lover, Sean, or her husband Tony had been given a fighting chance in the face of her adoration for the fireman from Gresham, Oregon.

She smiled one last time. Matt's face appeared both encouraging and dismal, if such a combination was possible. Doug had decided to drive based on the fact that Daniel was prone to road rage and Christian hated highway driving. As though to pacify, he'd reminded Matt that he had been a long haul truck driver before college. Matt chuckled and shook his friend's hand. "Just take care of my girl, that's all I ask."

They had traveled a little over a mile when Christian suddenly threw her hands up. "I can't do it!" She gaped at Doug as though she'd just been asked to commit a crime.

"Do what, girlfriend?" Doug slowed down as they approached an intersection.

"You've got to turn around. We have to bring Bear. He's got skills that we need. *Please!*" With an agreeable nod, Doug spun a U-turn, SUV roaring, as he pulled ahead of a line of traffic and made his way back to her front door.

Several minutes later, after collecting the dog, his lead, food, dish and bed, as well as a forgotten set of walkie talkies, they headed back out towards Daniel's condo which was conveniently on route to the Oregon turnoff. After his divorce, the gregarious probation officer had decided to move into *Columbia Estates*, the area's highly-touted singles townhouses, which not only had the status quo work-out room, swimming pool and tennis courts, but also offered a landlord-sponsored Sunday brunch in the community lodge as well as 'get-to-know-your-single-neighbor' potlucks. Daniel depended on his mother to prepare his weekly dish, but fibbing about his cooking ability hadn't hampered his dating acumen. The cheerful Latino was all smiles as he threw his gear into the back and climbed in the passenger's seat next to Doug.

They spent their first half hour hovering around safe conversations. Daniel was aware of her friend's sexual orientation, but didn't have complete comfort with the subject. Finally Doug broke the ice by saying, "Hey Daniel, you'll be glad to know that I booked individual rooms for us. My buddy works for Best Western corporate. He gave us a sweet deal: three rooms for the price of two all the way down. I figured you wouldn't want to share a room with a fag."

The gay man's self-effacing humor startled the probation officer, but in seconds he had joined in by saying, "I figured you wouldn't want to share a room with a spic, either."

Christian held up her hands, "Would you guys stop already? I get sick of the politically-correct bullshit, too, but really?" The two men grinned gleefully at one another from across the seats.

"I think we should talk about our strategy," she announced purposefully.

"Do we actually have one?" Doug asked, clearing a slower semi-truck as he headed onto the bridge over a wide swath of the Columbia River at the Washington-Oregon border.

"Well, sort of. Daniel, here, *discovered* an address where we think Stephanie might be staying."

"Yet what if the girl isn't there?"

"Then we're out of there as soon as possible. Listen, you don't want to mess with those Sliver boys." Doug cringed. "Assuming they are part of this. To say they are bad dudes is an understatement. Furthermore, if this gang of loser polygamists don't have anything to do with Whitney's death, why not let Stephanie hang out where she chooses?"

Christian nudged her partner. "Tell him what we found out." Soon Daniel had Doug up to speed on the story of their visit to the Clists. By the time he'd finished, and had included their impressions from the family photos, Doug was shaking his head in admiration.

"You guys do some damn good detective work."

Doug paused thoughtfully. "You know, out of all those Sliver kids, Joe was the nicest. He was the youngest of the clan. Jared is next. He must be about twenty-two. James is almost thirty now, if I'm remembering right. Jed would be next, then Jeremiah and finally John. It was James who beat me up more than a few times when we were in our teens. In the end, I think he wanted me."

"Whoa, enough information!" Daniel cried. "So, we hear we'll overnight in Salt Lake City."

"Yeah, I have to drop something off at the Temple, though we had to pull some strings to get that done, me being excommunicated and all. If we haul ass, we can get there by about ten tonight. I may need a driving break, but it's only seven now. We're making good time. Tropic is another five hours from Salt Lake, so I booked one night in Salt Lake in each direction. I've got a week off, so that gives us five days in the Bryce Canyon area. That should be enough time."

"What's the game plan once we get there? How do we get in and out?" Daniel pulled out a notebook, ready to take notes.

Her eyes lit with excitement, Christian tapped the map that lay across her lap. "There it is. The Paria river. So that's our way out."

"What about here?" Daniel pointed to a section on the map where the border seemed to be accessible.

Rummaging around in her papers, his friend pulled out another grainier Google Earth map. "Look at this plateau here." Her voice rose emphatically. "See how steep it is? My friend who lives down there, Juicy, says it's nearly sixty feet above the river, straight up. So, as I was saying, if Stephanie is there, we'll grab her and, if necessary, raft our way out."

Doug shook his head. "You're going to do what?"

"Hasn't she told you? She's a hotshot whitewater kayaker as in 'rock and roll'!" Daniel shivered. "Personally I hate the idea. I'll walk out, unless our friend here wants to pick me up."

"How do you know that Stephanie won't just come with us?" Doug asked, his eyebrows furrowing at the thought of the alternative.

"Stockholm Syndrome." His traveling companions barked simultaneously.

"What, like in the case of Elizabeth Smart?"

Christian nodded. "And Patricia Hearst and others. I know enough about Stephanie's deadbeat family to know that she believes that she has no one. I also read her juvenile log notes. She knew both Jared and Brandon. At one time, she and Jared were dating and it sounded serious, if you can be serious at fourteen. I think she also had a crush on Brandon. There's a picture on the Clist's family wall of a bunch of kids at a youth summer camp. It was probably taken two or three years ago, before the kid was sent up. He has his arm around Stephanie. She looks absolutely smitten."

"What the hell does that mean?" Daniel asked.

Christian rolled her eyes and reached forward to nudge Doug. "Do you see what I'm dealing with? Smitten, as in 'head over heels' as in 'lustfully in love'. It's an old-fashioned English term."

"Yeah, you're talking to a Mexican, sweetheart. Watch your language from now on!" Daniel laughed good-naturedly. He seemed to relish her teasing. The group shared another laugh. So far, things were going nicely, Christian thought as she gazed back down at the map.

"So there is an alternative to the river. Christian can dress up like a Mormon chick and trick them into thinking she wants to join their cult."

"I guess that's one way. I think she has the same thing in mind for you." The driver winked in the rearview mirror at Christian.

"No way. I'm not wearing that ridiculous underwear. My manly parts will suffocate." Daniel's face took on a look of horror.

"I wore it for years and obviously it hasn't stopped me," Doug joked in reply.

Christian cleared her throat. "Now, if the water is too high and we can't get in on the 'we are one of you' gig, maybe we could pretend that the car is broken down. We'll unscrew the distributor cap or take out a spark plug. Then we'll tell them that we are in Bryce to go hiking and we're stuck."

"This doesn't sound half as exciting as the second plan. The more I think about it, the better it sounds. Just think, I'll be posing as your husband. Now I'll really get to boss you around!" Christian took a swipe at Daniel's head.

"Don't get cocky." She immediately regretted her words.

"That's just what I might do." He grabbed her hand mid-air and gave it a kiss.

Watching their antics, Doug smiled knowingly. "Well, it looks like you two will do just fine. By the way, what's my role in this?"

"Driver par excellent and communication expert."

"First long-haul driving man banger to gay hairdresser to polygamist converter! I'm making progress." Daniel added.

"You guys are going to drive me crazy!" Christian closed her eyes to think. "Doug, if we play the victims of anti-polygamists, how do you think these people might react?"

"I don't know. If this clan is as crazy as it might be, anything could happen. I know that if my cousins are living there, you will have to tread carefully. Those guys have radar for anti-Mormons. You can't say anything that doesn't gel with church lingo, or they will see you are frauds immediately. You are going to have to be very, very careful. If you say you are recent converts, it will help. You can play dumb a bit easier. But you have to talk about your conversion. Remember those little Mormon nerds who used to knock on your doors as kids?"

Daniel's laughter filled the car. "When I was high school, a couple of those freaks stopped at the house one day. I was the only one home…rare thing indeed. I wound those kids up for hours. They thought they had me at first. Then I served them lemonade, but I spiked it with my Dad's stash of tequila. Man, those kids were so drunk."

Christian moaned. "You can be so wicked!"

Doug laughed. "Yeah. I was on my mission trip and…."

Christian dialed her phone as the men continued their conversation. Her call was brief. After leaving a message for the company's owner, she asked about the water levels and classification of the Paria River. When she hung up, she released a big sigh. "The water is really rough this time of year. She doesn't recommend rafting until after May 1, but we may have no choice."

Daniel's voice was laced with exasperation. "I thought we were coming down here to catch a killer, not catch our death."

"And rescue a girl." Christian added. "I think that Stephanie is the key to Whitney's murder."

* * *

The next few hours passed quickly. Conversation turned more animated as the coffee kicked in and the group became more comfortable with one another. The route through Oregon was fairly easy and Cabbage Hill, the primary mountain pass, was clear. After a few hours, everyone began to grow a little restless. As Boise came into view, Doug suggested that they stop for lunch. The consensus was immediate.

An hour later, they were back on the highway headed for Idaho Falls. The terrain soon changed. Rolling hills of wheat and farm land became forests of pine, alder and firs. The city of Idaho Falls was primarily populated by LDS church members and Doug had a few relatives who lived there. Dinner was a quick stop for hamburgers. Even Bear got a double whopper.

Finally after nearly seven hundred miles, Salt Lake City came into view. It was a stunning sight. The towering mountains encircled the vibrant city like majestic old crones, sharp-edged and yet serene, silently guarding Brigham Young's Promised Land. Here lived a tenacious people who had been heinously persecuted for their beliefs during a time when America was full of superstition and distrust. Eventually forced from the Midwest in the early 1800s, the Saints came to this place in search of peace and found great prosperity as well.

Christian had done her research, learning that the Mormons were more than just tenacious. This was a people who truly believed that they were the chosen ones. From the Quorum of Twelve came strictly interpreted creeds, gleaned from Joseph Smith's inspirational Book of Mormon.

At a time when the country was uncertain as to its future, where slaves were quietly rising against their oppressors and Indians still roamed the Great Plains, Joseph Smith was charismatic and cunning. He wrote the Book of Mormon as a way of defending Americans' place in the world. The thirteenth tribe of Israel had found its way across a terrible ocean and been rewarded by God. The Golden Tablets, in their strange and indecipherable way, had said so.

When religions were sprouting like sunflower seeds, the Church of Latter Day Saints stood out. It believed in a personal relationship with God, one that was not driven by a priest's blessing, the redemption of the confessional or a rich man's bribing tithing. Originally, plural marriage was just a rumor to the faith, but eventually a publication was released, which was, at one time, sanctioned by the great leader, that talked to the virtue of multiple wives.

According to the Mormon television channel, which specialized in the history of the religion, after Brigham Young had settled the Saints in the land of the Great Salt Lake, his minions began to practice 'the lifestyle'. A fundamental concept, it was backed by scriptures in the Old Testament, just like an eye for an eye or tooth for a tooth. Indeed, Lex Talonis, the Law of the Talon, was a creed by which the sisters and brothers abided. However, such barbaric concepts disturbed the more genteel of Americans. Resistance to polygamy came in the form of brutal attacks and public outcry. Finally after several decades of practicing plurality, the Mormons legally lost their lifestyle. In 1882, the United States government passed first law against the practice of polygamy called the Edmunds Act. Some Mormons abstained while others went into hiding.

With Daniel now at the wheel, Doug directed him into the center of town and eventually to Temple Square. As the glowing white quartz spires of the greatest Temple in Mormon history appeared, the group grew silent. There was no doubt that the building was inspiring even those who refused to believe. As though to welcome them, a statue of the Angel Moroni appeared, his sacred image heralding hope and resurrection. Christian finally found her tongue.

"That is absolutely stunning. It's like something you'd see in Europe. Look at the Gothic influences."

"Absolutely *Goth*!" Daniel replied with a chuckle. "I wondered how many pockets the Saints dipped into to build that thing."

"You are such a cynic," Christian shot back.

Doug shook his head. "You know, he's right. This beautiful example of Mormon faith was financed off the backs of hard-working folks. The expectation for active membership is a ten percent tithing. Plenty of families probably skipped dinner to buy this kind of inspiration."

"If this was your contribution to the world, however small, it's not a bad thing to think about on your deathbed."

"It took forty years to build. I'm sure there were a few dudes left wondering," Doug added. Clearly the only female was outnumbered. She shut her mouth.

As they drove up to the hotel, the weary sun had finally nestled into the surrounding hills for its night's slumber. Christian yawned, yearning for a cup of cocoa and a soft mattress. Tomorrow would be another long day.

* * *

The next morning, Christian got up early with Bear to go for a run around the city. Doug had already departed with the car to take care of his family business and left a message on her cell phone stating that he would be back and ready to hit the road no later than ten. She gave a knock on Daniel's door, but only heard a loud groan, so she set out to explore on her own.

Their hotel was just a few blocks from Temple Square and the morning was surprisingly warm for the mountainous area. Bear was thrilled to be out of the car and hotel room. Her dog trotted briskly beside her, smiling at his newfound freedom while sniffing into the clean air.

She'd always been intrigued by the Great Salt Lake, the largest inland body of salt water in the world. It seemed an anomaly of nature, like the Latter Day Saints themselves. Running toward the south end of the Temple complex, she marveled at the cleanliness and orderly procession of streets. Brigham Young had taken great care in planning the city.

Upon the arrival of the Saints, Young had gathered his Quorum of Twelve and announced that the Temple grounds would encompass forty acres divided into plats with each one of the council members owning an equal portion as their 'inheritances'. Later this decision was changed and ten acres remained upon which sat Temple Square. The city was nearly perfect in its original design, geometrically square and running east to west, though now elegant skyscrapers rose like sentry guards around the nucleus of Brigham's vision.

As they ran passed well-dressed young men and women on their way to work in the busy city, she thought about what she had learned about their faith. Persecuted for believing in the idea that one receives personal revelation from God, the Saints were run out of the Mid-West from Illinois to Missouri. Their homes were burned, their crops ruined and their families attacked. This blatant rejection by American society forced the straggling band of devotees to search west for their promise land. Like the flight of Israelites, they believe their reenactment of the Old Testament was proof of their worthiness and authenticity.

Soon Christian arrived at the west side of the Temple. It was an astonishing display of gardens and statuary, pathways and reflecting pools. She paused to take it all in. Here was something of magnificence and perhaps one of the greatest buildings to rest on American soil. She was truly awestruck by its beauty and didn't want to miss a detail. Wandering through the gardens was allowed and so she took a few minutes to admire the grounds. The winter had been mild and as a result, spring had arrived earlier than usual. Blossoming crab apple trees, early-blooming rosemary bushes and budding patches of tulips and daffodils filled her eyes with life and color.

Returning to the hotel with a happy dog in tow a few minutes later, she showered quickly, left a loving phone message to Matt and gathered her things. The crew climbed into the car for another long drive. This time, Christian was behind the wheel. Six hours later, they drove into the tiny town of Tropic, Utah. The scenery had been breathtaking during the way down to Bryce Canyon, underscoring the fact that the Saints had chosen one of the most pristine places in the world from which to speak their truth.

CHAPTER 12

"The sure sign! You have to know the secret handshake, so they believe you are who you say you are," Doug insisted. They were sitting in a small cafe in Cannonville named Pete's, which boasted of the best homemade pies in Utah. A six-foot high glass cylinder pie tank sat in the middle of the room, spinning slowly. Inside, fluffy white meringues, nearly a half of a foot high, sprang up like snow-covered mountain ranges while deep dish chocolate creams and baked apples created the lowlands of desserts. A long gray Formica-topped bar ran parallel to an open grill which produced excessive amounts of smoke and sound. Disheveled by time, the three world-weary waitresses all looked over sixty. Deep red booths, their patent leather upholstery worn by frequent use, ran the circumference of the small interior. Along the opposite wall from the entrance, a child's mechanical horse, a jukebox and a pin-ball machine were crowded together.

They had already finished their breakfasts of scrambled eggs with hash when Doug, turned in his seat, demonstrating the grip to Christian.

Daniel chuckled. "This reminds me of some Masonic ritual. I had a friend in high school whose Dad was a Mason. That's weird stuff, too."

"People love ritual. It taps into some deep subconscious desire to sit around a fire and chant."

Christian yanked her hand from Doug's. "Those men over there, they're watching us." She put hand up to her face, as if to wipe away a lock of hair as she spoke.

Doug flinched. "Man, this is a trigger for me. I don't care how nice Mormon people seem to be on the outside. I've had the holy shit kicked out of me by brothers just like those dudes. Check out the cowboy spurs on their boots. Bet you've never had one of those things stuck into the side of your calf."

Daniel glared in the men's direction, but got no visible response. Christian kicked him under the table, hoping to avoid a confrontation. Eventually her partner gave up the stink eye and reached into his backpack, pulling out a handful of paper. "I find this on the internet the day before we left. I just forgot about it until now. Look." Stealthily, he shoved a piece of paper toward her. On it were several photographs of two hands in a handshake.

"This is the 'Sure Sign of the Nail'. How do you know that someone is not the devil in disguise? The first token of…" she gave a little cry. "… Melchizedek Priesthood."

"That's how I found it. I've learned the 'Chrissie Google', as I call it."

Daniel glanced at Doug. "You see, if you spend enough time with this crazy girl, here, you will figure that you can find almost anything by Googling it."

"I'm getting the feeling that those kids got their wires crossed. This is a Mormon name, dating back to the Old Testament. I thought you said those kids were devil-worshippers."

Christian glanced up as the tired waitress dropped the check on their table. She grabbed it before the others could respond and slipped from the booth. As she approached the cash register, a beefy-looking rogue came up behind her. She turned slightly, catching his reflection of a greasy mirror which was mounted behind the cashier's area. He looked familiar somehow.

His mouth opened, offering a gleaming smile. "You folks from around here?" At least six foot three, the cowboy wore a dirty pair of dungarees, a leather jacket and a beat-up cowboy hat. He had a chiseled, handsome face, but for the weathered mark of the sun. His two friends had wandered out the door, apparently leaving him to pay.

"Actually no," Christian replied cautiously. "This is a wonderful town, though. We are hiking in Bryce Canyon."

The man stared over at Doug for a long time. Finally he nodded. "Yep. I thought I heard you talking about horseback riding a few minutes ago. We run our own show, you see, and thought you might be interested in checking out our trail rides." He pulled out a business card. It read, 'Harrison Outfitters.'

Christian prayed that her change of complexion didn't give away her carnal thoughts. This man was sending her signals of physical appreciation that she couldn't help but notice. "Hey, that's awesome," she managed.

The cowboy looked back over at her companions and eyed them thoughtfully. "Well, just want to be of help. Lots of people come here and use our competitors. We don't advertise in all the big magazines, but we got the best rates around. We can take you up the Paria River. It borders our land. You go right at the end of town, follow the road passed Sliver Boys' Ranch and eventually, you'll see our signs. And I do private rides, if you're interested." There was an awkward silence.

"What kind of horses?" Christian feigned interest.

"We got a few Arabians, for the better riders, but most of our trail horses are Appaloosa mares. Reliable, ya know?"

"What about kayaking? I hear the river is amazing."

The man gave a grave nod. "Guess so, if you do them belly rolls. I wouldn't get on one of our rivers this time of year for a million bucks, though. There's all kinds of eddies that will suck you to the other side of the earth. Anyway, hope we can be of help." With a tip of his hat, the man strolled leisurely out the door to join his friends. The men climbed into a fully-loaded Ford King Cab, resembling the trio from *Bonanza*.

Christian gave a loud sign of relief. The Sliver Ranch directions were the best thing that had happened to them so far. As Daniel approached her, she gave him a nod and pulled him aside so the waitress couldn't eavesdrop.

"Did you hear that?" she gasped in excitement. He shook his head, indicating a negative. "According to the Marlboro Man, our target's just around the corner."

* * *

After quickly checking into the Best Western Ruby Inn a few miles north in Tropic, they set out to scout the area. Following the directions to Harrison Outfitting had taken them by a turn-off that had very small sign indicating the way to Sliver Ranch. From the map, it appeared that the Paria River ran parallel with the road about a half a mile away, though a bend in the river two miles down appeared to bring it almost roadside had the gravely track continued. At one point, the slender reed of the river cut crossed the southeast corner of the rectangular acreage of the Sliver property.

The fact that Christian had ordered local area maps from the county assessor's office had impressed both of her traveling companions, but when Daniel pulled out an introduction letter from Joe Sliver to the Mormons, she was the one left speechless.

Doug pulled off at the bend in the road near the Sliver Ranch and motioned for them to get out. Bear was the first to jump out and immediately set off to mark a perfect fifty foot circle of territory around his protected. After each had retrieved a set of binoculars, they huddled surreptitiously behind a cluster of Ponderosa Pines. Behind them, grotesque rock formations, stalactites of rust-colored sandstone, stretched their craggy fingertips into a cerulean sky. The strange shapes, called hoodoos, looked like whimsical characters from an etchasketch. In the chilly mountain air, the late afternoon light cast eerie shadows across the Bryce Canyon wilderness. They gazed in appreciation at the red-striped cliffs of Kodachrome Basin, glowing hypnotically in the distance.

"This is my thought. Let's say that Stephanie is afraid to leave, isn't allowed to leave or otherwise refuses to leave. In any case, we will basically have to abduct her. Daniel and I will go in with this letter."

Daniel raised his eyebrows, nodding with approval. "As I was saying, the letter states that we are looking for a place to stay and I am Mr. Allred, a long-lost cousin of the Clists."

"How do you know that will fly?" Christian felt a sick sense of panic overtake her. The whole ruse seemed to be a mistake suddenly. "What if they don't believe us? These fundamentalists have a blood mentality. Their history of violence makes the Taliban look tame."

Daniel shrugged. "We'll think of something. So we say that we took the bus down and are looking for a place to stay, that Joe told us about their lifestyle and we felt like we'd fit right in. If we can't find Stephanie, we hike out at night. If we do find her, Doug and your friend, Juicy, can drop a raft off on the corner of the property line where the Paria River cuts through. We grab Stephanie and raft out."

Christian gave a fleetingly smile. "Let's hope that works." She put her head in her hands. "What have I got us into?"

Doug shook his head. "You find me a road that gets me to the pull-out. Otherwise you're stuck hiking out. Who knows if that's even possible? Look at the rock structures around here. Are you planning to climb a hoodoo, because I'm sure the hell not."

Daniel hadn't said anything for several minutes. Suddenly he released an exasperated breath. "Jesus H. Christ, will you look at that!"

"What?" Christian asked anxiously. An errant thatch of blue-black hair was swirling around her face in the stiff breeze, fighting the constraints of her baseball cap. In an act of childlike frustration, she yanked off the cap, doubling her efforts to procure a ponytail of sorts. Dressed in khakis and a dark brown jacket, she'd hoped to create a camouflage as she stood next to the tan-colored SUV which they had parked next to an outcropping of sandstone. Her traveling companions had dressed the same, and so, from anyone more than a quarter of a mile away, they were nearly invisible.

Daniel motioned to her binoculars. "Look to your far left. There's a low green building. There's a guy out there and he slapping around some woman. She's got a little kid clinging to her skirt and she looks like she just stepped off the set of a Spaghetti Western."

Doug responded with a low whistle. "No kidding. Check it out, man. There's a bunch of little kids and a pen of dogs, too. If those are guard dogs, neither of you are going to get out of there without a fight." As if he understood their words, Bear gave a low growl. Christian reached over to soothe him.

From what they could see, the Sign of the Nail Ranch was nearly a mile off the main road. A wooden fence, reinforced with thick metal posts and looped barbwire ran along the property as far as the eye could see. A rustic gate, wide enough to accommodate a semi-truck, was adorned with a three foot high emblem that resembled a pentagram surrounded by a circle. The star had two points facing upward rather than the typical one point. Doug mumbled that it looked like a Mormon Endowment Ceremony symbol as Daniel gave a grunt of disagreement.

"I don't know what an endowment ceremony is all about, but the pentagram is the sign of a witch. My grandmother taught me that much."

Christian put down the binoculars. "I'm beginning to wonder if this is a Satanic Cult disguised as a Mormon polygamist's camp..."

"Disguised as a cattle ranch," Daniel finished off.

Doug waved his hand. "No. Actually Joseph Smith was a Mason and used a lot of their secrets. These are ancient things, guys. People all over the planet borrow one another's symbols. The swastika, for example, is originally a Hindu sign for good luck. Hitler just twisted it around a bit."

"Twisted is a good word," Christian countered with a nod. "Okay, so here's what this is going to look like. We borrow some rafts from Juicy's rafting company. We drive in off this road here." Pulling out the map, she placed it on the hood of the car. Pointing to the left corner, she continued, "We'll drive up this way, it's a forest service access road, and hide the inflatable rafts in the bushes here, near the Sliver Ranch border." Doug and Daniel leaned over and studied her map. She had highlighted the roads in various colors.

"Are you that good at navigating whitewater because I don't have the slightest idea what to do." Daniel's tone rippled with doubt.

His partner huffed. "We can do this. I've called Juicy already and talked to her about it. I'll admit, about six hundred yards from the pull-out, there are a set of rapids that we don't want to test, but we'll pull out before we get that far."

"Juicy is who exactly?"

"Juicy, the whitewater guide. She's an old friend of mine. We did the "The River of No Return" in Idaho together a few years ago. Juicy knows her stuff. She did tell me that the Sliver land that borders the river is guarded day and night by dogs. I guess there are 'no trespassing' signs posted starting about a mile upriver from the ranch."

"Juicy. Hmm, does her appearance match her name?"

"Daniel, stop being a perv. She's over six feet tall and weighs more than you do. The woman is pure muscle and all lesbian."

Her partner looked utterly dejected. "Okay, so I guess that means no juicy fruit for me."

"On the contrary," Doug interrupted. "' Fruity' is exactly what she is." They had a laugh over that and then grew serious again. Daniel had his hand in his jacket pocket, unconsciously massaging his pocket pistol, a Raven Arms MP-25.

Doug warned his friends to crouch down as a pack of trail horses appeared to the east. "Looks like our cowboys from the restaurant," Daniel murmured, gazing through his binoculars at the slow moving procession.

"Let's get out of here," Christian urged, climbing back into the front seat. "I don't want the town folk talking about us. We can stop at Juicy's on the way back to pick up the gear. This needs to happen tomorrow. If that girl is in any danger, we need to get in and out as soon as possible. Doug, did you bring Daniel's underwear?"

Her partner looked from one to the other as they pulled onto the road. "Really? I have to wear those things?"

Doug grinned. "Well, we might as well break the news sooner than later. Daniel, ole' boy, you'll be wearing my Dad's underwear tomorrow and Miss Chrissie, here, will be wearing my deceased mother's undergarments as we Saints like to refer to them."

The Hispanic's caramel-colored skin paled, as he shook his head adamantly. "Now that....is just gross!"

Ten minutes later, they pulled up to Juicy's Joyrides, a rafting company that was housed in a small white building upon which several types of kayaks were perched. Set back from the road, there was scarcely enough room to turn around the SUV amongst the various trailers, boats and other rafting supplies. A tall, husky woman was standing on the steps of the building talking to a group of young people. She waved them into the door of her establishment, evidently to fill out paperwork, and then jogged up to Christian who was barely out of the car. Before anyone could say a word, Juicy had wrapped her comparatively petite friend into a bear hug, her broad, Slavic face beaming with happiness. Lifting her sunglasses off sun-kissed cheeks, she revealed a pair of warm brown eyes which sparkled with something between raw curiosity and simple practicality.

"How long has it been?" The large woman squeezed her bulky arms around Christian's slender frame joyfully.

Squeezing her friend in return, she grinned. "Too long, big sista!" The two women began an intense catch-up contest, filling one another in with her history since their last parting. Daniel and Doug stood back, waiting for the ritual to finish. Finally, after nearly five minutes, Juicy reached out a meaty, calloused hand, offering it to Doug, who was fiddling with his cell phone.

"Hey, guys, sorry. Let me introduce myself, I'm Juicy, sole owner and operator of this outfit." She shook both men's hands eagerly. Running her hand through a thick patch of short gray hair, she tugged on an earlobe and gestured to the car. "Let that dog out, will ya? Nobody needs to feel left out around here."

She opened SUV hatch and Bear bounded out. After giving Juicy a wet face, he wandered around the area, marking territory, although carefully as to not wet equipment. "Smart dog," the robust woman said after a minute of watching the animal. Then Juicy directed them over to a pile of gear that she'd organized ahead of time.

"This is all you should need. I have radio transmitters strapped into each of my bigger rafts, in case they get separated from one another on the rivers around here. You never know and these rafts cost a pretty penny, let me tell you. Anyway, there is a portable pump right here." She'd opened a plastic bin and pointed to the apparatus. "Plus there's a first aid kit, a two-way radio, extra paddles and lifejackets, a waterproof tarp, some power bars, bottled water, a couple of heat packs, then, just in case you run into any wild critters, a tranquilizer gun with plenty of darts." She gazed up the sky with a dubious expression. "When do you aim to do this thing?"

Christian looked nervously into her friend's concerned face. "We plan on going in tomorrow with the goal being to find Stephanie in the first twenty-four hours assuming she's there. Unless they have her in isolation, she should be around the property somewhere. After we find her, we're going to have to convince her to leave. I have no idea what this girl is like nor her state of mind. As far as I know, she doesn't have a clue that her best friend has been murdered. That information could cause any number of reactions. Still, the plan is to get her out of there in the next two days, hopefully during daylight hours."

Juicy's tan complexion darkened with an unknown emotion. "Listen to me, sweetheart. If you can't get out in a couple of days, we're coming for you. Also, you don't want to ride that river at night. Secondly, there's a big storm coming in at the end of the week. You do not, I repeat, do not want to be on that river if a mountain storm hits. There's no telling what could happen if you do."

After they finished loading up the gear, there was only enough room for three, which meant that Bear had to squeeze in at Christian's feet. The enormous dog groaned happily, his strong tail whipping the car door with pleasure, finding no inconvenience in the arrangements, though his master could hardly wait to get back to the hotel.

That night, they ordered in pizza. Christian didn't want the group to become a common topic of conversation in the small, close-knit communities along Highway 12. Though there were frequent tourists passing through, the time of year didn't bode well for a rafting party, much less one with a dog that was the size of a small pony.

* * *

Christian had avoided calling Matt for long enough. They'd been playing phone tag since she'd left town. The night before she'd left, he had been distant and cool. His recent phone message had sounded carefully constructed. Like a tower of dominoes, it appeared as though the relationship was on the verge of collapse. At first she thought he was suspicious, jealous perhaps. She couldn't really blame him. She'd insisted on the trip to Utah without giving him a choice in the matter. Guilt flooded her as she leveled her reactive nature to see things from his perspective. Had she put herself truly in his shoes, she would not have gone. Still, this was her moral choice, though in truth, she felt there was no choice at all. When it came to young women and their safety, Christian was pathetically addicted to the role of hero. She was led blindly by her desire to right a very wrong world.

He answered on the first ring. "Hi." His tone was flat.

"Hey, how are you?" she asked softly.

"Good. We won our last game. The team's going to the state semi-finals championship next weekend in Tacoma." His voice was subdued, despite such a triumph.

"I'm so proud of you, Matt. That's fantastic." A heavy silence ensued. She knew he was angry that she wouldn't be with him at the high school basketball finals. She didn't blame him.

Finally he mumbled, "You know, Christian, this isn't easy. This situation reminds me of when we first met, when you were trying so hard to prove that your intuition is all powerful. You're always hell bent on blaming some religion for the world's problems. The Mormons, for example, are good people. Joseph Smith believed that the black man was equal. Despite what people say, he ran for president on an anti-slavery platform and allowed blacks to vote in Utah before it was a state."

"What does that have to do with polygamy and these crazy fundamentalists?" She felt heat rise in her chest as her defensives were put on alert.

"Nothing, I guess. I just hear prejudice in your voice. You've never lived with prejudice, so you don't know how it feels."

Beads of sweat sprang from her pores as she took a deep breath. "That's not true. I live with it every day…with you, and before, with Tony. Did you know that one of my high school girlfriends refused to be in my wedding because I was marrying a Mexican? And Tony wasn't *a Mexican*. He was an American and a damn good one at that. Maybe only as a witness or vicariously, whatever, but I've lived it, believe me." There was another long silence. Finally she heard a sigh.

"I'm sorry, babe. It's just that…"

"What?"

"I miss you and frankly, something feels different between us."

She took a deep breath, wanting to agree, but knowing the timing was all wrong. "I'm sorry. This is hard. I miss you, too. I'll be home soon and we'll take some time together. I promise once I find this girl, I will let the authorities do the rest."

"We'll see," he answered evenly. "Either way, I love you."

She heard a knock on the door. Daniel had taken Bear out for a run and was evidently back. "I love you, too. Gotta go. Bye."

She opened the door. Daniel's dazzling smile immediately took her mind off things. She grinned as Bear raced past her to his water bowl. "How was it?"

"This place is beautiful. We should plan a trip back down, for pleasure I mean. I would love to hike these woods. Or cross country ski, like we did last year, remember?"

She felt herself blush. They had spent a long weekend at his family's cabin, over a year ago. She had felt so completely safe and at home with Daniel, though they hadn't known each other very long at the time. Ironically the only other man who'd ever given her such a sense of protection had been her father. "Yeah, that was a great time."

He pulled off his sweatshirt and his tee-shirt came with it. She gazed at his strong, sinewy arms and smooth chest. Except for a few clusters on his pectorals, the man was virtually hairless. Like Matt, she thought vaguely in surprise. Tony had been the opposite. She'd assumed that Daniel would be the same in that way as her deceased husband. Maybe Matt was right. Maybe she did tend toward prejudice. She averted her eyes, realizing that she'd been staring at him.

He seemed to read her discomfort. "I know," he joked. "I'm not eye candy, not like Matt."

"He has nothing on you, Daniel," she said shyly.

Daniel had turned a dark red. With an embarrassed grin, he said, "Want to have a drink with me?"

She could feel the heat in her body and was shocked at herself. He was pure temptation. Instead, she stuttered, "I've got to get some sleep. Thanks for taking Bear."

"Sure. No problem. See you in the morning." She watched as he turned and strolled down the sidewalk, whistling softly to himself.

Though she tried to go to sleep, her nerves got the best of her. Eventually after several attempts, tomorrow's probabilities became amphetamines to her anxiety. She got up and turned on the television, but the only choices were an old Marx Brothers movie and a Mormon talk show. When she couldn't stand another minute, Christian called Daniel and asked if she could come to his room to talk. Sleep was evading her for good reason. Suddenly their rescue ruse seemed overwhelmingly dangerous. Juicy had an old friend who was with the Garfield County sheriff's department. According to Juicy, he'd been watching the Slivers for some time. Three years ago, when Juicy had first come to town, a couple of guys from the ranch had roughed-up the rafting guide after discovering that she was gay. Brad had become furious and vowed to take the Sliver boys down at the first opportunity. The strange clan had kept to themselves after that, but in the past few months, unusual activity had been observed by the locals, including large trucks coming through town at night, only to be seen leaving the ranch in the early morning hours. Now suspicious, Brad and his law enforcement cronies were aching for a reason to enter the compound.

Knowing that Juicy and her cop friend had their backs was reassuring. Yet despite all of their preparations, when Daniel opened his door, her fragile courage hit a wall. Her partner had opened a bottle of Cuervo Gold tequila and was chasing it with a Bud Light. "I figured since we might not live to see the sunset tomorrow, I might as well tie one on for good luck."

"What are you talking about? These people aren't going to kill us, for God sakes." She wasn't sure she believed that.

Daniel eyed Christian blurrily. "Christ, if they killed that little girl, one of their own, what makes you think they aren't going to consider us live bait?"

"That isn't going to happen!" Christian felt feverish and frightened all of a sudden. She hadn't expected this kind of behavior from Daniel, not to mention the fact that he'd likely smell like alcohol the next day.

"Whatever you say." He caught his reflection in the mirror over the bed and smiled. "Will ya look at that guy?" He'd grown a short beard for the purposes of disguise and in the process, appeared distinguished rather than boyish. "And I've already tried on my fancy underwear. Man, are they uncomfortable! How can they stand wearing them, especially during the summer?"

"Don't ask me. I have to wear my bra over mine to be able to wear any at all."

"You don't have to wear a bra on my account," Daniel joked. Ignoring him, she grabbed the bottle and took a small swig of the tequila. The superior brand slid down her throat like hot silk. In moments, the alcohol started to take the edge off. Still, if the truth be told, she was terrified.

CHAPTER 13

The rosy dawn streamed through the cracks of the blinds, creating a soft pattern of pink rectangles on the hotel's otherwise dingy carpet. When the clock radio began to bleep its irritating reminder, Christian stirred, immediately noticing the beginning pangs of a headache. She'd left Daniel's room around eleven. He had fallen asleep in his clothes, after making a feeble pass at her. She had sat there, watching him sleep for a few more minutes, running the next day's scenario over and over in her mind. Eventually she'd traipsed back to her hotel room with Bear, thankful for the single shot of tequila, for sleep was finally her friend.

She took a leisurely shower and washed her hair, careful not to scrub too hard. She'd colored her hair an ebony hue. The semi-permanent product was guaranteed to last through six washings, but she didn't want to take any chances. Drying briskly, she gazed at her reflection, deciding against bronzer and mascara. She wanted to appear freshly scrubbed and innocent. Twisting her wet hair into a smooth knot at the nap of her neck, she pulled on the calf-length frumpy denim skirt and high-collared white blouse over the thick cotton undergarments. The legs of the Mormon symbol of purity rolled up on the ends. At least the Saint's short-sleeved top clung to her skin, supporting her breasts. The brassiere with cups the size of small melons was made lopsided when she slipped her cell phone into the lining of the monstrosity.

Pulling on her cowboy boots, the nervous probation officer slipped on her neoprene jacket, making sure to discard any indication of her proper name or profession. She had borrowed an old driver's license from a friend with the Richland Police Department, who'd found it while cleaning out some files. Her false name was Joslyn Allred, and, according to the I.D., she was thirty-five years old.

Christian opened the door to an astonishing magenta sky. Smudges of gold and mandarin were slightly visible as the sun, shy to its own flamboyance, crawled slowly up the voluminous wall of pink. The air was chilly and bit at her exposed skin. She'd turned on the weather channel as the coffeemaker dripped its caffeine fix. Snow was expected in the mountains and chains were advised.

After whispering a prayer, she stuffed a handful of dried rattlesnake strips into her coat pocket at the last minute. The probation officer closed her suitcase and, with dog and case in tow, left the hotel room.

By the time she'd reached his door, her skin already felt clammy under her thick woolen cardigan sweater. Against her left breast, the cell phone left a square shape, which she attempted to readjust from time to time. Her snakeskin boots skimmed the top of her skirt, so that only her hands and face were visible. She felt prim and righteous, especially after she'd added the garish gold cross that she'd received one Christmas from her cousin, Father Pete.

She knocked on Daniel's door. After a few minutes, he opened it, looking both sheepish and exhausted. "Sorry about the drinking," he muttered, but his partner immediately raised her hand.

"Listen, I got you into this and I don't blame you for having second thoughts. Do you have your gun?" She was ready to get down to business.

He squirmed slightly and pointed at his groin. "It's in there, in that horrible underwear. God, I just pray the safety switch doesn't fail. I'm not interested in becoming an eunuch any time soon."

There was another knock on the door. Doug arrived with Starbucks coffee and a bag of donuts. "Here's something you won't enjoy for the next few days." His tone was serious as he passed out the large steaming cups of java.

The three looked at each other with a tender mixture of compassion and trepidation. They had found friendship in the past seventy-two hours and now looked upon their ties as something bordering on symbiotic. "Here goes," Daniel announced. "As General Patton once said, 'Courage is fear holding on a minute longer.'" He gave one of his lopsided grins and stepped out the door with Doug, Christian and a three-legged dog in tow.

* * *

Nearly eight feet tall, the ominous-looking gate was made of thick wrought iron. They stood a few feet in front of it, shivering against one another in the bitter cold, unsure of their next step. Doug had dropped them at the end of the road and they'd walked the quarter mile in. A stiff breeze from the north was picking up tempo. Behind them a tall clump of pine trees swayed dramatically against a darkening sky. In the east, storm clouds gathered like bruises on the pale face of day. In the distance, a semi-truck groaned around a corner, but otherwise, the world was silent minus the hollow moan of the wind in their ears.

There was not a soul in sight. A hefty chain was wrapped around the double gate upon which an oversized padlock was firmly clasped. Daniel immediately began to look around the bushes at the base of the two-foot thick cement wall. "What are you doing?" Christian felt irritated by the ineffectiveness of their plan.

"When we were looking at them through binos yesterday, I noticed one guy talking on a walkie-talkie. I figure they've got one hidden somewhere around here for people who come in and out. They probably have a camera, so they know we're here. However, we can tell them that Joe told us about the walkie talkie."

"If we find one," she protested as a four-wheeler roared out of the woods in their direction. Missing the wall by mere inches, the machine came to a screaming stop at the gate. A man in a hooded coat and sunglasses turned off the racing motor, jumped off and sauntered towards them.

"Who are you two?" he barked, pulling a cell phone out of the pocket of his down parka.

Christian stepped back as Daniel stepped forward. They had rehearsed their parts several times. "Good morning. My name is Jeremiah Allred. I'm a friend of Joe Sliver's. Me and my wife here, we're on our way to Texas. Joe said maybe we could stay with you all here at the ranch." His put-on southern drawl was comical, but Christian forced her expression to remain pious. "We got a ride as far as Tropic from one of our church members. He's got himself a family reunion down here. So we were wondering if we could stay here for a night, until he's ready to head out again." Her partner broke into a friendly smile, apparently undaunted by the rancher's grim response.

The stocky fellow exuded the edgy, callous nature of a man who'd spent time behind bars. Though his sunglasses made his eyes impossible to read, his narrow face, beaten by years in the sun, relaxed after a couple of minutes. He wore faded blue jeans and a Yankees baseball hat on his head. The deep lines on his neck were like crevasses in the surrounding rock.

Daniel gazed calmly at the ground while the man read the letter. He eventually glanced up at them. His lascivious eye left Christian emotionally naked. "We got rules here on the ranch and we're not used to offering up hospitality. I'll check with the boss. Maybe you can stay a day or two. You know how to ride a horse?"

He gave a self-assured nod. "Yep. Rode as a kid. My grandpa was one of them horse whisperer types." The man nodded thoughtfully, as though to test Daniel's merit as soon as possible. The majestic Ponderosas groaned fitfully as another gust of wind sliced the frigid air. Christian did her best not to shiver, but the temperature had begun to drop.

The man meandered away for a moment and spoke into his cell phone. With the recreational vehicle's motor roaring, they couldn't pick up a word of his conversation. Pulling her close to him, Daniel wrapped his arms around her from behind. The night before, he'd told her that their marital roles would inevitably have to include some open displays of affection. She'd ignored him at the time, but now, with his arms around her and his warm breath on her neck, she relaxed a little and allowed him to support her. She was surprised at how natural it felt to be in his arms. He was only a few inches taller than her five foot nine, yet his arms and chest were muscular and steady against her back.

Eventually the man flipped his phone closed and walked casually back in their direction. He had an odd look on his face-something between a scowl and amusement. Gently Daniel released Christian as the man nodded to the four-wheeler. "Jared gave the okay to bring you in. Got a lot of work to get done today and a few of the guys are out at a cattle auction." Staring at the Latino, he added, "If you can ride a horse, you'll be expected to help out around here until you leave. Everybody does their part. My name is Curtis."

Daniel shook his hand and repeated his name as Christian dropped her head and mumbled hers again. She wasn't sure if Mormon women in polygamist clans shook hands, so she stuck with the demure act. It seemed to work.

"Let's go," Curtis ordered. "You, girl, on the back with me. Allred, you'll have to hang on back here." He pointed to the fender where Daniel would have to sit.

Christian climbed on first, thinking about what the man had just said. Jared was the youngest of the Sliver brothers-merely twenty or so, but it sounded as though he'd been left in charge. That could only be a good thing. She gave a pray of thanks for good timing.

The man took off at a slow crawl. Squeezed in behind him, her denim skirt rode up so that the lip of her undergarment peeked out conspiratorially. She tried to avoid leaning against the man, but for every bump in the pothole-marked road, she was jammed closer to him. Her breasts touched his back against her will. He smelled like machine oil, pine and smoke and a vague scent that reminded her of her grandmother's kitchen.

Snow fell slowly, like the tiny flower petals from a cherry tree. The air was starting to warm slightly, causing the flakes to melt as quickly as they landed. The road twisted and turned and began to crawl up a slight incline. Soon the mile-long track opened to the same clearing that they had viewed through the binoculars the day before. A long cinderblock building, resembling a set of barracks, sidled up to a large sheet metal building. Several small buildings, many of them which looked like old army portables, were placed haphazardly in a thick grove of trees.

He turned off the motor. Immediately a chorus of barking dogs resounded. Christian thought of Bear, who had been sitting in the back of Doug's car as her friend had driven away, looking terrified for his master. She cleared the machine, doing her best to move modestly as she did so. The sound of the river could be heard in the distance, a slight rustle of water against the roar of the wind. They followed the man toward the brown cinderblock building.

He opened the door and they stepped into a vestibule of sorts. Free-standing panels, in the style of office cubicles, created a narrow, twenty-foot entry wall on each side of the door. At the end of the last panel, which was covered in a bland beige fabric, they turned to the right and enter a large room which appeared to be a meeting area. At the north end of the room, there were rows of chairs. Castoffs of all varieties formed several semi-circles in front of which stood a raised platform. The lectern looked like it might have come from a school theater. Shorter than the ones normally used by adults, it appeared to have been painted several times in different colors. Behind the podium tacked high on the wall was a flag with unusual markings. She and Daniel exchanged glances as another interesting thing caught their eye. Behind the flag was an enormous blackboard upon which was written a family tree. The hierarchy of the organization appeared in white chalk. Noticing that the two were staring at the drawing, Curtis began to explain.

"This here is our prayer room. We got about thirty of us right now. We call ourselves 'The Saints of Lex Talonis'. Our church started in the old testament." Christian glanced over at Daniel. He seemed to ignore her gaze.

Curtis pointed to the flag which looked like it was made from black canvas. A red, six-inch band of swastikas bordered the three by four foot piece of fabric. A large yellow cross had been stitched in the middle. Layered over the cross were the initials "SOS" in a dark green lettering. "That table back there, that's where the men eat. The women and children eat on the other side of the building in the nursery. We got a kitchen connected to the nursery." He pointed to the opposite side from where they came in. "We got the offices through that door. Everybody sleeps in the cabins according to their families. We got seven men, nine women, well, nine since we lost a young woman, and seventeen kids. A couple of the men ain't married. Like Joe probably told you, we are cattle ranchers, but we got our beliefs. We get up at four every morning, have ourselves a church service, eat and then the men and older boys go to work. The women stay around here and take care of the chickens, milking cows, gardens and do some teaching to the little ones."

"That sounds like a lifestyle I could get used to." Daniel gave the man a nod of approval. Full of repressed excitement, Christian grabbed her counterfeit husband's hand and squeezed. They were at the right place, she wanted to scream.

Curtis's feral face lit up like a beacon of joy as Daniel continued, "Heck, I worked my grandpa's ranch for years and we did pretty much the same thing. My wife here, she don't really get it yet, but we can teach her. She growed up in the city, out in Oregon."

"Why are you going to Texas?" The man appeared irritated as he wiped a film of greasy sweat from his brow.

"We heard there was a new fundamentalist clan forming down there. We were hoping they'd let us join them. My sister's husband's daughter has been living with Warren and they said that's the next best place."

Christian wanted to kick her partner for making the Warren Jeff's reference, but it seemed to take hold in the man's mind like a brilliant solution. "You lookin' for the lifestyle?" he asked. His thick, caterpillar-like eyebrows dropped precipitously, hiding his beady black eyes.

Daniel took the cue. "We haven't been cleared yet. We got her step girl workin' on Jeffs for us, but we gotta wait until we hear. We've been calling every day, but then our phone ran out of minutes."

"We got the same thing going here, but better. Here you can make your own money. The Great Master and the Slivers, they pay pretty good. You don't have to give everything back. I got fifty bucks last week, after putting in my share for livin'. I got myself two wives now and three little ones, so that fifty bucks makes my girls mighty happy. Cheryl got to buy herself a new pair of reading glasses and Candice, my two-year-old, got her first pair of shoes." Curtis looked ready to burst with pride. He had obviously fallen on harder times.

Delicately smoothing her skirt, she nodded with approval as her eyes became cloudy with grief. Though it was an act, Christian had no trouble bringing on the tears. All that she had to do was think about her own dead baby. Then, as if planned for effect, an infant's cry could be heard somewhere in the building.

Daniel took the cue, gently putting his arm around her waist as Curtis looked on, apparently intrigued by the demure young woman's inexplicable change of mood. "My wife, she lost our baby just last month. Nearly full-term, she was. It wasn't her fault. The doc said she'd got something wrong goin' on down there," her partner explained as he gazed at her with genuine love in his eyes. He'd always wanted to play the role of her lover and now, despite the dangerous circumstances, he finally had the chance. Then he added, "Yep, that's why we came on down here. My darling' here, she finally agreed it's time for me to take myself another woman, for the sake of carrying on our family name."

"Allred is a famous Mormon name, all right. I knew me some Allreds back in Missouri. I came from there a few years back." Curtis yawned lazily, as though her predicament had tired him.

She gritted her teeth. The entire conversation made her want to retch, but she played along, using her disgust to further her distressed appearance. "I don't feel very well. Is there a place I might sit down?" If the truth be told, she was exhausted. The lack of sleep, all-consuming fear and the required role-playing was taking its toll.

"I'm not supposed to let you go anywhere until Jared gets here, but I guess I can show you to the ladies. They're on the other side of the wall back there, where the baby's crying. Sounds a bit like my little Abel," he grinned. "He's my second born son, nearly a year old now."

Daniel nodded. "So you have another child besides Candice and Abel?" Christian cheered inwardly. She'd already forgotten the name of the man's daughter, but her alert partner hadn't missed a beat.

"Yep. Got me the same type situation as you, brother. My first wife, Shelly, had our son, Cain, and then couldn't have another. I started seeing Cheryl after we found out. She was a waitress up at a restaurant in Cannonville. Anyway, I was seeing her on the side and she ended up pregnant, so we brought her on into the fold. Let me tell you, Shelly Mae wasn't too happy about it at first. She didn't like me marrying a fifteen-year-old. But damn, Cheryl is one hot little number, wait until you see her. She's already popped two kids and she's about three months along with my third."

Curtis had turned the corner and didn't see the anguished look on his face. In response to her tight grip, he pulled her hard and continued walking. They trudged passed the corridor of panels and continued around another corner into a small room with a desk. The man shrugged, seemingly embarrassed. "You gonna have to let me search you," he said, his tongue running over his lips. Christian gawked at her partner helplessly.

"What do you mean?" she whimpered.

"Jared said I gotta frisk you both. Now I ain't gonna touch your privates, so don't worry about that. But I gotta do it, or he won't let you stay. Pull off your coats," he ordered. Slowly she peeled off her jacket and stood with her legs apart. The man patted her back, waist and then told her to hike up her skirt. Her face turned crimson as he ran his hand up the inside of each thigh. Her heart was pounding so hard, it felt as though she might faint with the rush of blood. He barely missed the side of her breast where she'd tucked the phone. A tiny piece of engineering, it wasn't nearly as big as she imagined.

The Latino grimaced as the man patted him down. This time Curtis was more thorough. Christian held her partner's gaze as the man ran his hand up the back of her handsome partner's rear. The P.O.s stared into one another eyes, knowing should the gun be found, it was all over. Somehow, Curtis didn't catch it. Finally the excruciating exercise was over. Curtis gave a curt nod. "Through that door is the nursery. I'll step in for a minute and introduce you. Lunch is at noon." The cowboy looked back at Daniel. "I'll take you out to see the place while she's resting. We got fifty head a cattle and the boss is up north, fixing to buy some more."

He opened the door. In an instant, the bland, dim, haphazard world of The Saints of Lex Talonis was transformed. The open room was painted in bright colors. In one corner a group of children sat at a table, reading and writing. In another corner was a fenced-off area in which toddlers and mothers sat on a brightly colored carpet, playing with a variety of toys. There appeared to be over a dozen children or more, ranging from infants to preteens. A line of baby cots hugged the outer wall of the room while on the opposite wall, a small kitchenette accommodated a sink, a small refrigerator and a microwave oven. Several of the young women stared at the newcomers, as though seeing ghosts, but an older woman with gray-streaked hair and pencil-thin eyebrows stood up from the table.

"Curtis, you have brought us guests." Her tone was gracious. The noise in the room paused momentarily.

"Yes, Shelly. This is Jeremiah and Joslyn Allred. They are friends of Joe's. He thought they might stay with us for awhile." He handed her the letter from Joe, which had been stolen away in his hip pocket. Shelly read the letter carefully and then gave her husband a wary look.

"Don't worry, Shel. These people are like us. They're looking to join the lifestyle, too." Curtis looked entirely too pleased with himself, so though he was the reason that they had come here.

An attractive girl, with a head glowing in long, blonde ringlets and a ravishing smile, stepped forward and offered her hand. "Hello and welcome. My name is Cheryl." She looked at her husband longingly for a brief moment. Curtis colored as he introduced her. "This here is my other wife, Cheryl. She's been aching for some new faces around here. She's our little social butterfly." He grinned at the young woman as obvious desire spread over his craggy features.

Cheryl tipped her head back, laughing gleefully. Shelly, on the other hand, glowered with irritation. The polygamist ran his hand over his young wife's golden mane of sunlight as a little girl, who looked like a porcelain duplicate of her mother, ran forward and buried her head in her father's legs.

Leaning down, Curtis swept the precocious child into his arms. "And this here's my little angel, Candice. The rest of you ladies, I'll let you introduce Joslyn around. I got to take her man here out for awhile. What are we having for lunch?"

He looked directly back at Shelly. Obviously she was the woman in charge. "Hamhocks and green beans, just like you ordered, but I didn't have time to make a fresh batch of muffins. We're a bit short-handed with them other two being gone."

"Don't give me that. You got less people to cook for with Mel, the girl and James away. We'll be back." He set the little girl down and gestured to Daniel to follow him out.

Before he did, the probation officer drew his female companion toward him, planting a firm kiss on her mouth. "Behave yourself woman," he whispered huskily.

Curtis let out a loud croak of laughter. "Now that's my kind of man," he remarked, as he strode out the door. Mr. Allred turned and winked at Christian. It took all of her willpower not to want to kiss him back. Her body was falling fast to Daniel's advances. What had she been thinking?

* * *

Daniel had been gone for the entire day. Slowly the women of the compound had warmed up to Christian, though she did her best to appear shy and somewhat evasive. She'd offered only bits of Joslyn Allred's personal history, describing their journey from Washington and admitted to only recently becoming a Mormon, though she used the terms, 'sisters' and 'brothers', a lot. She soon learned that of the five young women in the nursery, all were married. She tried to memorize the names of the children, but the fear factor seemed to cloud her ability to think. References were made regarding men named Mel and James and eventually she learned that Jared's older brother had taken the other man, along with Jared's new wife, to Salt Lake City. There were whispers regarding the young woman's medical condition. There was no sign of Stephanie, Christian worried as regret began to nip at the back of her mind.

At first observation, the children seemed happy, like children who were well-fed and nurtured. Though their clothes were tattered and patched, they had plenty of toys and books, though some of the older children seemed to have perpetual frowns on their faces. However, most had been up since four in the morning and were required to milk cows, clean the chicken coops and split firewood before they could start school. She imagined that they felt as exhausted as she did.

As a whole, the clan members were quiet and well-mannered with one another. They all wore calf-length dresses of various pastels and had their hair tied back, except for Cheryl. She was the most outspoken of the group and seemed to thrive on attention. She giggled more freely and played with the toddlers. When asked by Shelly to assist an older boy, Toby, with his math problems, she just shook her head and cried cheerfully, "Sister Shelly, you know I don't know the first thing about math."

They ate dinner together around five. Christian had left to use the toilet twice in the six hours that she was with them. At one point, she stole back into the worship room and did her best to memorize the family tree. Mel's name was at the top along with the eldest Sliver's brother, James. Arrows pointed from James down to circles, which read Sally and Mary. She had not met those women until later in the day. They had been preparing the food and doing the laundry. From what she could gather, the chores were rotated so that no one got stuck with the hardest labors. Below James and his marital package were two more names side by side. On the left, Jared had two arrows going to his wives. Her heart nearly stopped when she read the name, *Stephanie*. Then she looked across at the other man's name. It read Steven. Next to a man named Ralph, there was only one female name and it was crossed out. She moved closer to try to read it, but heard voices. Startled, she fled back to the nursery before she could figure out what was written under the blacked-out circle.

Christian ate as much as she could at the meal without appearing to be greedy. The women had not invited her to eat lunch, but instead had left her to care for four infants who were fussy and fretful for the full hour that the women and older children were gone. Not accustom to caring for babies, the young probation officer felt overwhelmed. It was hard enough to pretend that she was someone else, but then to care for a nursery of crying babies almost took her over the edge.

Several times throughout the day, she thought about fleeing, finding Daniel and escaping as soon as possible. Her intuition was on overdrive. This place held dark secrets. Though seemingly content from the outside, she could see fear in the eyes of the older children. The babies were well-nourished, but were fretful and appeared to be confused. If communal setting were healthy for their inhabitants, why did these children have such flat affect and why did most of the mothers seem emotionally disconnected to their own offspring? Furthermore, she'd seen bruises on several of the older children. Two of the younger females, whom she guessed to be around twelve, were very withdrawn. She'd noticed small rings on each of these girls' wedding fingers. She wondered if they were already engaged.

The feeling of being trapped there was the most terrifying sensation. It dulled her responses. She was careful not to laugh, or ask too many questions. She was keenly aware of her gestures and movements. Compelled to constantly monitor the environment, she awaited positive social cues from the women, which never came. No one seemed at all interested in her. She was simply a fixture.

The routines, interactions and expectations were rigid. She was not allowed to leave the main building without telling someone, she was not allowed to take off her shoes, though her feet ached from hiking up the road in her boots and she was not allowed to take a cup of tea into the nursery. There was no music, television or telephones. The nearest neighbor was six miles away. As they talked amongst themselves, the women referred to their husbands as 'my master' and the head of the clan as "the Great Master". Though casual in her approach, Christian asked an older woman on how the clan dealt with medical emergencies. The obese brunette had only given her an amused smile. "You will learn. Generally we don't get sick here at the Saints of Lex Talonis. The Great Master sees to that. If as in Jared's wife's case, when the blood don't work, or we have a problematic pregnancy, we have a doctor in Salt Lake City who understands our ways."

Christian had thought back on her childhood as she'd bounced the screaming little boy, barely a year old, on her knee. Though she'd lost her parents and sister at the mere age of four, she'd gained a wonderful family with her maternal aunt and uncle and their two older boys and two little girls. Her male cousins were like brothers, always looking out for her. When her Uncle was promoted into international sales, they had traveled the globe to see him and spent one summer on the Mediterranean Sea on the east coast of Italy. She had sweet memories of her jovial, rambunctious family and wished suddenly that she could see them. Terror had a strange way of inciting a longing for all that is good.

Finally the men returned. Jared gave her a startled look, as though he recognized her. He explained that he was in charge while his brothers were away. His eyes glistened with a strange light as he spoke while his mannerisms were stiff and robotic. Christian plied him with her eyes, trying to develop a sense of trust. He eventually warmed up, adding that Joe had given them an excellent recommendation. Daniel played along, nodding and winking on occasion as though they shared a boy's secret.

The young man spoke hesitantly when explaining the clan's protocols and expectations, obviously uncomfortable with being placed in charge of things. There was a brief church service in which they were invited to attend. They followed him into the main room, but were forced to sit in the back. The prayers and absolutions took no more than fifteen minutes and then everyone rose and one by one, disappeared. She wondered if the religious aspect of this group was just a cover for having underage sex.

After the service, their host led them through a thicket of snow-sprinkled trees, swinging a large industrial flashlight to and fro. Christian had tried to talk to Daniel privately, but it was no use. She would have to wait until they were alone. They followed the younger man in the dark. He grunted with irritation as a branch swiped his face. "Watch out," he mumbled. "We haven't had a lot of time to cut down these branches. The weather's been pretty tough this winter. I had my wives working on it, but now that my little Stephanie is pregnant, I don't want her taking any chances." Her convictions had been right all along. It wasn't just a name on a chalkboard. Timidly, she stuttered, "I'm sorry. I don't believe I met your wife today."

Jared stopped sharply, swinging the flashlight into her face. "Nope. She's up in Salt Lake City, seeing her doctor. She'll be back in the morning." Christian smiled timidly in the spotlight, groping for Daniel's hand. His grasp was warm and reassuring. Between the icy breeze and her numbing fear, she hoped that her partner would rescue her from the place once and for all. All of a sudden, knowing that Stephanie was here and with child made the odds of taking her out of there an impossible wager.

They trudged a few more yards and arrived at a dilapidated cottage. It appeared to be made logs with crumbling shingles for a roof. "There's some firewood here," Jared stated as he pointed the light along the wall of the building. Daniel moved his flashlight in tandem to the younger man. "Got bottled water, some snack food and toilet paper. If you have to take a dump, you do it over there." To the right of the cabin was an old outhouse. The rustling sound of a small animal could be heard through the trees nearby.

"See you in the morning. If you want to come to services, be at the main building by five. Breakfast is at six and we ride out after that."

"Weird kid, scary place," Christian murmured after he was gone. Daniel was silent as he opened the door. The probation officers stepped silently into a small abode. A fireplace hugged one wall. Someone had already built a fire which crackled merrily, giving the room a sharp pine scent. There was a double bed on one side and a card table and two chairs on the other. A large blue star quilt covered the double bed and several candles were placed strategically around the space on pine shelves and the roughly-hewed stone hearth.

Her partner threw a couple of logs on the fire and sat down on the bed to take off his shoes. "Romantic, huh? This place is a tinderbox and probably crawling with spiders. Man, I could use a good slug of whiskey."

"That's only because you are still suffering from last night." She wasn't entirely sure how to deal with the situation. Matt would leave her in a nanosecond if he knew she was in a bedroom alone with Daniel. Ironically, she was calm, despite the awkwardness. She waited as he pulled off his coat, jeans and flannel shirt. He stood there, rubbing his hands in front of the fire in his Mormon garments.

She sat down on one of the chairs. "What in the hell have I gotten us into?"

Daniel turned back towards her. He'd pulled the gun out from his garments. Kneeling down, he slipped it under the bed. "If I hadn't done some surveillance training in the military, I wouldn't be here right now. That being said, we've got less than forty hours before we're out. Do you understand me? You've got to find that girl by then, otherwise we don't stand a chance."

A convulsive shiver shook Christian. She inhaled and tried to steady her mind. Maria had taught her some valuable skills over the past few months. She could only imagine what Daniel had learned from his grandmother. For once, she put her bravado aside and deferred to him.

"I think you're right. It's as though all of the women and kids are hypnotized. They are so unnatural with one another. All of them except Cheryl. She seems to have a bit of spunk in her. I'm going to try to spend more time with her."

Daniel crouched down next to her and took her hand. "Listen to me. I care about you. I should have never let us come here. If I thought we could get into that raft and get out of here tonight, I would carry you screaming and fighting to do it. They have guard dogs. We can't get out of here at night. The dogs are chained to the outer fence on long cords. They basically scout the perimeter at night and sleep during the day."

She gazed into his eyes for a long moment. It struck her that she'd never allowed herself to delve into those eyes for very long. His brown irises glittered with something deeper than affection. Blushing, he stood up and grabbed a bottle of water, chugging it down.

Christian glanced around the room, looking for some sign of normalcy. The small table next to her was covered in a blue cotton tablecloth. On it was a notebook and a pamphlet entitled, *Saints for Lex Talonis Handbook*. She picked it up idly, wondering how she was going to get the nerve to go outside to relieve herself. "I've got to pee and I'm not going to that horrible-looking outhouse. Will you be my look-out?"

Daniel shrugged. He looked like a guy from the olden days in his long underwear and thickening beard. "Go out by the side of the cabin. I'll stand at the door with my gun, just in case. Go on."

"Don't look." She crept down the wall of the building. Three feet from the door seemed far enough. The night was as black as iron filings, except for the full moon, which played hide and seek amongst the snow-clad clouds.

She nearly dove back into the room, slamming the door. Facing Daniel, an unexpected epiphany hit her like a proverbial ton of bricks. In the next second, she was in his arms.

CHAPTER 14

They'd finally crossed the line. Despite the exquisite thrill of their sexual connection, Christian was mortified at her immoral behavior. She had never cheated on any of her partners, but now the damage was done. Yet if she were truly honest with herself, her inner voice expressed no regrets. Daniel was amazing. She would never have guessed that the sexual energy was so intense between them, except that when the dam broke, the relief was unfathomable. After over nearly two years of waiting, she'd given in to him. They'd kissed and caressed in nearly every way possible. She let him undress her and as he stood her in front of the fire, he kissed every inch of her, holding his mouth to her sweet spot until she nearly collapsed from the pleasure. Then he'd taken his clothes. His body was taut and compact; his arms strengthened by years of military duty, his abdomen, six pack hard from hours at the gym. When he slipped off his underwear, she'd gasped. A man's erection never failed to surprise her with its insistent power. He lifted her as though she was a feather and carried her to the bed. Trembling with desire and frustration, she'd kissed him deeply, pressing her breasts against his muscular chest until first his fingers and then his mouth greedily found her swollen nipples. Soon he opened her legs and pressed himself into her, slowly at first and then harder as she heard herself begging for it. They came together, tears running down her face and then they started again. They had time to make up for. Afterwards, her body convulsing softly from the power of release, the morally distraught young woman had wept.

* * *

She lay still in his arms. In the glowing candlelight, her pale Celtic skin was white chocolate against his dark complexion. He stroked her, running a finger from her elegant neck down between her perfectly-formed breasts, the size of ripe grapefruits, until he had reached her navel. What had happened was an out-of-body experience.

And now the two years of waiting, the unfulfilled fantasies, the subtle rejections and the twisted heartache of witnessing of her other romantic relationships seemed insignificant with her in his arms. It had been worth every torturous second.

She had rolled away, wiping her tear-streaked face with the worn flannel sheet. Unsure of what to do, Daniel had simply rubbed her back and stroked her hair until she'd fallen asleep. His mouth still felt warm from her kisses. He yearned for her taste while trying to ignore the tumultuous mixture of guilt and desire that raced through his mind. Enjoy the moment. Don't think too hard about tomorrow. But for Christian and the chance at her love, he would have jumped off the moon.

In truth, though he had clearly failed virtue, in his heart, he had finally reached the pinnacle of success. Funnily enough, Daniel actually liked Matt and knew what it felt like to be the fool. His ex-wife had cheated on him several times. Each time he had taken her back, naively believing that loyalty would eventually bring love. That was until he'd met Christian. She'd changed everything for him. For the first time in his life, the street-smart boy from the ghetto had truly lost his senses. Beneath his Latin dignity and tormented pride, Daniel wanted Christian as badly as any man had ever wanted a woman.

* * *

She awoke with a start, her dream a tempestuous reminder of her situation. Her rational mind had been eclipsed by a yearning heart. She listened to the rhythm of Daniel's sleep, longing to run her hands over his body, to stir his magic.

Then guilt struck like a dagger and she felt any remaining strength drain from her limbs. She sat up and tried to get her bearings. The room was cold and the fire had gone out. Slipping from the covers, she fumbled to find her clothing. In the backpack, she'd packed toiletries, a pair of jeans, some socks and a couple of sweaters. She felt dirty from the prior day. Her teeth were coated and her face, grimy. Quietly she found the bottle of water that she'd left on the table. With a small towel and a bottle of camping soap, she slipped out of bed and did her best to scrub away the smell of fear and sex.

Pulling on her jeans and a thick, woolen sweater, she gazed down at Daniel. He slept with his right arm behind his head. His features were strong but symmetrical. His lips were full for a man; his square jaw was right out of a movie magazine. Why hadn't she seen the attraction before now? She knew in fact that she had, but that she'd ignored the feelings that had drifted in and out of her life for over two years. She was good at compartmentalizing, especially when it came to men in her life. She would always pick the man who didn't challenge her-whether it was emotionally like Tony, or intellectually like Matt. Daniel was a man capable on all fronts. She knew it and it terrified her.

Silently she grabbed her boots and her coat and carried them, along with her bag and the cell phone to the door. Daniel groaned in his sleep and rolled over. She didn't want to wake him, though her phone registered ten minutes to four. She hated herself and loved him. How could it be? She had been tricked by her own naivety. She had never allowed herself to see it before. How many hours had they spent together- talking, laughing, cajoling and contemplating life? How many times had she gazed into his eyes and knew that for it, the world was a better place?

She stepped outside. There was a faint glint of light in the space between the trees. She turned on the phone and waited. There was no signal. She turned it off and then on again, but still no signal. A burning lump grew in her throat. She had made Doug promise that they would wait for forty-eight hours before trying to rescue them. Now they had less than thirty hours left.

She wandered toward the sound of the river. Snow was dropping lightly and the woods were bright with the reflection of it. It was a fairyland of crystal and color. Her boots crunched as she made her way toward the horse barn, which appeared in the clearing, a dark red strip in an otherwise pale landscape.

Surreptitiously she opened a side door that led to the tack room. As she stepped inside, she breathed in the warm aroma of hay and horse sweat. A chorus of soft whinnies resounded and then, a low drone of someone sobbing. Softly she called out, "Who's there?"

The sobbing stopped immediately. Afraid to turn on a light, Christian fumbled for her miniature flashlight that was one of her many traveling items. The tiny beam didn't help much, but she stumbled forward between stalls, humming a tune that she'd learned long ago.

There were six horses in all. Some were lying down. The two that were standing snorted with curiosity as she passed. She gently patted their noses, murmuring reassurances. At the end was an open stall piled with straw. A small shoe appeared in the dim light as she swung it around. Then the sobbing started again, causing the pile of straw to tremble slightly.

She reached down and moved some of the straw. "Hello, little person, are you alright?"

Slowly, painstakingly, the ten-year-old boy known as Toby peeked his head out of the sticky yellow mass. He was filthy. "Please," he whimpered. "Don't let them know you found me."

Christian flushed with spontaneous anger. This child was obviously very frightened. She knelt down and handed him a granola bar from her pocket. "You look hungry and thirsty," she whispered, handing him what was left of the bottle of water.

She waited, watching while he wolfed down the bar. "Are you in trouble?" she asked, forcing a smile as his eyes had become saucers of worry.

Nodding, he timidly replied, "I didn't do my chores. You'd better go now. Daddy might find you. Then I'll be in more trouble. *Please* go!"

Reluctantly she left the child, exited the barn and jogged down toward the river as the sun was coming up in the east. It was a faded sun, fighting for its glory in the slate-blue sky amongst heavy clouds and mist. She reached the river in ten minutes and scanned the bank, looking for the red flag that Doug had promised to place near the hidden rafts. Her eyes moved back and forth, begging for an indication of their salvation. She pulled out her binoculars and peered out of the foliage with intense concentration. Eventually she spied something about seven hundred feet upriver that looked out of place. She focused on the spot until it was clear that the item was a small piece of red fabric. With a heavy sigh of relief, she raced back to the cabin, concerned that Daniel had awoken and found her gone. The frightened image of Toby was still fresh in her mind.

* * *

When she got back, it was nearly five. Daniel was still asleep. She laid some fresh firewood on the grate and stirred the coals until a spark lit. The fire slowly came to life. She peeled off her jeans and climbed back into bed. Shivering to the bone, she tried to keep her distance from Daniel, but in seconds he had rolled over and pulled her close. At first, she stiffed, but he sensed her discomfort and murmured, "I won't tell Matt," he promised, nuzzling her neck.

She frowned at him, though his eyes were still closed. "Of course we will tell Matt," she whispered, instantly regretting it.

His eyes popped open. He looked at her like a wounded puppy. "I'm sorry. I just want to do what you feel is right."

Before he could turn away, Christian cupped his face in her hands, staring directly into his liquid brown eyes. "Please listen to me. I didn't expect this. I don't know what's going on in my heart. I'm so confused, but…"

Daniel shook his head, apparently speechless.

"Listen please," she implored. "I can't fall in love with you. We work together, for heaven's sakes, and you're my partner! But now we have a mess to clean up."

"Hey, just because we work together doesn't mean we don't have feelings. We're human and I've made my bed…" Daniel stopped, suppressing an obvious smile.

She whimpered, attempting resistance. "We can't…" Before she could say another word, his mouth was on hers and she knew it was too late. This time, unlike the night before, she kissed back fervently, wanting him as desperately as he wanted her.

Her body throbbed. She had to stop before they went too far. Despite the years that she'd spent in a struggling marriage to Tony, and despite serious advances by a gorgeous professor during graduate school, she'd stayed strong and faithful. At the moment, she was disgusted with herself and felt like she was drowning in an ocean of desire. She needed someone to throw her a life ring and soon.

Daniel seemed to read her mind. After a few minutes, he pulled away. "This is torture," he mumbled, glancing at his watch. "We'd better get going. Did I tell you that Jared made me shake his hand yesterday? I did 'the sign of the nail'. It was perfect. I could tell by the look in his eyes, I'd passed the Saint's handshake test."

Christian offered a tender smile. "So what's our plan? Doug and Juicy will be here by ten tomorrow morning. I couldn't phone them, so they will probably be coming in with guns blazing."

"That won't work. They'd have to get a search warrant and there is no probable cause. We haven't seen anything unusual and the girls, if they are sixteen, according to Utah law, can marry if their parents give consent."

"Yeah, but Curtis admitted to getting together with Cheryl when she was barely fifteen."

"If you want my opinion, Cheryl was already pregnant before they got together. That's the story I heard from one of the other guys yesterday. Apparently Ralph, the workhorse, hates Curtis and made a joke about Candice being another guy's kid. A guy who isn't part of the SOS brigade." He snorted sarcastically. "Quite a group around here, huh? Furthermore, Cheryl's father apparently gave his consent before they tied the knot."

"Are you kidding me?"

"At this point, I'm not going to kid about anything. *Everything* seems far too serious." His eyes searched hers, laced with hope.

"So legal consent in Utah is sixteen? From what I could gather yesterday, all of those young women are at least eighteen. Only one of them has a child over four. The rest are either pregnant or have toddlers. That kid of Curtis's older wife is at least ten. The other two women who were working in the kitchen are in their thirties or late twenties. I couldn't identify what child belonged to which mother, but I doubt they're going to share that information this early in the game."

Daniel climbed out of bed. She could see his erection in the firelight. "Now you don't look. I need to use the facilities. I'll be back. Do you have my toothbrush?" She nodded, thinking how cute he was in the morning. His hair was tousled, like her own, which she felt the compulsive need to brush.

Christian watched him from the bed as he dressed and stepped out the door. In the distance, she could hear the sound of barking dogs. She thought of Bear again and felt the pang of symbiotic affection. How was her dog holding up with Doug? A creature of unusual intelligence, she knew that the canine would be anxious without her, though Doug had dog-sat for her on several occasions and loved Bear like his own three happy mutts.

Shoving worry from her mind, she quickly got out of bed, pulled on her clothes and began to brush her hair. Her cheeks felt raw from the cold, dry air. Today she would wear her hair down, she decided. If Cheryl could do it, so could she. Her thick mane fell in soft waves around her face and trailed down her back. The blue sweater was warmer than yesterday's blouse and gave her a stronger sense of security as she tucked the phone back into her bra. After years of not giving a toss about her appearance around Daniel, suddenly, stupidly, she now cared. She covered her lips with a clear gloss and smoothed her eyebrows. She was glad she hadn't looked in a mirror in a while.

A few minutes later, they were nearly to the main building. A dense fog had settled since Christian had been out and it took them awhile to find their way back to the nucleus of the compound. During their walk in, she explained about the lack of phone service, her heart-wrenching encounter with the little boy named Toby and the liberating discovery of the red flag. He, in turn, described the ranch, the men and their small cattle operation.

"Did you see any weapons yesterday?"

Christian took a deep breath, "No. Have you?"

He opened the door and ushered her in first. "Yep," he answered quietly. "Plenty."

* * *

The guard dogs began to howl shortly after breakfast. Her partner had left her and had taken the phone with him, hoping to make contact with Doug and Juicy from a different location on the ranch. She'd helped to clean up after breakfast, noticing her name on the chore board in the kitchen shortly afterwards. The little boy, Toby, was still on her mind, but he was nowhere to be seen. She'd been assigned to laundry duty with Cheryl and, after lunch, she was relegated to cleaning out the horse stalls. She really didn't mind either. It would give her an opportunity to snoop around a little more and time with the animals might just soothe her jagged nerves. Perhaps she would find the child, she thought absently, stuffing an apple and an extra breakfast roll in her apron pocket.

After their morning meal, Cheryl led her to the basement of the main house. It was a dark hole of a place, with a row of battered industrial washing machines and a couple of dryers. Parallel clotheslines, heaving with sheets and towels, were strung across the space, creating a claustrophobic maze. The smell of laundry detergent and bleach stung the probation officer's nose as she took minimal instruction from the woman. Compared to the prior day, the pretty girl was very quiet and reluctant to make eye contact. Christian noticed for the first time a fresh bruise on the younger woman's left cheek. Then, when she rolled up the sleeves of her white blouse to work, darker blemishes, like old burns, dotted her forearms. She kept her distance for the first hour, but then, as they began to team-fold sheets, she began to talk.

"I guess you must like it here. Curtis says you and your man are thinking on staying for awhile." Cheryl cocked her head and eyed her work companion with blatant curiosity. Christian quickly caught on. The probation officer been looking around the room, intrigued by what she hadn't found. Oddly there was none of the Mormon undergarments that she so dutifully wore. Instead underwire bras, lacy panties, traditional women's panties and men's boxer shorts were clipped to one clothesline in the back.

"Yes. We've been looking for a place to fit in. After we talked a bit to our old school friend, Joe, we realized that maybe we needed to find a fundamentalist group of our own. There ain't any up where we come from. We were headed for Texas, but since we found you first, if we can stay, we'd be just fine with it," Christian confirmed, wiping her brow. Her skin felt damp from the physical exertion of manual labor. Though this group seemed to eat nutritiously and in adequate amounts, the work on the ranch kept the women slim and fit. Cheryl smiled, her small straight teeth gleaming in the dim light.

"I guess if it suits you, then that's all the better for us. We lost ourselves a girl not long ago. I was really sad. I liked her. Maybe you and I can become friends. Let me say, if this is your calling and you prayed and God told you so, then you should stay. It's a better place than the streets at least, which is where I come from."

"I thought Curtis said you were working in town at a restaurant when he met you."

A dark crimson rose up Cheryl's neck and into her face. "Hmm. That's really nice of him to say that, but it's a lie. He brought me out from Omaha where I was working…well… let's just say I was working at night on my back with my clothes off." She gave a little snort.

"So what about Stephanie? What's her story?" Christian's gut told her that Cheryl was the type of woman to either hate you or love you and from everything inferred in the nursery the previous day, the voluptuous blonde had only expressed hatred for Stephanie Patterson.

The blonde stepped forward, eye-to-eye with the newcomer as she collected the corners of the sheet. "That Stephanie was trouble from the minute that she got here. She knew my friend, Whitney, and had come down here to find Whitney's brother. Our master wasn't here then, but Jared was all over it. He got married to her before we could find a way to get rid of her."

"Who is the great master then?" Christian asked innocently.

Cheryl had turned her back to put the sheet on a shelf. "You haven't met Mel yet. He's gorgeous, but don't tell Curtis I said so. He's from Washington, too. I guess he grew up with Jared and James."

"I get the feeling this isn't a Mormon congregation."

"Mormon? Who told you that?" Cheryl shook her head at Christian, as though she was a dumb child.

"We have our own teachings, based on our spiritual leader's philosophy. Our leader is an ordained minister. He got it done while he was in the joint and changed his ways. We believe in Lex Talonis as our fundamental truth, but there are a lot of other things we believe in. Some of it comes from the Old Testament, some of it from the Latter Day Saints' original stuff, but in a way, we are creating our own religion. Mostly we focus on the family and our relationship with the arch-angel, Melchizedek."

"Is James the leader here? I saw his name at the top of the chalkboard when we first arrived." Christian tried to keep her voice neutral, but the fear of the unknown gripped her again. This information was not what she'd expected. Maybe Cole Comely was involved after all.

"Not really. He's just the oldest. James is weak, if you know what I mean. He got messed up when they sent him to Afghanistan a few years back. He disappears now and then, like goes into the woods and pretends he's in a war again. Sometimes you'll hear him out there, shooting up the trees, when he's around that is. And his younger brother, Jared, is a total cracker. Got some psychiatrist to say he's a schizo, so he could get disability income. But wait until you meet Mel. There's something magical about the man. You can't help but trust him and do what he tells you to do. He's really smart, but there's more to it than that. He makes decisions and keep things rolling. For example, even though she's a pain in the butt, when Stephanie got sick last week, Mel insisted that we take her to a doctor. Jared was against it, but now, he's grateful as hell when he found out she has some blood problem."

"Rh factor blood type incompatibility," Christian murmured.

Turning back, the girl gazed at the other woman for a long moment. "You're smarter than you look!" Cheryl fluttered her long lashes and offered a genuine smile. "Stick with me, sister. We can get a little power of our own, even if it's only with the women folk."

* * *

Stephanie looked just like her photograph only healthier, Christian observed as they sat down to eat lunch. She'd positioned herself next to the younger woman, who was holding court with the others. After working all morning, the saint's version of Shepherd's Pie actually looked appealing. Under most circumstances, the ever-present fever of fear would have kept her appetite in hibernation, but the early morning run to the river and back along with her churning desire to make love to Daniel was more than her energy could bear. She gobbled as politely as possible and listened as Stephanie talked effusively about her trip to Salt Lake City. By the end of the first ten minutes of the pregnant girl's saga, the probation officer was annoyed and could easily understand Cheryl's negative opinion of her.

Stephanie was one of those females who loved center stage, but didn't have the personality or charisma to hold up to it. She obsessively flipped her thin, lanky, auburn hair, widened her closely-set eyes while gushing fountains of syrupy clichés. Everyone who crossed her path was a 'darling', a 'honey', or a 'sweetheart'. Even the phlebotomist who took her blood was *as adorable as they come*! If the world was a wonderful as Stephanie made it sound, there were no starving children in Africa and no 9/11s and car accidents didn't exist.

After twenty minutes, Christian thought she might puke at the uttering of one more superlative. She caught Cheryl's eye and nodded imperceptibly. Her new friend returned her gesture with a wide grin. "Told you so," she mouthed.

Christian considered the circumstances. Obviously there was no getting Stephanie out of there, unless they could prove her mother hadn't signed a release to allow her to marry Jared. The girl was barely sixteen, but that was good enough for Utah law. Growing discouragement crept under her skin like breeding lice. Who was she to come here with noble aspirations when she didn't know a thing about Stephanie? What made her think that life on the streets was better for this girl than here? Still, if she could convince her to go to her father's home to join Serena and start a new life, there might be some hope. Unfortunately the girl seemed enamored with the ranch and their way of life. Serena had warned the P.O. that her younger sister rarely listened to reason and at least on the ranch, the irritating young woman was well-fed and monogamous.

The day seemed to go on forever, though mucking out the barn gave Christian plenty of time to think. It was pleasant in there. The smell of fresh straw and horse dander filled her nostrils with reminders of her past. Though Amy's death had been tragic, visions of their youth together sprang like sprouts in the fertile valley of her memory. They had been the best of friends from the day that they'd met in third grade in Mrs. Daughtery's class. Amy was like a copper twin to her chocolate tones. Her best friend's bright, metallic-colored locks were long and straight like her own deep brown mop and their faces had similar features-pale, creamy skin, wide-set blue eyes and small noses, both with a spray of freckles like salt on popcorn.

Unlike some best friends, they had never been competitive with one another. Christian was an ice-skater of considerable talent while Amy was a trophy-winning equestrian. Amy was to visit her friend and her cousins in Italy during the summer of her fateful death. Had her friend kept her original plans to fly to Rome a week earlier, the accident with her horse would never had happened.

Between the guilt of betrayal, the exhaustive role-playing, the fear of discovery and the triggered memories, she was spent by the time Daniel arrived to get her for dinner. He was highly agitated, yanking her behind a stall while looking over his shoulder suspiciously. His voice was a hiss as he said, "You won't believe it, but I think that this Mel is Brandon Clist. Did you remember that Brandon's middle name is Melvin? Then, a couple of times, the short guy, Jared, called him Cancer. Anyway I told the guys I needed to take a dump. I went way out in the woods, near the river, and got reception. I called Andy Stimpson in detention and had him check for me. His physical characteristics are nearly a perfect match. He's grown some, and he looks older than his twenty years, but that's what prison will do to you. He has some bulk now, too, but again, there is nothing better to keep yourself busy in the institution than getting in shape."

Christian felt the surge of victory. This was exactly the outcome that she'd hoped for. Now it was just a matter of finding some evidence to put Brandon at the scene of the crime. The chance that the perpetrator had made a fatal error was the only leg she had to stand on. "Brandon had some scarring along his jaw and lower cheeks, like he'd had some childhood acne. Were those noticeable?"

Daniel shook his head. "He's grown a beard. The other problem is that he was really pissed that Jared gave approval to Curtis to let us stay. They got into it and I thought they would come to blows. Finally he frisked me. I was so glad I left the gun behind and had the cell phone shoved up inside my baseball cap. Obviously I couldn't ride with a gun nearly up my ass, but man, the dude stuck his hand far enough up that he would have found it."

Christian's heart had begun to race with trepidation as she stared into her new lover's face. He was rarely unnerved by people or events, but they were trapped with a cold-blooded psychopath and had no real protection.

"Did you convince him that we're credible? Did you get a hold of Doug? Are they coming to get us tomorrow? Can we get a search warrant?" Her rising voice beat a heavy staccato. Like brittle leaves in a violent wind storm, questions were spinning from her mind in a million different directions. She wanted out. Her gut told her that they only had a small window of time before Mel inquired as to their real identities. He didn't have access to identity computer systems, but who knew when and if Joe Sliver would fold.

"Shh, I hear someone." Daniel pulled her into an embrace, kissing her passionately as a man came around the corner. Pretending as though they were completely alone, he began to run his hands down her back and to her bottom, cupping it softly. She felt a crazy mixture of fear and passion, her body tingling with resistance and wanting.

"So you like to take your women in barns, like some animal!" A deep voice caressed the air with its own dark longing. Christian pulled away from him abruptly, as though shocked by the intrusion. Strong emotions gave color to her cheeks and she used the moment to hopefully show embarrassment at getting caught.

Daniel played it off. "Hey man, you guys don't let me get enough play time. I got to grab a little when I can." Her partner's sexual tone belied his anxiety. Spinning her around like a rag doll, he added, "Want you to meet my new boss, Joslyn. This is Mel."

The hair on the back of her neck rose and her breath became shallow as she searched for the appropriate response. Daniel was right. Unless her eyes were deceiving her, she was looking at the sexual predator legally known as Brandon Clist. Her intuition thrust instinctive knowing into her gut like a saber as she recognized a killer. The young man's eyes were cold and older than his years. She thought back on the juvenile detention photo taken when Brandon was only fifteen. He'd changed significantly, grown brawny in his budding manhood. Sporting a tidy beard, his skin was bronze from the life of ranching. Yet the eyes were the same and they held her captive longer than she wished.

In fact, she had met men like Brandon before. Over time, without question, she'd learned to listen to her inner voice. Timidly, she put out her hand to shake the man's before her. He was more handsome than his original photographs had obliged. His crystal blue eyes continued to graze her from head to toe, evaluating her as though she were livestock on the block, or a slave at auction. She shuddered involuntarily. "Oh, I'm catching a chill," she stuttered, attempting to portray her debilitating desire to disappear as mere shyness.

Mel continued to stare at her.

"So what's your story?" he demanded, his eyes flashing dangerously. "I don't like the idea of you just waltzing in here. Joe Sliver's not one of my favorite people and that tells me that you've got some convincing to do."

In that instant, an unexpected jolt of rage raced through Christian's veins, like lightening up the limbs of a tree. She wanted to slap the impertinent malcontent. Instead she gathered herself, looking directly into his eyes. Using all of the womanly wiles she could conjure, she gave him a little half smile, stood up a bit straighter and pressed her bosom in his direction.

Daniel pretended to be oblivious, reaching down to fiddle with his shoe as she murmured coaxingly, "Now Mr. Mel, I don't know why you would second-guess a newly converted Fundamentalist like myself. I've been saved! And a roll in the hay never hurt anyone." She winked and leaned forward to touch his arm. "I'm a bit sweaty from all this hard work. Do ya'll have a bathtub around here?"

She knew enough about offenders like Brandon to know the image of a woman naked in a bathtub would probably soften him, or if the truth be admitted, harden him in all the right places. She loathed giving him the fantasy, but she wasn't about to let him win.

He grinned. "My cabin has a nice big bathtub. I think there's some bubble bath in there, too. All the gals bathe in there from time to time."

With that, the man scratched his neatly trimmed beard, as though making a final decision. Finally he pointed them in the direction of a newly-built log cabin. Christian did her best to send signals to Daniel that read, '*don't you dare leave me alone with this piece of garbage.*' His interpretation was right on, because he said, "I could use a little scrub myself, honey." He nodded to Mel. "You're very generous. Both my girl and me haven't had a chance to bathe in a few days."

The small house was immaculate. It vaguely reminded Christian of the psychopath's childhood home in its cleanliness and austerity. However, there were no family photographs or other signs of human comforts. The couches were made of black leather, the end tables bare except for simple white ceramic lamps. The floor was beige wood floor while the walls smoothly plastered and painted white. The only picture on the wall was a photograph of Kodachrome Basin.

"You like?" their host asked eagerly. "I was sent up for a few years and learned carpentry skills while I did my time. I built this myself, for the most part."

Even devils need approval, Christian thought, as she coyly smiled, rose up slightly on her toes and tilted her chin upward. With the grace of a dancer, her posture became erect as she spun slowly in a circle, allowing him to experience her admiration. As she turned a second time, her gauze skirt, the only other one that she'd packed, lifted gently away her legs. Her former training as an ice-skater was often handy when it came to performing ballet movements. She could create the illusion of floating when she wanted to. The clan leader appeared temporarily spellbound. Daniel stood back, seemingly captivated as well.

Clearing his voice, her partner managed, "Such a nice place you got here. And you built it yourself. Maybe you can teach me some of those skills down the road. In the meantime, where's that bathroom. I'm dying to take a leak."

Mel nodded, pointing to a closed door. "In there. I got to get to a meeting. You two have yourself a great time." He narrowed his eyes at the Latino, as though to say, "Don't worry. I'll have no trouble imagining what you're up to while I'm gone."

They waited until he had left the house and had walked down the gravel path before Daniel groaned a sigh of relief. "Go have your bath. I'm going to search this place from top to bottom while I can."

She nodded and slipped into the neat white room. The hygiene was that of a hospital, only without the germs. There was an old-fashioned claw foot tub, a small fiberglass shower, a sink and a toilet. Following her partner's lead, the probation officer opened the wooden cabinet below the sink. It was filled with tidy stacks of toilet paper rolls, a bottle of Draino and some scrubbing powder. She bent down and peered into the back of the frame. Something had caught her eye. She pulled out several rolls of Charmin' and gasped so loudly that Daniel came running into the room.

"What is it?"

"Oh my god, look at that and don't touch!" As she removed the last row of paper rolls, it became clear what they were looking at. Unless she was mistaken, shoved into the crevasse was a hammer with a strange shape on the top. As they leaned in further, he gave a loud gasp. They were staring an oyster-spat hammer.

"Jesus," he murmured. "Are you sure?"

"Don't touch it. Wait outside. I need to think." She could barely stand to undress for the thought that the evil nemesis would burst in any minute. They were in the presence of the very thing that could stop this insanity, but the next step seemed as elusive as the first one had been. She tried to relax and let her thoughts settle into some kind of a plan. Exhaustion had become a leech on her system and her ability to concentrate had drained away. Starting the bath, she climbed in and tried to focus on the process of soaping, moving as though she were doing the Tai Chi of bathing. Her heartbeat finally slowed and her inner rhythm took over.

Meanwhile, Daniel was standing outside the door, impatiently awaiting his turn. He whispered through the crack in the door as she scrubbed the scum of the sicko's stares from her skin.

"We've got it. We've found the weapon and have cause to arrest. As soon as we get out of here tonight, we'll start the process of obtaining a search warrant. We have a motive, a weapon and a suspect."

"We can't place him at the scene, God damn it. And he's probably wiped the tool clean." She grabbed a clean towel from the top shelf above the toilet. "We've got to hurry. Come on in," she replied, quickly drying off.

"Skin oil soaks into wood. We can get a sample, I just know it." Daniel countered, stepping through the door while yanking off his shirt.

"Don't think we can take that thing out of here ourselves. I don't want my prints on it. Not to mention the fact that if we run now, without explanation, he'll figure us out. He'll know that we found the weapon and hide it again, or get rid of it completely. You need to go out tonight and send a text to Doug to give us a little more time. We need to hide that thing ourselves, later, when he doesn't suspect it. Then we need to find an excuse to leave. You need to get in a fight with someone. That will get us kicked out of here."

Daniel bent down to peel off his shoes and socks. "Are you crazy? They'd rather shoot me than look at me. I'm a wetback to them. You should hear the way they talk to me. Anyway, are you nearly done in there? We've got less than twenty minutes before we have to be in to eat and I'm starving." His voice was wound tight with worry.

Christian grimaced. "Me, too, but the hot water feels awesome. Climb in there and look the other way so I can get dressed."

Dutiful for a second, he turned back around, just as she had dropped the towel and was reaching for her undergarments. They both froze as he tried to look away, but simply couldn't. "I'm sorry…" he stammered; now slowly moving his gaze from her eyes downward. "You're just so damn hot."

He stepped forward and pulled her toward him. His skin was the color of milk chocolate and his cut chest was as smooth as suede. Suddenly, his mouth was on hers, tender and yet demanding. Before she could resist, his mouth dipped to her breast. She closed her eyes as stinging tears of guilt and happiness began to roll down her cheeks. Slowly, in spite of herself, she reached down and lifted his face back to hers.

A loud noise, like a shotgun, sounded. He withdrew from her instantly. Falling back against the wall, she was left shaking with pleasure as he disappeared to investigate. She dressed quickly and came out of the room,

"What was that?" She was hardly able to speak.

"No clue." Without another word, he slipped passed her into the bathroom, where he took his turn scouring the days grim away. She waited impatiently, wondering what kind of emotional hell was awaiting her future. The next step was hanging between them like a paper-thin veil as they raced to get back to the main house in time for dinner. Christian felt the flush of desire still tingling under her skin as she sat down at the table. The other women looked at her like she was a snake in the grass.

CHAPTER 15

Matt couldn't sleep. Climbing out of bed, he left the lonely bedroom and went to the front door to get the morning newspaper. Meandering out, he grimaced, his bare feet smarting against the sharp gravel on the driveway. He shook his head, trying to clear the cobwebs. His ability to concentrate was vanishing like the stars at sunrise. Standing on the edge of the property, he watched as a glowing ball of light peeked out from the west. The sky was a burning crimson canvas with streaks of gold, illuminated as though by electrical current. In the distance, verdant green stripes of newly planted vineyards butted up against the pale gray back of Candy Mountain. Rattlesnake Ridge was a dark, slumbering bear in the horizon. It was breathtaking sight, like so many of the sunrises in his small Pacific Northwestern town.

He hadn't heard from Christian in over forty-eight hours. He'd called Doug and he'd reported the same. They had called each fifteen times if not more in the past day, both berating themselves for allowing her to partake in such a wild goose-chase.

Two days prior, his lover's client, Cole Comely, had been successful at one thing in his short and turbulent life. He had managed to kill himself. The note that he'd left was a horrifying explanation of a murder of a young girl and his servitude to a master of the darkness. He had named his master, Cancer, as the primary suspect in the death of Whitney Clist. The finger-pointing was nothing new, except that he also said that a blue Ford pick-up with Utah plates had been used in the transporting of the girl's body. After a DOL search, Matt had learned from Christian's co-worker, Stella, that the car was registered to a Mel Clist.

Matt knew something else was wrong. The feeling went beyond his lover's physical safety. He could feel her pulling away, like an atmospheric shift, the calm before the storm. It was a sense that he'd always about people from an early age, fed by racial rejection and chronic disrespect. He had grown up in a place where black people were expected to stay 'in *their* place'. His intuition was keen and he didn't trust Christian's partner one bit.

Daniel had always been friendly toward him, even before he'd started dating Christian. The men knew one another when Matt had worked in detention. Both were members of a pool league that met at a popular tavern on Tuesday nights after work. When they'd made their relationship public, his lover's work mate had become less engaging, though his gregarious personality still shone through. He'd always known that the Latino had feelings for Christian, but he'd never believed that she had feelings for him in return. With a deep sign, Matt turned and headed down the trail for home. If his gut was right, he'd guessed wrong.

When he opened the door from the garage, the phone was ringing. He ran over and caught it before the answering message kicked in.

"Hello," he said, caught breathless.

"Matt. It's Scott. I got your message. This is nuts. Why did you let her go down there?"

Matt chuckled humorlessly at Christian's adopted brother's accusation. "You know as well as I do, when Christian puts her mind to something, there's not a superhero in the world that can stop her from doing it."

A loud groan could be heard from the other end of the line. "I know. But she normally listens to you. What the hell's going on?" Matt gave Scott, a hotshot attorney whose career included an illustrious Act I in the violent crimes division of the King County Prosecutor's office, the lowdown. The sharp, forty-something Seattleite, who had been a big brother to the young woman since she had lost her biological family at the age of four, was on the verge of calling in the FBI after he heard the details.

"So you know that she's gone to some kind of a lunatic fundamentalist compound, and that it is possible that a girl might be there who knows who murdered Whitney, yet now there is new evidence to suggest that the killer is in the Tri-Cities? Has a warrant been issued by the kid's parole officer so he can be picked up?"

"Your sister is convinced that this sex offender, Brandon Clist, is back in Utah. The original emails were traced to an internet café in a little town called Cannonville, near Bryce Canyon. That's the general vicinity where she and her buddies were headed."

"So she's traveling with Doug and Daniel? What did they think they were going to accomplish by going down there?"

Matt gave a heavy sigh and sat down on the bed, feeling the weight of mountains descend. "Christian believed that the victim's best friend was being held on this ranch against her will. She also had this idea that she would know more than anyone about the murder."

"I need to talk to Juicy."

"That's her friend who owns the rafting company?"

"Yep. She rents everything from snowmobiles to ATVs. The rafting part of her company is seasonal. Anyway, we go way back. She's a family friend. Her gang of thieves down there includes the sheriff's department, so I'm guessing that they are watching the compound from afar. Unfortunately, they are probably betting that the leaders have plenty of weapons, so they're probably in no hurry to ambush them. I have the ranch up on Google Live Earth, though and from what I can tell, it appears that all the vehicles have been accounted for. There is no sign of a blue pick-up. I see about six men on horseback, riding towards some cattle that look to have strayed. I can see a number of small cabins and a large building that must be a barn. I see a bunch of people who look like women based on their clothes. There are a few small bodies running around a climbing gym of some sort.

Hmm. The property is basically self-contained. The Paria River runs along on north-eastern border of the property and that's a fierce little stream, let me tell you. The river drops away and a steep incline carves out the north to south line. The highway runs along the southwest border, but again, the land rises. It looks like half the property sits on a plateau above the river and highway. There really no way out of there unless you go through the gate or down the river."

Matt dug through a file folder that he'd found in the back of Christian's desk. Groaning loudly, he replied, "I can see that now. I just found a map that she was using to plan their strategy. It looks like a copy from a forest service manual."

"Do you see anything about a rescue operation?"

He snorted. "I had no idea how much work she's put into this. She must work while I'm sleeping. She's got all kinds of notes on the area, a list of supplies, including guns, a plan for escape via the river, and three different phone numbers for Juicy." His voice trailed off. Fear and helpless had silenced him momentarily. Scott picked up on his terror.

"Take a deep breath, buddy. That's the way my little sis works. She's very creative and determined. When we were kids, she used to make us play spy games. She conjured up all kinds of stories and we solved a couple of serious mysteries. One included getting the police to arrest a sexual perpetrator who lived a couple of doors down. She had spied on him for weeks and figured out what he was up to with a couple of the younger neighbor boys. Once Chrissie puts her mind to something, she doesn't let go."

"Tell me about it." His tone bristled with sarcasm.

"You should have called me. Tell me what her working board says on it." Scott's voice was taut with tension.

Matt shook his head. This was not his fault. He stepped over to the large white board. "Here goes. At the top, she's written Brandon slash Cancer. Under their names is a list of suspects: Clist's father, Cole Comely, Joe Sliver and some kid named Lobos. Miasma is also there, but crossed out. Seems that douche bag had a solid alibi. He was at the hospital with his grandmother the night that Whitney was killed. Brandon's name is the only one that she's circled. She has the murder weapon identified as a tool used in the propagation of oysters and next to it, in parentheses, the Clist beach house? As for murder scene, she has listed the cabin, church parking lot, Cole Comely's bedroom and then a blank. She has scribbled a bunch of notes in the margins, most of which I can't decipher."

"What about the police? What else do they have on these people?"

"Look buddy, I'm a school teacher. This stuff isn't my gig. If you want answers, you need to call Stella, or someone who has a bit more knowledge. In the meantime, we must figure out a way to get her out of there." Matt felt a black panic looming in his peripheral vision. As though losing his sight, it threatened all things sacred. "One more thing. She and I got into it before she left. I have the feeling that we're on the skids, for the long haul. I guess what I'm saying is, I don't know how much influence I have with her at this point."

"Sorry, Matt. She's still living in the past, and I don't just mean over Tony's death. Christian is…" There was a long pause. "Never mind. What does Harry say about the case? Does he know anything? We worked together on the last case."

"As I said, call them, call whoever, but one of those calls needs to be the call that rescues them. I've got a bad feeling and it isn't getting any better."

A bulldog on a bone, Scott was relentless. "So give me Juicy's numbers. I've got Harry's, but he isn't going to do much good."

"You're the big deal ex-prosecutor. Don't you have anybody with some power that you can call?" Matt muttered, ready to strangle the man whom, for Christian, walked on water.

"I'll do everything I can. You know that. Christian's my blood. But I'm not going to call my friends in the FBI and send them down to a viper's nest without having my ducks in a row. What else did Christian tell you?" Scott added, his voice charged with emotion. Matt could almost see the worry on the man's face.

"Not a lot. I do know that Brandon's family told Christian that he was in Indonesia. That was the last place she knew about, but of course she didn't believe them." Like opening a freezer door, a cold slap of air hit Matt as he digested what he'd just said. "He's there, with her. I'm certain of it."

Scott's end was silent. Finally he mumbled, "Give me the numbers now."

"Okay." Matt recited a series of phone numbers. "Call Harry, too, and I'll call our locals. There's some new information that might just get them into gear. Apparently just after they left for Utah, a new piece of information started circulating. The janitor from the Mormon Church finally came forward to say he remembered seeing a blue truck slowly driving by the stake house a couple of nights before Whitney's death. The weather was really bad that night, so the roads were slick. People were traveling with caution. Then there was a separate police report regarding a road rage incident in early January. A woman reported being followed by a blue pick-up near Columbia Trail. She said the truck appeared to be following a red motorcycle. They only remembered it because when they tried to get around the truck, the driver waved a gun at her. She was scared and managed to get most of his license plate number. Four of the letters that the driver wrote down match a truck registered to Clist."

Scott gave a loud sigh. "Columbia Trail. Isn't that the road to your place?"

"Yes. And you're also right about your next question. Your sister's Ducadi is red." In the next second, a vividly dangerous scenario entered Matt's mind. If Brandon Clist was at the compound and if he had been the one driving the blue pick-up, her life was definitely in jeopardy. Snapping back to reality, he heard Scott's voice, but hadn't registered the words.

"Sorry, could you say that again."

The older man's voice was razor sharp as he hissed, "That guy is dead meat."

* * *

Something wasn't right about the new couple. Mel contemplated that thought as he led his clan through evening prayers. Leaving Jared in charge was the protocol, though the kid didn't have any more sense than a newborn calf. Recently his nephew had been flexing his muscles, calling Texas to report in behind Mel's back. That would not happen again, he thought as frustration turned to fury. He slammed his hand into his fist to emphasize God's word, though in truth he was seeking internal relief. Staring out into the small crowd, his angry eyes zeroed in on Jared. The kid seemed clueless. He grinned back at the speaker like all was well. Unfortunately Mel was stuck with him, though the kid didn't fit his idea of a protégé. To manage the compound required intelligence, ruthlessness and pragmatism, qualities of which the leader excelled. As Mel instructed his people to take a moment for silent prayer, he considered what he'd heard earlier from the women.

The sisters had reported that Joslyn was quiet and rather dull. To their credit, they'd used her to do the most labor intensive tasks and she'd measured up. Indeed, Mel found the woman, Joslyn, to be intriguing and sexy. Perhaps she just reminded him of the one of many hookers he'd hired after he'd been released from prison. He must have had a hundred if he'd had one.

Hastily finishing up his sermon, Mel excused himself to his cabin. Once inside, he tried to call his contact in Salt Lake City, but there was no answer. He went to the bathroom and started the shower. Climbing in, he allowed the hot water to drain off the mental residue of day. Staring at the white fiberglass wall, his mind surged with a singular obsession. What if that piece of crap Moloch had told someone about Whitney before he died? What if he left a note and confessed the whole damn thing? Cursing, he picked up the soap dish and flung it against the shower stall. It bounced off the side wall, mocking him with its resistance. His blood pressure began to climb as he picked it up again and flung it out of the stall and against the bathtub. Now it shattered. Bits of glass spun through the air in slow motion.

He knew that his follower had been out of his mind with worry the last time that they'd visited. The idiotic vampire wannabe had been very upset about his encounter with his probation officer, begging Mel to do something about her. Mel had tried by using his many resources, but the last he'd heard, every attempt at eliminating her had been unsuccessful.

As he climbed into bed, he thought about the new woman again. She might be a nice piece of meat, too, though he would take it slow with her. That damn wetback always had his eye on her and there was no doubt that the guy could probably beat his ass. Though not extremely tall, Mr. Allred was solid muscle and had quick reflexes. He'd caught that runaway calf earlier in the day and brought him back like he'd retrieved a small dog. Obviously, it was an advantage to the ranch to have him around.

* * *

Christian awoke early and slipped out before Daniel stirred. She wanted to check on the child again. She hadn't seen him since the morning before. First she ran to the river, carefully climbed the thick-bodied oak near its bank and hanging precariously from a branch twenty feet up, she tied the yellow ribbon. Before they'd landed in S.O.S. hell, they'd agreed with Doug and Juicy that if they needed to extend their stay and had made phone contact, the ribbon would be the signal that they would remain until further notice. As she hurried along, her thoughts went to her partner and Matt and the soul-searing guilt. The sooner that she confessed to Matt, the better. Daniel had disagreed. Over a heated discussion the night before, they had butted heads as they normally did, though this time, she was aroused and wanted him. Before the night was over, she and Daniel had nearly crossed the line again. She physically ached for him. It took all of her will power to stop to his desire. No matter how often she imagined Matt, his face would soon retreat from her mind's eye.

In the distance, the dogs were barking. The sound seemed to echo loudly as she forced herself to move faster. Yet even the run hadn't brought her temperature to comfort level. She thought of Clist and how his eyes had unclad her when he'd come into the kitchen as she was cleaning up after dinner. He seemed taken with her, asking her about her childhood and later, her relationship with Daniel. At one point, he'd introduced her to the four German Shepherds. She'd forgotten to take the breakfast muffin out of her pocket, and smelling it, the dogs became greedy for a treat. After asking permission, she'd fed the dogs, hoping that she was making points with the canines for the future.

She stumbled over a rock, nearly falling to her knees. Her heart dropped into her heels for a moment as she steadied herself. A sharp crack shot through the air. At first she thought it was gunfire, but then a drum roll sounded and the dull metallic sky instantly lit up with a shock of lightening. Then she heard a faint noise and she found herself changing direction and moving toward an outbuilding that she hadn't noticed before.

The dawn lit up again as electricity snaked through the bruised sky above. She raced out of the trees as buckets of rain sluiced from the heavens. The diminutive shelter appeared before her like a sepia photograph, tinged in browns against a flat backdrop of pewter rain. She shoved open the door, seeking relief from the deluge. The room was only about six feet by six feet. In the center of the room above which was a gaping hole in the roof sat a pail. The tinkling sound of falling water against metal echoed in the cramped space, a solo in a symphony of nature's sounds. The rain pattered, the thunder rumbled and then came the strange keening again. As her eyes adjusted to the murky darkness, Christian saw a cot lining one corner. Upon it was a hump the size of a small goat. She wrung out her hair, shook out her parka and slowly moved toward the mound.

"Hello?"

There was a short silence and then a hiccupped sob. "Go away," squeaked a frail voice.

"Can't I stay until it stops raining? I'm getting wet out there." In truth, rivets of rain were running down her face and her clothing was drenched.

The quilt-covered mound moved slight and a corner flapped up. "You will get in trouble. Mel will beat you."

The child slowly sat up. Christian could see that he was Toby, the little boy for whom she'd been searching. His face was stained with streaks of dirty tears. He was shivering violently. "Please. HE WILL HURT YOU."

She peered closer at the boy, gently pulling back the blanket to see that he was nearly naked. Flat purple lines marked his chubby thighs.

"Oh, Toby, did Mel beat you?"

"Yeah, last night, after he came to get me."

"Why would he do that?"

"Because I bit him."

"Bit him? Where, sweetheart?" Christian tenderly pressed her hand to the boy's cheek.

An odd little giggle escaped the boy as he replied, "On his thingy."

After a few minutes of reassurance, the motherly woman promised the boy that she'd bring him some food and stepped out of the shack. The rain had slowed to a dribble and their cabin was not far away. As she jogged through the trees, she saw a person and two of the German Shepherds in the woods about forty feet in front of her. She tried to veer off to the right, but the dogs started barking and loped toward her. She stood completely still, knowing that the animals had been trained to attack. Praying that they could smell her scent, she steadied herself and tried to appear calm. The first dog was nearly on her when she recognized his markings and called out his name. He slowed his pace as his nose went up into the air. Wiping her tears, she straightened up and tried to mimic normalcy. The dogs slowed and began to sniff at her legs. The person approached. In moments, she could see that it was Mel.

"Hey, it's the beautiful Miss Joslyn. What are you doing out here so early in the morning?" Suspicion marked his pale blue eyes as he came closer. He appeared older than she remembered, unshaven and disheveled. "Just out for my morning run. I'm a marathon runner, or did I already mention that?" Strangely, she found that she enjoyed lying to Mel. After all, she'd never run an entire marathon in her life.

He leaned closer to her, as though to sniff her as well. He was dressed completely in camouflage. A thick billed hunting cap covered his head. She hoped that her appearance gave the indication that she was telling the truth. He looked over her shoulder, preoccupied with something.

"Where did you come from?" he asked, adjusting his cap against the weakening rain.

Pointing east, away from the river and the hut, she said, "I did a big loop from the cabin. Probably a couple of miles."

"I would suggest that the next time you want to go for a run, you come get me first. We have some wild animals around here and there are some dangerous sinkholes that you could fall into if you're not careful."

Glancing at her watch, she shook her head in agreement. "Yes, sir. Should I wake you the next time I want to go for a run then? Say the day after tomorrow?"

He grinned lasciviously. "You can wake me up any time, baby." Offering a fleeting smile, she turned and ran as fast as she could back to the cabin. Daniel was already awake and poking at the fire.

"Where in the hell have you been?"

Christian felt hot tears on her cheeks as she explained.

"We're getting out of here," Daniel insisted angrily.

Her gut wrenched as she remembered the yellow ribbon. "I put the marker out this morning. If he sees that, he might think the call was to confirm that we need more time."

Daniel grabbed her, kissing her hard before he spoke, "We are in danger and I'm not letting anything happen to you. When we get back from the morning service, we are going to make a plan."

They hustled over to the main building and slipped in just as Mel began to recite the morning service. She watched in awe as the group nodded and recited simultaneously. She was reminded of Mrs. Stanford's funeral. The flat expressions on the people's faces, the lack of challenge to their authority and the deep lull of his hypnotic gibberish was enough to convince her that they were his sheep and he, the wolf in their clothing.

"Lex Talonis," he repeated, his voice rising up and cresting like a soft wave. "An eye for an eye, blood for blood. We must always respond with the Lex Talonis. For knowledge is power, and in the release of the greatest gift, pleasure, we shall overcome our weariness and submit more to our Lord."

The pervert continued to talk about the concept of sexual desire and the power of procreation. The young man's eyes glanced around the room until they landed like lasers on Christian's face. She gave a weak smile, as though to agree with whatever hyperbole he was selling, but she could hear no more. She knew in her gut that he had killed Whitney. She just needed to prove it.

He finally let his eyes stray from hers and towards the other members of his cast. It had only been seconds that he had looked into her soul, but she had, too, looked into his and was certain that her epiphany was the answer to this dangerous and delirious mystery.

CHAPTER 16

It was nearly eight o'clock. Breakfast was over. She was in the kitchen, cleaning up and stuffing food in her apron pockets for Toby. Mary and Shelly Mae had already started preparations for dinner. The hind end of a recently butchered pig was in the oven and loaves of wheat berry bread dough were slowly rising in the three bread machines on the long counter. Steam fogged the windows and left a pasty dampness in the air. Pale green metal cabinets, taken from old military barracks, were stacked in corners for storage. The ranch women were very conscientious about stockpiling food. During her childhood, all of the LDS families whom Christian had known had stored food in their basements, under their beds and in most of their closets. The Sign of the Nail Ranch was no exception.

As she dried the last of the dishes, she glanced again at the clock on the wall. She and Daniel had made a plan. Time was running out and they had to get out before Mel suspected something. Worried that Juicy and her team of deputies would arrive with guns blazing, they decided that they would leave on the rafts that afternoon. There was alleged child abuse, the murder weapon and underage marriage issues that would suffice to convince authorities to issue a warrant now. Daniel would leave on horseback, telling the men that he'd seen a breach in the western fence and was afraid the cattle might escape and fall into the river. Once on his own, he would meet her at cabin to collect their belongings. They would ride to the drop-in from there.

Bone-chilling rain from the night before, along with the melting snow runoff had made the river waters treacherous, but that remained their only other escape route. The contact point with Doug and Juicy was less than four miles down the river after all.

She would feign illness after lunch and ask permission to rest in their cabin. Hopefully she could convince her work partners to let her go. Generally the women were quite rigid about work, but she could force herself to vomit if necessary.

Just then Stephanie ran into the room and asked, "Can someone please come to the nursery and help me for a few minutes?"

Christian stepped forward. "I will." This was her last chance to talk to her privately. She hadn't decided what she would say to the younger woman. Revealing her identity to such a frivolous and attention-seeking prima donna clearly challenged common sense. The only thing that Christian knew to do was to make mention of Whitney's death in an offhanded way, acting innocent to the girls' connection.

Stephanie was visibly distressed as they entered the nursery. The babies were crying and one of the older children had spilled a large glass of juice. "Change that one. She's just taken a dump. I'll puke if I have to do it," the younger girl ordered bossily. She bent over to wipe some juice from the floor. As she did, Christian noticed an enormous tattoo in the middle of her back as her tee-shirt rode up her torso. The tramp stamp image nearly took the probation officer's breath away. The leering face of a devil smiled out at her. The words, "the devil made me do it" were written above the image in old English script. Yet below the cartoon-like face was the most revealing message of all. It said simply, "Brandon."

In order to hide her surprise, Christian threw out a snide comment. "What will you do when your baby needs changing?" she asked, averting her gaze.

Stephanie spun around, eyeing her critically. "Look bitch. If you haven't noticed, Mel has the hots for me. If I don't want to change dirty diapers, I won't and I don't give a flying fuck which baby needs it."

Christian scooped up the tiny baby girl. She was an adorable infant with long brown lashes and a crown of curly dark hair. "Shh, little darling. Shh. You're fine. Here, does that feel better." She pulled off the diaper, which was soaked through, and wiped the baby's bottom clean. Like the other infants, she had terrible diaper rash. There was a consensus among the young mothers in the nursery that diapers were a hassle and that children should only be changed when they had defecated. Therefore, the children sat in wet diapers a good part of the time.

Stephanie was obviously in a sour mood, but Christian didn't know when she would get another chance to talk to her. She blurted, "I'm just glad to be here, dirty diapers and all. That place I came from in Washington, it's become very violent. Why this pretty Mormon girl, Whitney Clist, was murdered just a couple of months ago. No one can figure out why. She was such an outstanding young lady; people loved her."

Glancing over, she watched curiously as the girl's face grew dark with a strange fury. In that moment, Christian recognized jealousy, envy and hatred. "I knew Whitney a long time ago. She wasn't always so great." A looming silence pervaded as Stephanie stopped mid-sentence.

They were momentarily interrupted by the two older women who had been cooking on the day of the imposter's arrival. Placing the baby in a swing, the probation officer turned the knob, which started the contraption swinging to and fro. Swiftly, she grabbed a small hand towel and mopped up the juice. Stephanie pretended to be busy at the children's table. The older of the two women, Mary, murmured that the stables was her assignment for the day.

Christian nodded dutifully. She slipped over to the table and handed Stephanie a folded piece of paper. She then left the large room for the kitchen where she hurried out the back door. As she stepped out, she could hear Cheryl and Shelly arguing loudly in the laundry room below.

She walked hastily toward the barn where she was on duty for a second day. Once out of sight, she dropped to her knees and began to sob uncontrollably. She was an idiot to have come here, to try to remedy the evils of the world. Taking on an alias, coming here on a false pretense, and finding comfort in the arms of another man…naked shame pressed against her skin like dry ice. She began to pray feverishly, asking God to make right so many wrongs. She'd always wanted to do the honorable thing and it now seemed as though every choice that she'd made was the opposite of good. Infidelity, lying and impersonation, seduction and passivity in the face of evil were all sins according to her upbringing. She had hurt too many people and felt overwhelmed by the stranger whom she'd become. Certainly Mel was the very image of Satan personified, but from the stories that she'd heard, the lives of the women had been exercises in torture prior to their arrival on the ranch. Abuse and suffering abound in the shadows of these women's lives. In the coupling of their trauma histories with isolation, insidious religiosity and ruthless dogma driven by an all-male autocracy, their very selves had been transformed. No longer were the female members able to maintain the power of individual thought nor truly have awareness of their personal wants and desires. They were truly the victims of the Stockholm Syndrome. In a terrifying way, the Sliver Ranch had become a sort of paradise for most of them. Who was she to question fate?

Rising off the forest floor, she stumbled in the direction of the hut where she'd last seen Toby. She had not wanted to reveal her knowledge until she knew that he was still there. Interfering with Mel's decision did not seem a wise choice just yet. Opening the battered door of the hut, she waited as her eyes adjusted to the darkness. Toby was still the corner of the room on the cot. He'd been crying and wiped his face hastily.

"Hello," she called. "I have some food and clothing for you and I'm going to take you back to your mother." The boy's eyes grew into large lobes of fear as the sound of footsteps descended behind her.

"What are you doing here?" the man hissed. With great flourish, he made his face into a wicked caricature from his favorite old horror movie. Heaving with insidious power, he behaved as though possessed. This was the part of his act that he most enjoyed. Joslyn's head jerked in his direction. Suddenly he knew who she was. She'd worked at the juvie when his nephew was in trouble. Rage shot through his veins as he realized that she'd tricked him, that he was the fool. No one made him out to be the fool. Not the old lady and her pathetic son, not the self-important bastard at summer camp and certainly not a woman had the nerve to sneak on to *his* property into *his* world and dare pretend to be someone else in *his* presence! Against the wall, the little boy whimpered fretfully.

"Out!" Mel's anger was volcanic in intensity. Spittle flew from his open mouth as the frightened child leapt to the floor. Almost colliding with the wall, the boy raced out of the door and into the woods. In that next moment, the woman came at him with vengeance of her own.

She was upon him then, like a feral cat, scratching at his face as she tried to move around him and out the door. He reached out and grabbed her as she attempted to slide by. She screamed as chunks of her hair came out in his hands. Whirling around, he dove at her, tackling her to the ground, holding her arms and clamping down on her breast with his teeth. She reacted by rolling sideways and kneeing him in the groin, so that he release his mouth. He roared, gasping for air. She kicked him in the shin and said his name. Electricity slid up his back as she screamed, "And you're a killer!" Shaking with fury, he slapped her over and over until she was limp. Throwing her over his shoulder, he carried her out to the truck and threw her in the back. Now she'd really have a price to pay.

* * *

Daniel had convinced Curtis and Jared to let him go alone to fix the break in the fence. During the night, several head of cattle had wandered near the ravine, so they headed in the opposite direction to collect them. He waited until the other men were out of sight before he turned his horse around, heading in the direction of Mel's cabin. He had a few extra minutes before he was to meet up with Christian.

Fortunately their illustrious leader, as Curtis so often liked to call him, had apparently left for town to collect supplies and wouldn't be back until late afternoon. The clan had a communal blood drive every third Thursday. They drew blood on the premises and Mel delivered it in large ice chests to the Red Cross, according to Ralph, a former army medic, who was in charge of the procedure.

Enthusiastic about the blood drive, Mel had encouraged the clan to eat well that day in order to prepare. Everyone seemed willing to contribute after he'd lavishly praised them while adding that it was their civic duty to help others. Once again, Draconian Order had been the theme for the morning's sermon, as Mel reiterated the importance of the law, Lex Talonis. His rigid expectations were perfectly aligned to the commandment that their blood be given to others so that their power could be passed beyond the walls of Sliver Ranch. Noble-minded thinking, spiritual commitment and self-discipline were the virtues that had made the Saints greater than the average man, he had stressed, while under their breath, his clan had mumbled unwittingly in agreement.

Daniel considered the megalomaniac who seemed to have a Svengali-like hold over the Saints of Lex Talonis. Over the past few days, he'd observed the group carefully and had begun to understand the spell that Clist had cast. These were the unwanted and disenfranchised; troubled souls with dark secrets that they longed to discard. There was Ralph, an army medic who had been dishonorably discharged, Curtis, a longtime con, Stephanie, a homeless runaway, Cheryl, a former prostitute, Jesse, an illegal alien, Steven, a mentally retarded man, and Jared, who, according to clan rumor, had been diagnosed schizophrenic. He'd read some information on cult mentality before they'd arrived. There was no doubt in his mind that this group of misfits was the perfect recipe for Mel's success.

The sun was high in the sky by the time he'd found his way to the edge of the clearing where the cabins had been built. Fortunately Mel's place was fairly protected by a thicket of Ponderosas, which gave Daniel a place to put the horse without drawing attention to her. The woods were silent as he climbed off the sweating animal. He looked around for a source of water, but could find none. He made a note to water the creature once he was done with his investigation.

The cottage looked like something from a Disneyland theme park, he thought, slowly making his way around the building, peering into the windows to be sure he was alone. The log cabin-style abode had small, colorful signs in the yard which read 'Beware' and 'Strangers are not welcome'. Painted on rustic wood, the script was very ornate and reminiscent of style one might find in an old English pub. Strange clay gnomes were perched in the surrounding trees while a life-sized grizzly bear, carved from an enormous tree trunk, stood near the front door. He hadn't noticed the yard art when they'd come to the house the first time, but then again, he'd been deep in fantasy over the vision of a naked Christian in a bathtub at the time.

A black crow swooped down to scold him from a nearby nest, causing him to startle. His palms suddenly felt sweaty from the creepiness of the place. Surprised to find the back door unlocked, he double-checked that his gun safety was off and slowly turned the knob.

"Hello," he cried as loudly as seemed necessary. There was no answer. The men had told them that the women took turns cleaning Mel's cabin, since he had no wife, but from what Christian had said, that rotation was not yet on the calendar for the week.

He hovered momentarily in the kitchen, scanning the room for any cameras, though he hadn't noticed any the last time they'd been in there. He smiled to himself, remembering the vision of Christian naked and glowing from the bath. The pleasure of the sight had nearly disabled him, his desire so intense that he had to force himself away from her. He had to keep some sense of honor. If she wanted him, it would be her call now.

He looked around for the signs of a safe or lockbox. Slipping into the living room, he glanced down the hall. The home was a one bedroom and bath with a simple living/kitchen area. Clean and lacking in décor, Daniel suspected that there was more to the place than met the eye. He noticed the corner of a braided rug turned up and took the cue.

Pushing back the small coffee table, he rolled back the rug to reveal a small crack in the Pergo floor indicating a crawl space. He ran his nails along the edge until he could get a grip and was able to pull up a one foot by one foot section of the fabricated flooring.

Sure enough, in the narrow space below was a metal lockbox the size of an ice cooler. He stood and looked out of the front window. The horse was contently chewing on some wild grass. From where he stood, there was a road to the left, which was clear for about three hundred feet. Still, he would have to be fast.

He yanked out the box and opened it. There were three or four books on satanic rites and ceremonies, one entitled, *The Book of Melchizedek* and another, *The Devil's Handbook*. There was also a manila envelope. Quickly he dumped out its contents. Gasping, he froze. There, at his feet, was a picture of Whitney Clist, another man and Mel. The girl was naked and tied to a bed. On her body was painted several symbols in what appeared to be blood. The men had on black robes, the type that monks might wear. On their foreheads were painted the Sanskrit sign of light and Hitler's symbol of national power, the swastika.

Fear burned through his body like a jolt from an electric socket. His stomach spun with disgust as he glanced through the remaining photographs. Images of sexual-sadistic torture were the bulk of his find. His mind raced with the shock of disturbing realization. He had to get Christian and get the hell out of there. Tucking a few of the photos into his inside coat pocket, he slipped the box back into the hole, covered it with the rug, and adjusted the table. Glancing around, he made sure that he'd not left any trace of his invasion and raced out of the back door and to the horse, who only glared at him with annoyance.

* * *

It was pitch black and achingly cold. She shivered while the terrifying struggle drilled its way into her memory. As she was prone to eidetic imagery, the type of memory known for its film-like recall, she could see it again in her head in living color. He had come up from behind as she'd stepped in to talk to Toby. At first she'd thought she could simply pass it off, as though she'd simply stumbled upon the child while investigating the building. But his face had turned into a crimson, twisted mass of rage as he'd shouted that he knew who she was…an imposter. And she would now have to pay. He'd lunged at her, his smallish hands gripping her arms as he threw her to the floor. The child was screaming, indeed loud enough to have brought help, but the slow motion of the assault had brought no one and she knew that she would be raped and killed if she didn't get out. Gratefully he'd sent Toby running. With adrenaline as fuel, she recalled all of her training from the police academy and the many self-defense classes. He had ripped at her clothing, threw up her skirt and tried to negotiate his way into her private parts, but the Mormon underwear was a surprisingly helpful deterrent.

Growling like an animal in heat, he'd flung her against the wall, but her words had halted him momentarily. She remembered her own voice then. As a child, she had a clear voice, medium pitched and yet soft. Now her tone rang with strength driven by revenge. "And I know who you are, too, you pathetic pervert."

The young man had only growled with an unknown emotion. She'd wanted to add, "If you hurt me, there will be a thousand men who come after you," but his fist had interceded. Perhaps that was a good thing. They say you are not supposed to titillate a rapist's rage.

She touched the side of her lip. Swollen and bloody, it throbbed with pain, but her teeth all felt solid in her gums. She'd tried to run, but he'd caught her and threw her in the truck outside. Driving her to the cabin, he'd forced her to write a note to "Mr. Allred" explaining that she was hitching a ride into town with Curtis, at which point she was going to get help and that he should wait there for her.

She did her best to use a different handwriting, but Mel had found some notes in her bag. Gripping her hair and yanking it from time to time, he told her that if she thought to leave any clues, he could kill her on the spot and leave her raped and bloodied body for her boyfriend to find. She had obeyed. And she'd prayed that Daniel would get there soon. He had taken the gun that morning. They'd planned to meet, but not until much later. Forcing her by the hair into the truck, he'd driven down a dirt road for about fifteen minutes before coming to a stop. Continuing to pretend that she was unconscious, she'd allowed him to lift her out of the car. He groaned at her deadweight and mumbled that he'd be back to get a taste of her later.

She'd managed to slip off her silver bracelet, throwing it onto the ground as he trudged with her in his arms through the trees. She could smell his body odor, which was a ripe combination of garlic and expensive cologne. When he stopped, she though he would shoot her, but instead he laid her down and shoved her. Then she'd fallen like Alice down the rabbit hole and hit hard twice.

Drifting in and out of reality for some time, Christian eventually opened her eyes and carefully sat up. The only light was a trail of silvery reflection from somewhere high above. He had left a canteen of water and a sack of Doritos, an afterthought from his pickup truck's bed. She would have no regrets. When his hands had gripped her tender parts, her mind had flailed with refusal and she had wished for death. He would have rape her, but her scathing identification must have killed his libido. Making fun of him had nearly cost her life, at least he'd left her free of sexual assault. The thought of sadistic torture, rape and a painful death was an imminent reality.

Gazing up, she could see that the hole was at least twenty feet down, but she'd first smashed against a ledge of sorts before gravity flung her to the bottom like a rag doll. The fact that he'd also tossed in some sustenance was a strange anomaly. He must believe that she would die. Perhaps he had thought that the water would prolong her decline and had found some pleasure in that concept. On the other hand, maybe he was coming back to substantiate his threat.

The pit was safe from certain predators, but there were snakes. She had heard them moving, awaking to the spring warmth, their nests beginning to rustle with new life. The rattlesnakes' offspring are more lethal than their adult counterparts by the mere fact that they have no control over the amount of poison that they release from their sacs of defense.

She sighed heavily, testing her limbs again to see if anything had been broken during her fall. She felt battered, but all parts appeared to be in working order. Her head felt the size of a watermelon and was squishy on one side where a rock had torn into the side of her skull. She tried to concentrate, to weigh her options, which amounted to about none. Slowly a throbbing sensation on the side of her left breast took center stage to the other wounds. A violent shiver shook her to the bone as she recalled the struggle again. His damning words reverberated in her brain, "You taste good. I might just eat you."

Reaching up to feel for a foothold, she walked her way around the pit, which was nearly ten feet in diameter. Something slithered over her foot and then was gone. The snake didn't frighten her. Her rattlesnake bite as a child had made her immune for the most part. The strangest part of the mystery was that snakes seemed to be hypnotized by her very presence, as though she were some Indian magician who used the power of movement to keep them at bay.

She laughed and shivered simultaneously. Sunset was not far away, but she would not be afraid. A strange giddiness overcame her as she realized that they would be looking for her soon. Daniel would get out and instigate a rescue team, unless Mel found him first. She moved around the narrow hole again, looking for a foot hold. Now a crack of sunlight seeped into the space, illuminating the slimy walls. To her left movement, tiny feet skittered. Moles and other creatures of the dark had made this hollow their home. The pit was actually a deep wash-out, a sink hole that inevitably filled when the river was at flood stage. The glacier waters from high up in the mountains surrounding Salt Lake City had not yet begun to melt, but she could hear the slight trickle of falling water, as though the tunnel to her left led to an underground stream. After the attack, he had blindfolded her, but from the topography, she was fairly certain that he hadn't left the Sliver Ranch property.

A memory came back around for a second time. His voice had been like something from a horror movie. She thought of all the degenerates before him…Son of Sam, Ted Bundy, the I-5 Killer, and Jeffrey Dahmer. And then he recognized her. She could tell that he enjoyed his torture more once he'd figured it out. Why did her society produce such evil? Had bad people always existed or was this some kind of aberration of modern mankind?

* * *

Mel brushed his hands against his sides as though he had just finished working in dirt. Glancing up, he scanned the cerulean sky. A Red tail hawk swooped lazily in the horizon, drifting through the swaying trees. To the east, Kodachrome Basin glittered like a Mayan city of gold. A slight haze hovered in the north, indicating another possible storm. Yet he was in no hurry. By the time anyone found Joslyn, it would appear as though she'd fallen into the pit. Many of the S.O.S. clan had commented on her early morning runs and he had warned her at least once in front of the women about the danger of running in the woods. Perhaps he would offer to take Allred to the authorities to request assistance tonight. But on the way, Mr. Allred would meet his fate. Noone at the ranch would know the difference either. The leader would simply explain that he'd driven him into town and dropped him at Louie's Bar and Grill. The old guy who owned the restaurant would vouch for him. He was scared shitless of the clan leader. If the woman's body was never found, why would anyone point at finger at him?

He thought back on his first conquest years ago. That victory had whetted his appetite, but it was a long time before he was to act again. Years of incarceration had limited his access and means, but not his imagination. Yet he was a man of principles. Murder born of necessity was his motto.

Rubbing his crotch softly, Mel thought about his ideal protégé. He missed him, but he knew that Brandon had to stay away from the ranch until he'd finished off the probation officer. The younger man's last call had indicated he'd hadn't garnered the courage, but there was time. In fact, the master still had much to teach the younger man. There was a system to killing. It required self-control and careful planning. One needed to act rationally. Unlike most killers, he had actually read up on the subject, studying diligently while at the institution. Learning about predators' habits, the art of deception and the ways to cover one's tracks, he had thought through the process each time, each time except the one time.

He considered the Seaside murder again. Confident that he'd never get caught, he was shocked to discover that Whitney had witnessed the drowning. Shame on her for keeping a secret until he'd got out of prison and was getting his life back on track. She had thought that to blackmail him would stop his advances. Sighing heavily, he shoved aside his longing. At least that threat was eradicated.

Jerking the pick-up into high gear, Mel raced up the road and took the next gravel turn toward his cabin. Shoving the truck into park, he ran in and foraged through the metal box that he kept under the living room floorboards. Jogging back out, he jumped into the vehicle and drove towards the main house. For now, he would have to act like everything was normal. If the spic suspected him of anything, there could be trouble. The gun on his hip felt reassuring as he skidded to a stop. Then he remembered something that Curtis had said about the Mexican. *"That wetback is as slippery as deer guts on a doorknob."* Despite Curtis's limited intellect, sometimes the old con hit the nail on the head. That statement worried him. If that bitch was a copper, Allred must be her accomplice. He leaned over and pulled out the 32M, loading the barrels with care. He would not take any chances. He would bring that brown-skinned piece of trash into his confidence and spin his magic. Then he'd take his revenge.

With a grin of satisfaction, he glanced at his watch. It was nearly dinner time. The man should be back soon, he thought determinedly. He would confront him, kill him and put his body in the back of the truck for proper disposal.

Edging up to the guest cabin's window, he peered in. The room was dark, though it appeared as though someone had lit the fire again. He glanced over at the bed. There was a body in it. That bastard, Allred, had probably ditched on his work and come back to nap. Instantly a brilliant idea came to him. There had been an electrical problem in the small dwelling a few months back. Old wiring had forced them to disconnect the circuits for fear of an electrical fire. However, he had learned a thing or two about electricity while in the joint. He moved away from the window and went to the front door. Finding a heavy branch which had broken in the last storm, he slowly dragged it over and placed it in front of the opening. The door opened out for reasons like this, he realized, smiling with grim satisfaction. Fortunately, the narrow windows of the cabin were too small for any man to climb out of.

On the east corner of the building was the old electrical box. Quietly he opened it and connected several wires, causing sparks to fly. As a small fire started in the box, he ran over and climbed the large elm tree that hung over the A-frame. He was like a monkey at work. Slipping up the trunk and balancing on the branch above, he walked out to where he was near reach of the chimney. He took off his thick down jacket and with perfect aim, flung it on top of the tiny brick opening, which would cause the room to fill with smoke.

By the time he'd climbed down and looked into the window to see if his victim had awakened, it was too smoky to see anything. The fire on the east side of the hut was climbing up the dry log wall and catching the edge of the parched roof. Waiting until the building was nearly up in flames, he went to his truck and hooked up the hose to the large water trough that was a permanent fixture in the back of the vehicle in case of wild fire. Spreading a thick blanket of water around the perimeter of the inferno, he took out his walkie-talkie and called for help. The men were on the other side of the property. It would be a while before they arrived. In the meantime, he would dig a small trench to prevent the fire from spreading. By the time help arrived, the wetback's body would be burned beyond recognition.

* * *

The sunset was a bright red glow behind them as they drove back to the main house. Famished and exhausted, the men were an hour late for dinner. Mel had told them that he believed the Allreds were in the cabin asleep, explaining that he'd come upon the fire too late, but had heard screaming from within. The log which had held the door had burned away just as the men arrived. There was no explanation as to why the victims hadn't bolted from the flames.

If the authorities came snooping around, the Saints would be prepped. Sadly the young couple had been sound asleep, probably not used to the hard work of ranch living, when the electrical fire broke out. He led the men into the dining room. Once again, he felt like he was back in the game, a quarterback running for a touchdown. Under his breath, he murmured, "Now that was *fun*."

CHAPTER 17

Daniel flew through the trees, kicking the poor Arabian like he was a bandit on the lam. He had always loved the Westerns and had fancied himself a cowboy as a kid. Indeed, the make-believe of little boys was long gone. They were in serious trouble. Overhearing Ralph and Curtis's conversation that morning after breakfast had confirmed his worst nightmare. The two men had placed a bet as to how much longer it would be before Mel got a piece from the 'new girl'. Apparently more than two days was a long shot. Their joking was grim as they acknowledged that their wives were a little safer now that the pretty Joslyn had caught the boss's eye.

The the old woman P.O.'s gut wrenched with unfamiliar pain. If ever he'd felt the desire to actually kill someone, it was now. Mel was a sickening excuse for a human being. Christian's midnight tears over the little boy had taken him aback and confirmed what he'd believed since their arrival. It wasn't just teenage girls who were in harm's way at Sliver Ranch. He thought again about her note. When he'd returned to the cabin, she'd left it there on the bed, explaining that plans had changed because she'd been able to hitch a ride into town. Strangely, she did not mention Juicy or Doug, or the rafts. Still if she'd been in a hurry to go, at least she had a safe way to escape.

She never ceased to amaze him. He'd known her for nearly three years and still there were surprises. She was the type of girl who took up windsurfing because it was there, without a fear in the world. She'd dove on the Great Barrier Reef, climbed the Egyptian pyramids and bungee-jumped off some bridge in South America. He wouldn't put it passed her to act on impulse if the situation so required.

Before he'd left the cabin, Toby had arrived. Crying hysterically, the boy was unable to tell Daniel what was bothering him. Eventually the probation officer had tucked the child into the bed, assuring him that his mother would come to get him soon.

He brought the snorting horse to a pounding stop near the edge of the property. There a small crevice, big enough for one man, bordering the river. It would take him to freedom. He had little time. Christian's note was confirmation that he must leave. She was convinced there was more going on at the ranch than met the eye. After finding the photographs, so was he. Christian was one smart cookie. Now she would meet him at Juicy's, or if that was impossible, call from a public place. He pulled the note from his pocket and read it again. This time he noticed something different about her handwriting. Her tendency to forget to dot 'i's was notorious around the office. In the note, every one of those vowels had big circles above them. He nearly crumbled with the realization that he'd missed it. She was not en route to safety at all.

Daniel was petrified and unsure as to how to proceed. The ranchers had a cache of weapons that numbered in the dozens. A stand-off was not completely unlikely and therefore a gun battle, terrifyingly possible. The erotic memories of his time with Christian garnered his attention as he checked the surroundings. Their brief romance had been the sweetest time of his life, despite the circumstances, or perhaps because of them. He had touched her and loved her in a way that he'd never dreamed would be possible. Now the dream appeared to be ending as fast as it had begun. If they came out of this alive, he would do everything in his power to win her love. It was worth the heartache of rejection, he decided. Glancing up the river one last time for the markers left by Juicy, he swallowed hard. Insurmountable as this next exercise appeared to be, he had an overwhelming reason to be successful. It was called a life with Christian Vargas.

He tied the animal known as Quicksilver to a tree limb, loose enough to the river for the creature to escape and access water. That he had to steer a small rubber raft to safety on Level 4 whitewater was the next overwhelming step. Daniel pressed on. Squeezing through the narrow opening in the rocks, he padded silently a quarter of a mile to the designated entry point. The plateau was only eight feet above the river over the edge of the cliff to the shallow inlet below became a challenge. Still Juicy had been clear when she'd said that scaling the wall would be impossible without climbing equipment and plenty of experience. Comparatively, she'd added, rafting would be a piece of cake. He hadn't believed a word of it, nor had he ever truly scaled a wall of such height, but he managed in seconds?

The expectation of the team was fourteen minutes from river entry to landing. Four miles down was the turn-out. In between was a single level three rapids and during the spring, one level four. Fortunately there were no falls and because the river was so high, a highly unlikely chance of being sucked into any deep potholes. Juicy said the way to get through it was to stay in the middle. It was a narrow river, so that wasn't saying much. His heart pounded like a bass drum in his chest as he rapidly pumped the plastic bubble shaped like a miniature accordion. After five minutes, it finally looked like he was making some progress. He continued, sweating draining off his face and running into his eyes.

A cool breeze dried the perspiration from his face as he pushed in the plug with a sigh of satisfaction. Testing the tautness of the thick rubber, he found the raft's air content satisfactory. Now he must face this alone, with little time, if he was to save his beloved. He tried to slow his breathing, to lift himself out of the mental fog of fear that clouded any semblance of concentration. Shoving the boat halfway into the water, he climbed in and grabbed the double-sided paddle. Slowly the raft moved into the Paria. Along the shoreline, sunbeams sliced like lasers through the thick clumps of Ponderosas, sending ripples of light across the water. The late-afternoon sky was a powdery blue and there wasn't a cloud for a hundred miles.

After a few minutes, the river sloped westward. On his left, a wall of pink sandstone rose like a prison wall on the far bank. After a quarter of a mile or so, the water became frothy as the river curved keenly to the right. He could hear an intensifying pounding as he paddled around corner and without warning, abruptly dropped off a three foot ledge before straightening out. Water sluiced in, but not enough to be concerned. His stomach now in his shoes, he shook the chilling droplets out of his hair and face, cursing Juicy for giving no warning as to that 'fall'. He tried to slow his breathing as the river opened up, becoming a shimmering sheet of dark green glass. A striking vista loomed in front of him momentarily, like a scene from a sci-fi movie, the rocks formed strange knobby shapes against the horizon. Hoodoos, that's what Christian had called them. Recognition of something besides fear helped to steady his nerves. He could still think.

For another half mile the towering cliffs filled his vision in glowing colors of rust, gold and ochre. Just when he thought he might relax, an ominous-looking pothole loomed ahead. Furiously he paddled to the left, dodging the hole by a few feet. A long eddy flowed near the boulder-choked bank as he skirted another larger ledge of rock on his right. Maneuvering the raft to the left, he paddled viciously, digging in and leaning forward into the waves that churned like a bubbling witch's brew. Entering the main chute, he began to tremble uncontrollably as the roar of the rapids grew nearer. The spray of water obscured his vision as he felt the boat twist and moan against the current. The raft hurled forward, moving in the fierce cauldron like a rollercoaster with no brakes. The water suddenly shot over the boat, its frigid assault stealing his breath and drenching him. His limbs felt frozen with cold as an icy panic began to overtake him. He was no longer in control. Instead the brutal desires of nature had taken over. He closed his eyes as he felt the raft lurching and bucking, a bronco ride out of control. Then it hit him. He had been a budding bronco rider as a kid, competing a couple of times in the Benton Franklin County Fair. As soon as the memories consoled him, the rapids disappeared behind him and the water smoothed out again.

Relaxing at the knowledge that he'd survived the test, Daniel checked his watch. He'd been traveling nearly ten minutes and the worst of it was over. Breathing deeply for the first time since hitting the water, he paddled furiously now for the last set of rapids. He could do this. As he approached, something appeared his peripheral vision. He glanced to his left. In the trees was a stunning four-point buck. The creature raised his tremendous head as though to nod hello.

In the next instant, he was flung out of the boat and sucked down. Blackness obliterated light as air became a lost commodity. He kicked hard, remembering that fighting a whirlpool would only make it worse. His chest expanded, aching painfully with a screaming desire for air. He forced himself to stop flailing. For what felt like an eternity he paused, and then knew that he was going to die here, that he simply couldn't hold out any longer. As that thought left his tormented mind and was traded for surrender, Daniel shot up through the water like a cannon ball, landing on his face on the side of the riverbank. Gasping, crying, thanking Jesus, he scurried like a crab up the bank and then dropped his head again until a quiet joy of surviving collided with despair.

CHAPTER 18

The next thing that Daniel remembered was being hauled into the backseat of a car as Juicy and Doug bickered amiably about what to do with him. The gay man was afraid that he was experiencing hypothermia while Juicy insisted that he just needed a good shot of whiskey. Perched on the top of the back seat above him, a hairy sentry guard groaned happily. Bear's chunky black tail beat a steady rhythm as he leaned over to lick his master's friend. The long wet tongue got a reaction and eventually Daniel raised his head, mumbling, "We have to find Christian."

Doug and Juicy looked at him dumbly. "That's what we were afraid of." A half an hour later, they realized the gravity of the situation. If, by any chance, Christian had left the compound, she had not made it to a telephone, or to Juicy's home which was the plan if they got split up. Though Juicy had turned up the car heater to blasting and wrapped the shivering P.O. in a cozy down sleeping bag, Daniel wasn't prepared for the trauma of the near drowning and his lover's disappearance. Then his memory jogged, remembering the stolen photos, which he'd wrapped hastily in a torn piece of plastic. Handing them over without another word, he watched as Juicy glanced through the package at the top photograph. With an ugly grimace, she mumbled, "Good work," placing them carefully into the glove compartment.

Doug passed him a carafe of hot coffee while Juicy handed him a bottle of Jack Daniels. Bouncing and bumping in Juicy's jeep across the open terrain, Doug's voice was high-pitched with words of worry. Juicy finally slammed on the brakes as they approached the edge of a gravel road.

"Listen to me, both of you. We're calling in the troops now. My buddy, the guy you met at the coffee shop in Tropic, he and the rest of the sheriff's posse are on stand-by." She grabbed her cell phone from the dashboard and threw it at Doug, "Look up Harrison on speed dial."

* * *

An hour later, they were poised like a posse at the OK Corral not far from the place where the original trio had first spied on Sliver Ranch. In addition to the three of them and the dog, there were six sheriff deputies, and a sharp-shooter who had once been a Green Beret. Three men had come on horseback. The rest arrived on four wheelers. The sky was nearly dark as night was fast approaching. The mountain air had grown chilly. In the distance, the landscape's geometric knobs of rock shadowed the group like a host of faceless Easter Island statues.

Small flashlights were pulled from pockets, their pinpoints dancing across the faces of strangers like mini searchlights. The constant low hum of determined voices gave Daniel a sense of reassurance, though he anguished. Where was Christian? He forced his mind to stay calm, but the image of Brandon, Mel, Cancer whatever his name was, would not leave his mind. He shuddered, not wanting to consider deplorable consequences.

Juicy explained that she'd received a call from Christian's brother, Scott, the night before and that he'd been in contact with the Utah attorney general as well as state patrol. Scott was left with no other choice but to make waves where it counts.

"Scott is on his way down here as we speak," Juicy explained to Harrison and his band of deputies. "Jurisdiction is tricky, but the Utah state authorities want to cooperate. Polygamists are not their favorite cup of tea. Besides, the Sliver brothers have been under surveillance for a few months for other illegal activities. Apparently one of them owns a brothel in Salt Lake City. That's just the kind of thing that gets the LDS elders all stirred up."

The men had gathered around a large map stretched out on the front end of Juicy's SUV. Each of them held a tiny two-way radio set to a matching frequency. As the designated lead, Harrison barked orders, pointing to the various entry points, explained that two of his men would climb the western wall, Doug and Daniel would enter from the road and another three come in from the river. The plan was to go in at sunrise and start a clandestine search for Christian and if possible, the little boy, whom Daniel explained had been abused by the sect's leader.

"In the meantime, Scott's working with the proper authorities to secure search warrants for the compound as well as probable cause arrest warrants for both Jared Sliver and Brandon Clist," Juicy added, a bitter tone to her mellow tenor voice.

"According to Scott's contact up in the prosecutor's office in Benton County, they've tracked an account from a series of cellular phone calls at the ranch to Brandon Clist," Doug offered up. "However there's a problem. According to Scott's last phone call, Brandon Clist is in Benton County jail. Apparently he was extradited from Texas about a week ago for failing to register as a sex offender. Furthermore, there was an intercepted call that came from the ranch. The message was from someone known as Cancer. Apparently they were planning a special meeting next Friday in the desert just south of Pendleton."

Daniel swallowed hard as a voice in his head began to scream for answers. Who in the hell was Mel? He put his hands, calling for attention. "Hey guys, listen up. This is what we've got. A guy who calls himself Cancer, who contacts young men and recruits them for some satanic ritual stuff. Case in point: Cole Comely and Thomas Witherspoon. Then we have a ranch full of polygamists with a guy who calls himself Mel, who we now know is not Brandon Clist. We have some interesting overlaps between the Sign of the Nail Ranch and their church Lex Talonis and the satanic blood ritual, evidenced by the cutting on Whitney and the empty container found in the desert outside the Tri-Cities. Finally we've got a meeting that's coming up outside of Pendleton. I say a surveillance team is assigned to Brandon. If he's getting bailed out of jail any time soon, he will lead you to at least one of your perps. In the meantime, I'm going to rescue my partner." Before anyone could interrupt, Scott jumped out of an arriving jeep. They filled him in quickly on the last developments. In seconds he was on the phone to Oz Rellim. "Make sure Clist is out of the pokey and keep a team on him. There is a meeting coming up near Pendleton. Your guys need to be there."

The team was jacked up by the integration of information. The questions came fast and hard. Pushing the minor questions aside, Daniel explained what he knew about the sect's lay-out and behavioral patterns. Eventually the men agreed on the details of the rescue operation. "The rest of us will sleep here in turns until four. The sun starts to rise about an hour later. Ben and Carl will position themselves by the western perimeter here." Harrison pointed to the map. "That will insure quicker access in. Be prepared to enter the compound at five. Daniel can get them in. Take turns sleeping so you can keep an eye on the road coming out of the compound, in case Mel or whatever his name is decides to leave with Christian or the boy. Jack, Stuart and Stim will over the south side, heading out for the river in a few hours. Juicy, I think you should go back into town and wait with Scott."

"Not a chance," Scott replied. "I'm right there for my sister."

The deputy shrugged. "Have it your way. You can ride with me and Roy in from the east. I know a place where we can get through. These two here," he paused to point at Doug and Daniel, "You go straight in, toward the buildings. Stim and the rest will cover the river, in case Mel decides that's his way out. Everyone has a walkie-talkie. Stay in touch. As soon as someone finds Christian and the boy, we call one another and get out. If the big shots arrive in time with arrest warrants, they can do their thing. Our goal is get them out.

Period. No heroics, do you understand me?" Solemn nods circled the group like falling dominoes.

Daniel's mind raced ahead as he blurted, "There are dogs."

"We've got that taken care of. Each team will carry a small tranquilizing gun." In the lantern light, Harrison smiled over at the probation officer for the first time. "Sorry," he mumbled. "I didn't recognize you at first. Glad you made it out. That river's no friend this time of year."

The Latino nodded, still stunned by his harrowing experience. Fortunately the whiskey had taken hold. Slowly he moved toward the map and began pointing to landmarks. "Here, where the fence meets the wall is where I cut the electricity this morning. Just in case. And here, that is the leader's cabin. Like I said, he's called 'Mel' by the Saints. Over here is the shed were they keep their guns and ammunition. I also found a blue pick-up in there yesterday, stashed in the far back. It was covered with a tarp, but the keys were in the ignition and it looked like it was still drivable." He leaned closer and carefully studied the map. To his surprise, the cabin where they had slept had disappeared.

Nodding to Daniel, the cowboy continued with his instruction. "So in other words, there's no time to lose. That asshole might take off with her. That's why we need to make our move as soon as possible," Scott interrupted, his deep baritone rumbling with concern.

Juicy unloaded supplies from the back of her rig and said good-bye. The horseback riders left next, disappearing into the dark landscape like phantom actors from an old western. One by one, the men gathered their thoughts as they settled down for the night. Hidden behind an enormous outcropping, they clustered around a small camp fire that Juicy had built while the others had conversed. Daniel had been given dry clothes and a freeze-dried packet of camp grub. The river guide had also brought the team a pile of sleeping bags and several canteens of coffee as well as power bars for the morning.

Bear huddled between his two male companions, moaning fitfully. The warmth from the big dog's body was a welcomed addition to the waning heat from the fire. Daniel looked over at Doug, who'd not said much since they'd arrived. He wondered if he was out of his element, afraid somehow that his gestures or conversation might give his sexual orientation away. Mountain men probably tolerated the thought of a lesbian better than a gay man. Leaning toward Doug, he whispered, "Thanks, buddy, for getting me out of harm's way. I thought that river was going to have me for breakfast."

"Hey, man, you are one brave dude. You couldn't convince me to do that for the million dollar winning lotto ticket," the man replied with a heavy sigh. "I just can't stop thinking about Christian in there with that lunatic. You know, she's one of my best friends. I'd do *just* about anything for her."

"Yeah, I know what you mean. I would, too. Hell, I'd never have climbed in that freaking raft otherwise." There was a long pause as the worry of her well-being weighed heavily in their minds.

"You guys hooked up," Doug remarked matter-a-fact.

Daniel squirmed, recalling his promise to keep their romantic interlude private. Yet during the past week, he had bonded with the man sitting next to him, an unlikely friend to be sure. Doug was a man whom he'd otherwise have written off for being too 'different' than himself.

"How'd you know?"

Doug chuckled softly. "If I were straight, I'd have never let that opportunity pass me up. She's a gem. And she's tough. Matt, he's great guy, too, but I know that woman pretty well and she's not totally satisfied in that relationship. Every time we hang together, your name comes up."

Daniel felt a little thrill race through him. He wondered if hope was a concept that he could contemplate. "Really, she talks about me?"

Doug reached out to stroke Bear, who was finally snoring contentedly. "Yep. All the time." They sat in silence, worry consuming them when there was beep from a phone.

Reaching into his coat pocket, Scott flipped open a small razor phone.

"Hey, Oz. What'd you find out?" Daniel could not see his friend's face in the darkness, but the one-sided conversation was prolonged. He waited, watching in the man, sensing a major shift in the case. "No shit. That means...oh god, we've got to hurry."

He snapped the phone and released a heavy sigh. "Brandon Clist just spilled his guts. The guy at the ranch is his uncle. They looked him up. He's wanted by the FBI for extortion and possibly murder. His code name is Cancer."

"What do you mean? The kid looks exactly like this uncle." Daniel felt the terror before the words left his mouth.

"Yeah. Gary Melvin Clist is only about ten years older than Brandon. It would be easy to confuse the two."

Daniel nearly cried. "I know all about Mel Clist. He spent six years at McNeil Island for a kidnapping, sexual abuse, and more."

"Apparently the uncle is a certifiable sociopath. And we've compared photos. He's the kid's doppelganger."

"Dopple what?"

"His look-a-like. Brandon's the spitting image of this guy."

"What else did the parents say? Can they confirm that the Mel from the ranch is this uncle?"

Scott shook his head. "Rellim didn't elaborate. He was only able to talk to them for a few minutes. He said that the mom has been hospitalized. They've lost their daughter, Daniel, and their son is facing some new charges as a result of his association with this freak. Apparently Gary Melvin Clist's prints were found on the outside wall of the stake house."

* * *

The morning air was as cold as an ice box. Daniel felt the ache of poor rest and river battering in his bones as he opened his eyes to a rosy dawn. The air was acrid with the smell of smoke. Sitting up, he laughed when Bear began to lick his face eagerly, his tail flapping with doggy anticipation. Then he remembered that bad news of the night before. How he'd found the ability to sleep at all was a miracle.

Somewhere in the far distance, a low whistle from a train, or a long haul truck sounded. Doug was standing a few yards away, his back to them, urinating against a tree. Anxious to get going, Daniel slipped from the sleeping bag to join him, keeping a respectful space between them. He soon trudged back to the fire where Harrison was boiling water for coffee. Doug had already returned to the fire where he knelt next to Bear, feeding him from a bag of dog food.

"So does everyone have an idea how we're going to handle things if they pull out their weapons?" the brawny man named Roy asked ominously.

"It won't get that far. The deal was, if our girl didn't make it to the rendezvous rafting point by four o'clock yesterday, I would leave. She would then go to Mel and show him a note that we crafted, which basically stated that I was leaving her for my old flame. I blame her for all kinds of things and tell her that she's better off at the ranch with people who will take care of her."

"But that was before you got her bogus note." Scott had lit a cigarette and was pacing nervously.

"Yeah, I know." Daniel felt like weeping, but had the fortitude to know better. "Scott, she was determined to get statements from a couple of the younger mothers who have indicated that they're not too happy at Slivers' Ranch and are looking for a way to get out with their kids. You've got to see this place to believe it. There is no, I repeat, no way to communicate to the outside world unless Mel or Jared deem it necessary. From what I could gather, the only woman who's been allowed out in the past six months was a girl named Stephanie, the one who we were first here to find, and that's only because she's got some issues with her pregnancy *and* she bangs Mel on the side."

* * *

Mel meticulously burned the Asetic Bible, a book of black magic known only to a few. He couldn't part with the pictures, but the book was giving him trouble recently. What he'd never admitted to anyone was his superstitious nature. He looked for signs and most of the time, read them correctly. When he'd returned to the house, a black crow had dove at him like a bomber pilot, nearly taking out his eye. He didn't know what the experience meant at first, but when he went in to get his gun, the book was sitting on his coffee table. That was not its normal spot. He'd obviously left it out in a forgotten moment. He used many of the passages in his sermons. Slowly he was getting the Saints to understand the philosophy, a unique combination of Asetian and Satanic principles, with a bit of fundamentalism thrown in. The group had begun to succumb to his program. He thought a lot about the omens before setting the large oil drum alit and dumping the book, as well as the rope, the blood-stained clothes and the woman's ID into the blaze. Joslyn's betrayal, Toby's assault on his manhood, the necessity of Moloch's murder, keenly portrayed as a suicide and now the black crow's attack were esoteric warnings. It muddled his mind and sent surges of anger through his veins. Furthermore, he also sensed that he was forgetting something important.

He stared into the flames as they licked at the chilly morning air. Chanting a few lines from his self-authored prayer book, *The Saints of Lex Talonis* Handbook, he thought about his father. Few people in the family talked about Leo. He was a strong, quiet man who had died while mining in northern Idaho. Mel and his brother had been with their Dad that day. The old silver mine was on their property, a fluke, but one that paid off from time to time. They had built the long ladder into the bottom of the cavern and had used a wooden bucket to haul out the rubble. Gerry and his Dad usually went down. It was Mel's job to sort the rocks into piles. When the cave-in occurred on that fateful day in 1984, Gerry had just left on his mission. There was no one to help get his dad out. He'd listened to Leo's screams for over an hour. Only a kid of seven and unable to drive the truck as the keys were in his father's pocket, he was dumbstruck as to what to do. The mine was a long way from their home. Finally, when his dad's terrifying screams had subsided, Mel had run the four miles back to the house. His mother and her sister, who was also his father's wife, had come with a posse of neighbors, but by then, it was too late. Leo had died in the place he believed would give him a new life.

The worse part of it was that his mother had sent him to live with relatives. That was the beginning of his hatred for women. That stupid evil woman named Joan had put him into a cellar to sleep. Didn't she know that it reminded him of a mine? Full of spooky heirlooms and piled-high boxes, he had to navigate his way to the back of the dark space to find the tiny cot. There were no windows and it smelled worse than a mine. His nightmarish screams were never answered by night and his older cousin enjoyed molesting him by day. By the time that he'd returned home, two years later, he was a different boy.

The burning was a ritual in itself. With the pages dissolving into smoke, he realized that he was offering this sacrifice to his father's memory. He had learned much from his old man. He'd learned that family was a priority and that the ways of the fundamentalist church were advantageous, especially to men. However, he didn't agree with everything that the old Mormon faith had to offer. Watching his brother disappear like the smoke before him, into the brethren of the Latter Day Saints, while disavowing his polygamist legacy was a horrible thing to witness. Mel was determined, therefore, to create his father's family again, only his way.

His blood condition was something that came later. He had to have fresh blood to survive. Over time, Mel had learned to accept his condition and in turn, worship the greatest spirit known to mankind. Together, he and Brandon had witnessed Satan as their savior. In fact he often thought that the angel

Melchizedek, his true namesake, was sent to manifest his power, not unlike Moroni to Jesus. The simple concepts understood by the satanic religion were practiced in the Mormon temple, under a different name, but not without similar meaning or message.

The clan had seemed upset the night before. The Saints had been taught to keep quiet, not ask questions, but their master could feel some dissention in the ranks. Curtis had appreciated Allred's help, if that was the bastard's real name. He told the clan to pray for the couple who had died in the fire, but some of the clan looked suspicious. To make things worse, the kid, Toby, had disappeared as well.

Worry gnawed like an infected spider bite. Allred was a spy, just like his woman, and though there had never been a reason for authorities to come on to his property, there was a chance that they would now. The pit was a long way out and she would be dead soon, if she wasn't already. The twenty foot fall should have done it, but then again, a person could never be sure.

He listened, his ears perked by a rustling sound in the woods. His hearing had become acute while in prison. There was always a gangbanger or pervert ready to sneak up on you in there, to get their jerk-off jollies, or otherwise physically harass the other prisoners. The guards were just as bad. He'd seen another prisoner buggered by a guard gangbang more than once during his incarceration. There was the sound again. It was a quiet splashing, like paddles on water. The fire was nearly out. He grabbed a bucket of water and plunged it into the drum. Then he ran in to get his gun.

* * *

Christian couldn't breathe. Her attempt at scaling the slippery wall of the pit had failed and she'd fallen backwards, landing flat on her back. The concept of dying in this horrible place began to take hold. She had been certain that Mel would come back for her, why she wasn't sure. She remembered him saying something about wanting another chance at her lifeblood, whatever that meant. Her brain felt scrambled, but then again, she was hungry and wounded. She had to find a way out, but without a rope or something to hang on to…and where was Daniel?

Her skin was clammy and cold to the touch. Shock was setting in now; she knew the signs. Her heart rate had finally slowed down, but her breathing was different. Oxygen was infinitely hard to come by. She forced herself through a progressive relaxation. Starting with her head, she mentally instructed body parts to relax. It helped conserve energy, perhaps, but only reminded her of how cold she was. The Mormon underwear was a blessing now, she realized, peering up at the smiling moon, which peeked faintly through a thick cloud cover. Hunger was a constant companion and thirst was becoming a pressing problem. She heard a faint buzzing in her ears. The mosquitoes were out early, she thought, as the sound increased. Shivering, she rolled up in a ball, trying to conserve body heat. The ground was damp and sticky.

The buzzing faded into a muted hum. Shapeless shadows began to shift against a soft glow on the opposite wall from where she lay. She succumbed to any fear, allowing the paralyzing inner tension to sweep from her body like a wave. Resistance never worked anyway. The anomaly started to shift as her curiosity increased. Rolling out of her ball, she gazed intently at the other side of the hole. The amorphous light congealed into small flickers which now danced merrily like fairies in a Disney cartoon. Fireflies? An image gradually evolved from the light. She strained to see and then cried out as a shimmering vision of her father appeared.

"Do not give up, little one." His voice sounded as though from a tunnel. "Your friend, Maria, has helped to make you strong. See your power, hang on. The man is not the boy."

With that, the vision faded away. Tears rolled down her cheeks. The pit seemed darker than ever and she wondered if seeing her father this time was a sign that her own death was imminent. She thought about Maria then, the funny little shaman with her secret recipes and magic potions- the snake meat, the death doll and the mystical laying of cards that so often revealed truths. Her last reading, where the devil card had appeared, should have been her warning. And yet the old woman had not foreseen her death, only the overcoming of evil.

She heard the sound of a gunshot. Listening and attentive, she also heard the sound of trickling water, the deep groan of a long-haul truck and the gentle patter of rain above. The dogs. She vaguely wondered if they might befriend her; perhaps lead someone to her rescue. And Daniel would not leave her here to die. He would know that the note was a fake.

Shivering against the cold, her feet felt like bricks of ice. Her eyes had adjusted somewhat, so she followed the sound of the water, moving her hands along the circular wall until she found a horizontal opening the size of a small log. Reaching her hand into it, she felt a narrow band of water which seemed to be moving away from her. She wondered if this was an underground stream and where it might lead. She thought about the Paria River, considering that perhaps the pit was an old wash-out and that the river was close by.

Cupping her hands, she scooped some water and drank greedily. It was refreshing, though spiced with an earthy mineral flavor. Better than no water at all, she acknowledged, realizing that if she could keep her body heat stable and had water to drink, she could actually last down here for a few days. That thought gave her courage and a sense of accountability to survive.

The probation officer had faced death many times before. Always, fate had passed her by. Her palm's lifeline was long and pronounced, though marked by unusual slashes, like stitches scored across a deep scar. She would overcome this, like the childhood snake bite, the near drowning, the fire at her aunt's home, and the vicious assault by the youth pastor-cum-killer a year prior. Her life was fraught with these things, like some people endured frequent illness, financial ruin or mental instability. It was not a matter of questioning destiny, but rather accepting it.

Suddenly an odd thought came to her. The Saints had been preparing for their monthly blood drive. According to the women, they gave blood to the Red Cross, but the drawing of it occurred at the ranch. Mel then delivered it to the local Red Cross facility.

She became agitated as the word, porphyria, came to mind. It was a medical condition that produced the need for blood consumption, it along with the affliction known as sanguine. She couldn't remember the exact medical explanation of the term, but the vampire cults often referred to their physical and psychic need for blood. If Mel was same man who had communicated to Miasma and Moloch, the Saints' blood drive could be a ruse for other intentions. She felt the bile rising into her throat as a remote image of the psychopath, guzzling the recovered jug found in the desert, came to mind. She'd seen a television show once on porphyria and people who drank animal blood in order to live.

Her heart began to race as she remembered something that Toby had said to her in the children's room the first day, when she was helping him with his studies. He had been rubbing a small wound on his neck when Christian had asked what had happened. He'd just grinned and said something about nocturnal feeders. She'd thought perhaps he was referring to a spider bite, but the marks had looked suspiciously like that of a human mouth. How could she have been so naïve! The vampire theme had been in her face since the beginning, when little Cole Comely had arrived in her life. If this group were satanic devotees and their leader, a practicing porphyriac, then it was no wonder the kid had a bite mark. Her brain pounded for more memories. There had been other signs, a lack of a cross at any one of the women's throats, no iconic displays of Jesus, no King James Bibles.

After consuming a significant amount of the cool water, she felt another shift in the atmosphere. This time it was related to the arrival of morning. One bird began her song, and then another, in a joyous greeting of a new day. A steady light began to filter down through the darkness. Exhaustion tugged at her spirits, but she was determined to remain hopeful. Perhaps she had slept a bit. Time was such a slippery friend...sometimes behaving like a tired old woman and other times, on fire, like a toddler who'd just learned to run. If nothing else, time definitely had a mind of its own.

Her thoughts continued to wander while a low rumble emerged from the depths of her coat. She was so hungry. Shivering, she suddenly remembered that her jacket had an inner pocket. Slipping her hand into the fabric's lining, she pulled back the Velcro closure and fumbled for the packet of dried rattlesnake meat. Laughing with irony, she shoved a long shriveled piece of the sour-tasting stash into her mouth. What would her teasing friends say now?

Closing her eyes and chewing slowly, she tried to recall her father, considered her relationship with Daniel, convinced herself to break up with Matt, and vowed to start spending more time with her brother, Scott. She knew that her mind was seeking every excuse to avoid terror, a skill in which she'd grown proficient. Just as she began to wonder why her mother rarely visited her in her dreams, she heard the sound of a dog barking.

CHAPTER 19

The river was high. The snow melt had begun a few weeks earlier, creating a dangerous passage for anyone who thought that whitewater rafting in early spring was a feat to be attempted. Mel continued his journey to the water's edge. He had collected the three dogs beforehand. He always felt more secure with the animals by his side. Pulling a gun wasn't like in the movies. To really do it well, one needed a distraction.

He whistled sharply as the Rottweiler rushed ahead. He was a brute of a canine. More than once, he'd scared off the sheriff's department simply by letting Lestat off his leash. Laughing, he thought about the progress he'd made at the ranch. He'd arrived less than a year ago, a wayward relative, looking for a place to rest and a hand-out. Yet the ex-con in him knew how to manipulate his prey. It was like a cat playing with a mouse until it got hungry. In less than three weeks, he'd convinced, James, the shell-shocked idiot from his brother's wife's side, to lend him some money. Next came the brothel in Salt Lake City and then, within another month, he'd organized his real gravy train-the drugs moving from Washington to Utah. The money from the drug trade and the brothel enabled him to pay back the cousin and buy out the remaining loan on the ranch. Then his nephew, Brandon, arrived, fresh from the institution. He, too, was anxious to conform to his uncle's control. As a reward for his innate intelligence, he'd put Brandon in charge of the first website, Melchizedek's Missionaries, where he drew a number of juvenile offenders, lost little girls in search of a daddy and prior sex offenders as members. Yet there was more work to do and now that damn probation officer and her pal had put a damper on his progress. If the sheriff's department decided to investigate, he could be caught for some illegal doings.

The guns weren't all registered and the kid, Toby, might be a squealer.

He reached down into his pants pocket and pulled out the woman's phone. Fortunately he'd found a phone charger and been able to get the thing working again. Flipping through the numbers, he decided to text message the four people who had left her messages as well as the first five people on her phone list. There was a series of beseeching messages from a man named Matt. There were two messages from a deep-voiced guy named Harry, inquiring as how the rafting expedition was progressing. There was a message from a woman, again, asking how much longer she should expect her to be away, and then an infuriated voice mail from a man named Scott, who'd demanded to know what in the hell she was doing down in Utah. Not one of the messages gave him an indication as to why she and Allred had come to the ranch.

The text message he sent out simply read: *Got as far as Oregon City last night. My mister bailed on me. See you soon.* He'd already thrown her backpack into the old rubber raft, poked it with a few holes and threw it into the river the night before.

When the authorities found the dilapidated boat and pack, who would they blame? She'd notified her friends after all. The cell phone should have gone into the backpack, but damn, he couldn't think of everything, especially with the wetback to handle. Instead, he simply threw the phone as far as he could into the river. Smiling, he imagined the woman's slow death. She would probably live at least a few more days, unless his snakes got to her.

* * *

Stephanie was scared. Cancer had slapped her hard, blaming her for the troubles. Threatening her again and again, he'd forced himself on her from behind. Nothing had felt right since then. Her baby hadn't moved in over twenty-four hours and she was pretty sure that was a bad sign. Gingerly she unfolded the letter that had come to her from Joslyn's pocket. She didn't know how Serena would know the boring chick with the pretty blue eyes. Joslyn had said that she'd met her older sister through Joe Sliver, which was the only connection that made any sense. Still, it seemed strange that she had held onto the letter for the entire trip down to Utah. Stephanie had a habit of losing things, and didn't believe other women were any different.

Dear Stephanie,

I miss you so much. I hope that you are doing well. I finally got clean. It took a stranger to get me out of J-Man's house and into treatment. I didn't think I could do it, but I guess three weeks clean and sober shows I can!

I decided that after I'm done in here, I'm going back home. You should come with me. Dad has called me a lot of times and has sent me an airplane ticket, too. As soon as I graduate from this place, hopefully in another couple of weeks, I'm flying back there. Dad said if I do what I'm supposed to, he'll pay for me to go back to school. I was thinking maybe I'd be a nurse someday.

Dad wants you to call him. He loves us, Stephie and wants us to be safe. I miss you so much, little sister, and know if we try, we can make something of ourselves.

If you will call and tell us where you are, then I'll have Dad send you a ticket right away. Please, come home! I'm a Rivercrest Rehab 509 339-2934. I can take calls from 4 to 6.

Lots of love, your sister, Serena

Her throat tightened as she read. Her sister was the only person who had ever protected her. She'd been a hero in the younger girl's eyes, until she'd got into the gang and drugs. Stephanie sighed as a deep shiver ran through her. Hot tears stung behind her closed lids. Her dad had tried over the years, sending them money, which their mother had used for new hair extensions, acrylic nails and a bright blue second-hand sports car. Connie was a grade A slut; one of those women who couldn't live without a man. Their little trailer in east Pasco was home to a revolving circus of predators.

Some kind, some mean and some deviant, they all eventually learned to hate Connie Patterson. She was an evil soul in her heart, which was why Stephanie had turned to the Mormon Church in the first place.

Sadly, she'd never quite fit in with the Latter Day Saints crowd, though she loved Brandon Clist with all of her heart and was determined to make things work out. In the end, it was obvious that he had never felt the same for her. And she'd paid a steep price for that knowledge. Joining the Saints to be closer to him had been a waste of time. First Whitney and then Brandon, both gone, leaving her with crazy Jared and wicked Mel. Maybe her sister was right. Maybe she should leave. All it would take was a call from her doctor's office. The lady doctor in Tropic had always said that Stephanie had other choices.

Maybe she would leave after the baby came. She smiled as her belly began to roll with life. "Whew! You had me scared for a minute, you busy little girl," she said softly as she patted her abdomen. Stephanie suddenly recalled that was what her dad had often said to her when she was young.

* * *

Scott felt sick. There weren't many things that riled him. Over time, particularly after six years in the King County Prosecutor's office, in the Felony Division, he'd grown as tough as weeds. His stamina and attention to detail didn't compare to his no-nonsense approach to crime. No one got passed him, or to him. No one except the young woman he called 'sister'.

Christian had come into his life at time when the advent of adolescence loomed and family loyalty was quickly becoming a distant afterthought. Starting middle school was the only thing on his mind that summer; the only thing until the rosy-cheeked, solemn-faced child arrived. Though her parents and sister had drowned, Christian had been found clinging to a life preserver. It is a strange bit of luck that she survived. The mayday call from her father's sinking sloop was never heard. Instead, a small freighter had lost power and was listing off the coast of Oregon. The search and rescue team initially thought that the child was drifting garbage until they'd come close enough to see her dark brown locks and pale, determined little face. A plucky, petite four-year-old, she had worn a wetsuit and cold weather sailing gear. She shouldn't have survived that day, but then again she shouldn't have lived the day that she was bitten by a rattlesnake over a year earlier.

Our little trooper, as his father had nicknamed her, was stoic and undemanding. Only twice in all the time that he'd known his young cousin had he seen her truly weep: once when her best friend had died and again when she'd buried her premature infant. Ironically, her arrival that summer marked the longest drought that Portland seen in one hundred years. Clearly ahead of her peers, the tiny brunette knew how to speak a bit of French, wore clothes like a miniature fashion model and refused to eat anything but bananas, English crumpets and cucumbers. His own mother, with a brood of four, put Scott in charge of the child. To his utter surprise, the little girl wasn't, as one might expect, a bore, nor was she a burden.

In fact, his 'sister' had always had a weird sixth sense. As an older child, she'd conversed with animals like they were human, and had often reported strange dreams that upset the entire family. During her elementary years, she would disappear for hours, only to arrive home with a new treasure or story to tell. She was an excellent athlete, but her real gift was her mind. Only sometimes, the very asset that provided unusual revelation would backfire in its analysis. Chrissie had guessed wrong this time. Brandon Clist was Mr. Rogers compared to the guy they were really dealing with. Scott's jaw clenched again as his brain raced for solutions. Mel Clist was a psychopathic killer and his beloved sister was his new conquest.

He said a silent prayer to the God of generosity. After all, time was of the essence.

* * *

"Where's the dog?" Doug asked, glancing around with concern.

"What?" Daniel's eyes were smarting from the sight in front of him. Thirty feet to his right, where the cabin should have been, was a tall pile of blackened stone. The lingering tang of fire burned his nostrils as he sniffed the air, realizing what he was seeing. Spindly wisps of smoke, like the fingers of ghosts reaching out of the ground, were visible near the old fireplace. The tree nearest to the cabin was scorched on one side, though the other was still green, as though someone had tried to save the old pine.

His recent home of the past two days was burned to the ground. He knew he'd smelled fire the night before. The glowing sheen in the evening's sky had been smoke on sunset. Yet this morning, the pallor of the day was as gray as the cabin's remains. *Please God, tell me that Chrissie isn't in there.*

Doug repeated himself, this time emphatically. "Where is Bear?"

Daniel spun around, grabbing his new friend's arm. "Look at that. That's where we slept. She could have been in there last night. The dog will stay with us. He's trained." The probation officer took off at a gallop to the crumbled northern wall where the bed would have been. The place was still dangerous. He knew a little about fires, had worked as a wilderness volunteer in college, but that was nothing compared to what he found.

"Careful! Watch out for hot spots," Doug hissed, whistling a low note, trying to coax the dog from the trees. He stepped gingerly into the ash and rumble, his own gut feeling the fear of incineration. An honorary tombstone, the fireplace stood like a primitive obelisk in the haze. There was nothing left of the furniture except the metal frame of the bed, warped by intense heat. Then he saw what looked like bones. He swallowed hard, tears prevented him from seeing anything else. Falling to his haunches, he wept for her. Doug's eventual whisper came as an explosion.

"These are too small to belong to Christian. Look at this set of rib bones."

"How in the hell do you know that?"

"Take my word for it. I worked in the animal lab at Pacific Northwest Laboratories before I became a hairdresser. These bones are not human." As the statement dawned on him, Daniel's face blackened with a new fury. If Mel Clist was standing in front of him now, he would kill him with his bare hands.

* * *

The search and rescue team had climbed through the fence and were walking the perimeter of the property, preparing to block off possible escape routes, when the three-legged dog appeared in the younger man's binocular view. "I see that dog, northwest twenty degrees out near that grove of trees," Carl nudged his brother and pointed due north.

Ben searched until he found the animal. "Right. He's moving fast. I say, let's follow him." Both were strong runners, able to keep up at a distance for a while. The canine was fast, but stopped every few yards to sniff the ground. Then he simply vanished.

Carl stopped, pasting the binoculars to his face and turning slowly in a one-eighty degree arc. "I can't see him anywhere. Radio that Hispanic guy. He's supposed to have the dog with him."

Ben pulled the walkie-talkie from his belt, pushed the button and spoke. "Daniel, are you there?"

"I hear you."

"We just saw the dog. He's running towards a ravine on the northwest corner of the property."

"Got it. I know the area. There's a steep ravine that drops to the river. I'm on my way." He took off running, yelling over his shoulder at Doug to follow.

After the men called Daniel, they continued due north. They jogged along for awhile, their eyes, eagle-like, darting across the landscape. They were trained hunters and knew how to survive in the wilderness. Ben, the older one, had served in as a sniper in Iraq and was prepared for just about anything. His younger brother was a rock climber and had scaled a few world renowned peaks in his time. Both were thrilled by the opportunity to investigate the Sign of the Nail Ranch. They had been there several times in the past, doing what was their own brand of reconnaissance. The cult was an aberration in their tight-knit community. Raised LDS, the men hated anyone or anything that made their faith look bad. Polygamists were the bane of a modern Mormon's ideology.

Panting heavily, Ben yelled to Carl, "There, movement over there."

They jogged another three hundred yards as a blue truck careered around the corner, squealing to a halt in front of them.

* * *

Christian awoke to the keening sound, a melodic tune echoed through the forest as clearly as if it were a great concert hall. Somewhere, in the distance, the child's voice wove like threads of silk through the woolly baritones. As the sound grew closer, she realized that it wasn't a child at all, but an airplane flying overhead. For a moment she imagined her brother coming to save her, but angrily tossed the illusion aside.

She felt the sensation of ancient memory as the faint sound of a dog's bark reached her. Her voice rose against her will. A simultaneous longing for rescue fought against a fear that Mel was returning with a cadre of evil conspirators. But the dog barked again and she knew his welcomed voice. Screaming now, she released all of her remaining energy for their find. They must be able to hear her. Her throat ached like a Brillo pad of pain now.

Then a mounting hope was crushed again by fear as the loud pop of a gun repeated itself and a roar of engine sounded. Dropping to her knees, Christian rolled to the wall nearest to her. There was a short silence and then a muffled voice echoed against the cylinder of rock, "You still alive down there?" There was a long pause. He was obviously waiting for her to answer. She pressed against the outcropping, which she'd tried to climb earlier.

Temporary darkness filled the space above as a body tumbled down the shaft, bashing against the wall to her left. There was a heavy thud as a man who would have been her rescuer landed. Mortified thoughts climbed around her brain as she realized the poor man's fate. Bile rose in her throat, but she forced herself to remain silent. Conjuring courage, she slid over to the dead man as another body dropped down the hole like a rock in a pond.

Cringing in terror, she waited for several minutes to pass. The engine roared to life, the sound of spitting gravel followed and then there was silence. Assured that her nemesis was gone, Christian rolled away from the wall and stood up. Placing two fingers in her mouth, she whistled long and shrill. She had no doubt her dog had known to hide from danger. In seconds, Bear stood quietly at the edge of the pit, his husky, black shape the reassuring sign of salvation. Then she moved to the most important task at hand.

The closest man was on his side. She heaved him over and immediately saw that he had no face. Dizziness swept over her momentarily. Oddly she felt the desire to lie down and go to sleep. This was just a bad dream. However, the other man was moaning softly, forcing her to act. He'd been shot in the chest, but the bullet hadn't killed him yet. She searched both of them for a radio or cell phone. Finding a small phone in the dead man's coat pocket, she assured the other one that she would get help. Opening the survivor's down jacket, she yanked back his flannel shirt and checked the wound. The bleeding was minor, but she worried about internal hemorrhaging.

Carefully she lifted his head and shoved her coat under it. She whispered as if to a tired child, repeating that she would get help; that he must breathe slowly and try to stay calm. His eyes were closed, but his hand moved slightly against her, giving her a sense of hope. Tugging against dead weight, she pulled off the corpse's coat and placed it over the other man's legs. Concerned that shock would set in soon, she had to move quickly or he would undoubtedly perish.

Frantically she tried to get the phone to work, but it was no use. They were out of reception's range. Adrenaline pounded in her ears as the power of purpose gave her mind a focus. She was always better under stress. When it came to fight or flight, Christian always chose the former. Meanwhile Bear whined anxiously from above.

"Bear, I want you to help me. I'm going to climb out." The dog whined agreeably. With great effort, she pulled off both men's belts, moving as gently as possible with the wounded man. "Do you have anything like rope or cording?" she whispered to him, but he was unable to respond. She searched and eventually found a sizable piece of nylon rope in the dead man's coat pocket.

Christian gazed up at the shaft with inexorable determination. It was now or never. Quickly, she made a sailor's knot and wove the rope through the belt buckle and looped the other man's belt through the first belt, leaving the buckle on one end. Then she pulled off her socks and knotted them around the rope. Her makeshift line was approximately eighteen feet when fully extended.

Now the true test would come. Calling her pet, she explained that when she threw up the makeshift rope, he was to find a solid place to hook it. She had taught the canine special commands and had no doubt that Bear would respond. He had been trained in all types of rescue techniques. This was one that she'd recently taught him, after an attempt to rescue some stranded rock climbers.

Her first toss was horrible. "Stupid," she grumbled as the belt bucket careened down and hit her directly in the top of the head. Cursing, she tried again and again. It took seventeen throws, but finally the dog grabbed the bucket in his teeth and pulled away. The socks stretched precariously as the dog dragged the line. In a few minutes, Bear returned to the edge of the shaft and sat down. Christian yanked and yanked again. The hook seemed solid. Climbing up onto the outcropping, she looked down at the man on the floor. "I'll be back as soon as possible." The advancing crunch of feet stopped her. Then there was an eager whine from Bear, his shadow looming over the hole as another face appeared.

His warm voice echoed down the cavity of hell. "Christian, are you down there?"

"Daniel, oh, my god, you found me! Do you have a phone? We need help!"

Second later, after the relieved probation officer had pulled his partner from the grips of death, he made the call.

"Hello, this is Daniel. I'm at the northwest side of the property. We need help."

"Where are you?" A deep voice rumbled with steadfast determination.

"I'm not sure exactly, northwest approximately twenty degrees, I can hear water." He glanced around. "The sun is low in the sky, to the left of me. I know the river is close, but I can't see it. I'm in a ravine."

There was a long pause. Eventually the trooper replied, "I know approximately where you are. Stay there. I'll send Ben and Carl over. They're closest to you."

His voice gave a hiccup of despair. "I think your guys are already here. Both have been shot. Christian says it was Mel who shot them. One of your guys is barely hanging on."

"The other?"

"The other is dead."

* * *

The jeep squealed to a stop as Juicy screamed, "Get in. The paramedics are already on their way. There's been a shooting."

Scott nodded thanks to the pilot, said he'd be back when he could and climbed in. Juicy's face was a mask of torment as she raced down the highway, filling him in on Harrison's call and subsequent events.

"Our guys on the river couldn't make it in. We can't reach Doug. Daniel has found Christian. The sheriff's department has called in back up. Your call to the attorney general must have helped. The staters are on their way with search warrants."

"Is Christian alright?" he managed to croak.

"Some bruises, dehydration, maybe hypothermia. A couple of men from Brad Harrison's team were shot. The one is dead and the other has lost a lot of blood. The sheriff's department is at the ranch's main house. They've rounded up everyone in sight, but the main dude, Mel, is nowhere to be found."

"How many of them are there?" Scott asked, trying his best not to seem unconcerned about her friends. Thank god his sister was alright. He dialed Matt's number to leave a message. Then he called his friend, who worked in the Utah State Attorney General's office, to inquire as to the issuance of the search warrant.

Paul Jackson answered on the first ring. "Based on what we know, there are grounds for child abuse and child pornography as well as sexual assaults. We've separated the men from the women. Man, the kids are terrified though. We had to get the victim's advocates in before they would talk. They've seen some ugly things. That guy, Cancer, tells them that he's some kind of an angel, Melchid...I don't know. Those people are a bunch of freaks, let me tell you. We'll get them for enough felonies to put them away for awhile."

Juicy was driving down the highway at one hundred miles an hour. When she got to a turn-off, she nearly rolled the jeep, but continued on where they approached a fenced area and an open gate. Doug was waiting for her along with a lone sheriff's vehicle.

The guy yelled, "Follow me." Juicy put the jeep back into overdrive and sped up the narrow gravel road, continuing on for another couple of miles. Soon the lights from a cluster of vehicles appeared in the near distance.

Another sheriff's deputy vehicle blocked the road. A square tub of a man stepped forward as Juicy slowed the jeep. "You here with Harrison and his crew?"

Scott leaned forward and barked, "Let us through *now*." The man's eyes grew wide, but he nodded and moved to the side.

Juicy glanced over at Scott, eyebrows raised, squealed forward another fifteen feet and slammed on the brakes. "Now I know where your sister gets it from."

The attorney bristled, his topaz eyes smoldering with a dark emotion as they jumped out of the jeep. "This is bullshit, Juicy, and you know it. My contacts told me that this place should have been infiltrated months ago."

"Well it was, sort of. Remember, our little community doesn't have much in the way of manpower and most of the time, Mormons suckled from Mother Denial's bosom anyway," Juicy explained, her sharp eyes carefully observing the scene.

"Where are they?"

Before they could an answer, a grim-faced Daniel came forward, pushing the fat deputy out of the way. He gave the briefest of smiles and put out his hand, "Nice to see you guys. Chrissie's over there. She refuses to move until they pull up the victims. They're airlifting Ben Gallagher to Garfield Memorial Hospital. His younger brother, Carl, is gone. I'm so sorry I brought her here." The handsome Latino's eyes gleamed with despair.

Scott replied quietly, "Hey buddy, this isn't your fault."

Just then, Christian appeared, her dog glued to her side, as though holding her up. She moved slowly towards them, but Juicy saved her the effort, rushing forward to pull her petite friend into her arms. "And I thought I knew you," she cried, pulling away long enough to wipe tears from her eyes. "I swear, boys, sometimes I think this girl has a death wish."

Daniel looked down, surreptitiously wiping his eyes. Her brother held her next, squeezing her until she squealed.

"Ouch. Take it easy. I fell a long way down." She pointed over to a deep hole where one deputy was preparing to scale down the wall.

Juicy gave a low growl. "Lucky that you didn't bring a gun, or that perp would be the dead one right now."

Scott gazed over at her, genuine surprise shaping his chiseled features. "I'd say damn lucky. We're going to make this one pay."

Christian was lightheaded. She felt herself begin to crumble, but Daniel was there to catch her. She looked at him as his lips quickly brushed hers. "You still like me now?" She felt as listless as an old coat on bent hanger. Her long, thick hair was tangled with bits of brush and weeds. Her skirt was covered with slime, the coat with dog hair.

Tears rose in his eyes. "You're going to be alright."

Burying her head into his chest, she nodded, pressing herself against him for a long moment. Her strength slowly returned as he allowed her to hang on, wrapping his protective frame around her, stroking her head.

Finally he whispered, "Man, you need a bath. You are one stinky chick."

Torn between relief and distress, she burrowed her face deeper into the dense fabric of his jacket. Aware that the others were waiting, she unlatched from Daniel and reached out to grab Scott's hand. Without another word, she walked him over to the edge of the pit. "He threw me in here." She choked back tears as she continued, "Then he shot them." A group of four paramedics surrounded one stretcher where Ben lay as another group pulled up Carl's body. In the distance, the buzz of a helicopter could be heard. The rescue team and a few guys from the sheriff's department were standing to the left in an open area where they had stretched out some red fabric to indicate where the chopper should land.

Juicy and Daniel were talking near another deputy who was on the phone. "They're coming in with the warrant now," he shouted to Scott over the noise. He caught Christian's anguished gaze and offered another tender smile.

Scott hugged Christian again. "I'm so sorry," he whispered. "Now let me do what I came here for. I'm going to get that monster." He squeezed her hand and moved hastily toward the fat deputy. As Christian began to follow him, he shook his head adamantly. "You, go with Juicy, follow the medics back to the hospital now. No arguments. Do you understand me? NOW."

"But what about the…"

"I know about the murder weapon and the pornography. Daniel filled me in."

"What porno?"

The brother waved her off. "Your heroic partner will explain later. Now get out of hell out of here. I'll come to the hospital as soon as I can. Get some food and water. And have someone look at that cut on your temple."

Scott nodded to Juicy who grabbed her friend's arm and marched her back to the jeep. Daniel disappeared into a deputy's car. Like a funeral procession, they slowly drove back to the main road where Juicy turned off onto the highway to follow the ambulance as the others turned back into the hellish world of The Saints.

After a few miles of silence, Juicy turned in awe, gazing at the wily survivor next to her. "Okay. Spill your guts. I want to hear every cotton-picking' detail."

CHAPTER 20

Mel was driving like a lunatic. They'd left shortly before dawn. He'd seen a suspicious raft on the river and told her to collect her things. He wasn't going to leave without her. He needed a decoy. He said a pregnant 'wife' was always a good bet.

She only had a few seconds to gather her possessions. In fact, Stephanie had very little to her name. A locket from her father for her tenth birthday, her grandmother's ruby ring and the letter from her sister were stuffed in the large Barnes and Noble book tote that she called a purse. The sisters at the ranch had burned her Abercrombie jeans and skimpy tee-shirts. It didn't really matter now anyway. Her ass had grown so big during her pregnancy, it was doubtful she'd ever fit into a size 2 again.

Mel had loaded the truck with a few supplies from the barn. A couple of sleeping bags, a tent, rain gear, some camping cookware and a small generator were stuffed in the back. He grumbled about having to leave the dogs, especially Lestat, but said that he had no choice. She didn't see the guns, but she knew that they were somewhere in the truck. The Great Master never traveled without his guns.

She felt deeply afraid now. Her baby was due any time. She was supposed to go to the doctor again the day after tomorrow. For a moment, she wondered if the doctor would notice if she didn't come to the appointment. Maybe the good woman would report that Stephanie had never shown. Maybe she'd called the police and they would come looking for them.

Stephanie dared to look at Mel. He had an ugly snarl on his face, seemingly oblivious to her presence. The metal-gray sheen of rain on the glass made it difficult to see out. He was furious that the weather had changed. They weren't far from Salt Lake City now. He would probably make them stay at 26B. Shuddering, she remembered the last time that she was there. He'd forced her to have sex with a couple of his friends. They were dressed all in black, with hoods over their faces. She was sickened by the experience. Though she'd turned tricks on and off for years, these guys were a bunch of pigs. They kept chanting weird sayings and joking about using her as a sacrifice. The one guy couldn't get it up, and got pissed about it. She had endured several vicious slaps until Mel had stepped in.

Without a phone or computer, she had no way of calling for help. Her best friend was dead. Her boyfriend had disappeared and her mom never responded to her letters. Maybe her sister would help, if she could get the phone for a minute without Mel noticing. She'd spied his cell phone on the truck's dashboard.

There wasn't much point in calling back to the ranch. Jared was checked out most of the time. Besides, what could he do? As for the rest of them, she was pretty sure that the women despised her. It didn't matter. She hated them, too, especially Cheryl, and only tolerated them because she'd had nowhere else to go. Brandon had promised to come back for her. He'd said that they'd run away after the baby was born. But now that seemed unlikely.

The rain snaked down in torrents. The truck started to fishtail as slippery sheets of water created resistance. Mel swore under his breath, trying to keep the vehicle steady. Stephanie was dying to take a pee. Just then, a truck stop came into view. Mel grunted to himself and pulled off the highway. "We'll eat here," he said, pulling out a grocery bag from the king cab's back seat. "I want you to go into the bathroom, lock the door and put this shit on your hair. Make it quick."

He handed her a box of Clairol hair dye. Her normally auburn locks would soon be the color of asphalt. Yuck, she thought, not daring to complain. She'd gone through her gothic stage years ago. "It takes at least twenty minutes for this stuff to soak in." She tried to keep her voice calm.

He pondered her answer. "I'll order some food to go. What do you want?"

The girl mumbled that a ham sandwich and coffee would be fine. She waited for him to climb out. Following closely behind, she suddenly stopped. "I can't do this without a towel. Is there one in the rig?"

Nodding in frustration, streams of water running down his face, he tossed her the keys. "On the backseat. Like I said, be quick."

Her heart was pounding as she turned back to the truck. Second thoughts loomed. Mel was dangerous adversary, but the girl had balls. She'd ingratiated herself to him long enough. Unlike the other women at the ranch, she didn't believe in his supposed power. It was all a game. Besides, if Brandon wasn't coming back, what was the point in staying on the ranch?

That was it. She'd made up her mind. Grabbing the towel and the phone in one fell swoop, Stephanie climbed out, lifting the towel over her head to stave off the rain.

Mel didn't notice her take the phone. Opening the greasy door of the truck stop restaurant with a hasty yank, he shoved her inside. "Get it done fast. Don't try to dry your hair. Just put the hood back up and meet me back at the truck. You have twenty minutes."

She nodded, eyes downcast, and made her way down the littered hallway to the restrooms. As she stepped around stacks of beer boxes, she noticed a small exit sign on her right. Several truckers were leaving the area as they'd driven in. Her hitchhiking skills would have to come in handy.

Feeling Mel's eyes on her back, Stephanie pushed open the door marked 'Ladies Spa'. The owner of the truck stop had a stupid sense of humor, she thought, quickly scanning the small space for company. She'd showered in more truck stops than she could count. They were normally sprayed down once a week with disinfectant, but the women who used them often left their mark. Rusted, dirty razors, empty shampoo bottles and, occasionally, a used tampon on the floor were normal finds, but here and there, Stephanie had found real treasures.

She waited sixty seconds and reopened the door. Mel was gone. Glancing towards the back exit, she took a deep breath and ran. Pushing open the back door, she felt the cold slap of rain as she searched for a truck. To her right, a Cisco truck was slowly pulling out to get on the highway. She ran up to the enormous vehicle and slammed her hand against the side. The driver looked surprised, but rolled down the window. "Help me, please. I'm afraid. I need to get out of here."

The man looked over at his companion, a woman of about sixty. "Get in next to her." She ran around the side, glancing back to see if Mel had appeared. So far so good, she thought as the woman hauled her, dripping wet, into the cab. Stephanie shook violently with fear until the truck had pulled onto the road and made its way for a few miles. She looked at the kindly woman beside her, who had found a towel and was mopping her face. "There now, girl. Let me dry you. Harvey, turn on the heat, for god sakes! Can't you see the girl is with child!" Stephanie shivered against the plump, motherly woman and slowly relaxed as she began to tell her story.

* * *

It was late evening by the time Christian had wolfed down a hamburger and allowed Garfield Memorial Hospital's E.R. staff to admit her to a bed. The doctor on duty had insisted on a triage duo of intravenous cocktails. She was dehydrated and had sprained her ankle in the fall. Once the medical team had warmed her to normal temperature and Juicy had convinced her that Ben was improving, the young woman promptly fell asleep.

About eight the next morning, she awoke to Scott and Juicy talking quietly next to her bed. She sat up, momentarily embarrassed by her compromising situation, though she was happy to see that sometime during the night, the I.V. had been removed. Their smiles were huge as she said good morning, but she couldn't wait another minute. As she shoved the covers back, her brother handed her a bag from Target. "Here's some clean clothes, sis. We'll order you some coffee."

"Ben?"

"He's going to make it," Scott replied. She breathed a sigh of relief and hobbling to the bathroom, turned back once to smile at the two of them, simply happy to be alive.

Christian took her time in the shower, scrubbing off the scum of her horrific experience with the hottest water that she could muster. She pulled a toothbrush and hairbrush from the bag, along with a set of new clothes. Her brother knew her well. The sports bra and panties, the Levi Strauss 501s, the wooly black turtleneck sweater and Adidas running shoes all fit perfectly. Her artificial hair color hadn't faded much, but with a touch of mascara and lip gloss, among a few other thoughtful purchases, she almost felt like herself again. By the time she'd showered and dressed, the coffee had arrived in the form of a double latte from the lobby coffee stand. The three of them sipped on their coffees, awaiting the discharge papers and catching up on the latest news.

"Mel is gone, as is Stephanie. At first, the clan members all swore that monster hadn't been on the ranch for weeks, but as of this morning, we have some confessions. Some woman named Cheryl has started to spill the beans." Scott looked exhausted after the long night, but seemed exhilarated by the new development.

"Additionally, the large cache of guns has been confiscated, but there wasn't a Magnum in the bunch," Juicy added. "Carl and Ben were shot with that brand of handgun. The deputies were scouring the property for more contraband. One room in the main house was locked up tight, but Cheryl knew where to find a key. Inside were several refrigerators filled with liters of blood, as well as blood-drawing equipment. She also explained that the group collected their own blood for the Great Master. Apparently, unbeknownst to the rest of the clan, he has some strange blood disease. He's a freak and drinks the stuff."

Then Daniel walked in. "How's our patient?" he smiled broadly and handed over a bag of fresh donuts. Christian beamed at the sight of him.

"I couldn't be better now," she said quietly. Her partner's eyes met hers for a long moment. The room grew still with the others' realization that rules of this young couple's relationship had now blurred for the better.

Juicy grinned. "Well now, I'd say there's plenty of good juju in this room at the moment."

Christian was grateful when the discharge nurse stepped in a second later and broke the spell. They finished their business and headed out to the car. On the way, Christian leaned into Daniel and whispered, "Thanks for being my hero."

He put his arm around her waist. "I wish I didn't have to tell you this, Chrissie, but the little boy, Toby, is unaccounted for. There was a fire and..." She bit her lip, holding her tears as he told her about the reports of more child abuse by Mel, his face growing stormy with revenge. "That guy is going down, Chrissie. I promise you that. There was a call this morning. Cancer is with the Salt Lake City police as we speak."

Bear was waiting in the car when they reached the parking lot. The dog nearly knocked his owner over with joy when she opened the door. After she'd given her dog the appropriate greetings, they piled in to drive to the local sheriff's office where detectives awaited them. It took nearly two hours for Christian and Daniel to complete their interviews. Then they headed back out to the ranch with the detectives in tow.

Once they had parked, Daniel and Scott meandered over to the main building. A couple of Harrison's deputies were standing near a storage building, sorting through more guns. Using a metal detector, they'd discovered a buried bunker with several hundred unregistered weapons. The clan members swore that they were unaware of the stash, though the state was attempting to pin it on Jared.

Doug and Juicy wandered down to the river, leaving Christian to her own tortured thoughts. Her friends all knew her well enough to leave well enough alone. Yellow tape skirted the perimeter of the main house. The guard dogs had been quarantined for a lack of vaccination records. The women and children had been escorted off the ranch early that morning and transferred to a shelter while the men had been taken to the jail in Tropic for questioning. The district attorney was holding them on a number of charges including sex with minors, kidnapping, trafficking and several other felonies.

Despite the oppressive gloom of the haunted place, spring was awakening. Nature had conspired with God to remind her that there was still a world of life to be had. Birds flitted cheerfully from tree to tree and slender green sprouts of grass jutted up along the well-worn pathways. Yet there was a strange hush over the place, the veritable calm before the fear of a storm. Christian knew that she had to return to the barn where she'd first met the little boy named Toby. She hurried away in the direction of the large metal structure.

The grief had begun to feel too hard to bear, yet she knew that her affinity for horses would help ease her internal distress. The barn door was slightly ajar when she arrived. There was a sign on it that read, "Do not enter; police investigation." Harrison had promised to care for the livestock until further arrangements could be made.

Ignoring the warning, she pushed the door open and stepped inside. Breathing deeply, she took in the sweet scent of hay and the damp, musty odor of horse sweat. Though at first they couldn't see her, the horses began to make soft sounds in response to her verbal greeting. She wandered from stall to stall, using a crutch to steady her while patting the animals softly on the noses.

A high-pitched sound came from below her feet as though from a tunnel. Christian kicked at the straw-covered ground. Her toe hit something sharp. She bent down and brushed away the remaining debris. There, beneath her, was a handle for a trapdoor. Grabbing the cold metal, she heaved it open. Beneath her was a small cell, a virtual bomb shelter. Like oozing blood on a deep wound, a savage vision matted her thoughts. Perhaps this was a dumping ground for Mel's torture victims. A holocaustic nightmare of barbaric portions might await her. She shook the image of piles of dead children from her mind as glittering eyes flashed at her in the murky darkness. To her joy, there was Toby.

* * *

Sunday's arrival brought the first true day of spring in the Kodachrome Basin, portending a pleasant day's drive. Doug, Daniel, Scott and Christian were leaving early that morning. After a collection of emotional good-byes to Juicy, Harrison and his men, the exhausted team headed for home.

* * *

After two weeks back at home with Matt, Christian was guilty of slippery conversations and avoidance in the bedroom. He was careful around her, understanding from the others that she'd been put through a virtual tour of hell. Yet she knew he didn't feel a tremendous sense of sympathy. It was an ordeal, to be sure, but one she had freely chosen.

Basketball state finals were in full swing. He was in and out of town, giving her space, respectful of her moods. Matt thought, perhaps, that she was suffering from some form of trauma reaction. In fact, she was struggling with ambivalence. Mel had been charged with several felonies. She sensed that it was only a matter of time, before the man would face a long time in prison. She'd done enough and was strictly ordered away from the continuing investigation. In the meantime, Christian could think of only one man, and his name was on the door of their shared office.

At work, things had returned to their normal routine. Daniel maintained a poker face around their colleagues, but saying and doing small favors that indicated his growing and open sense of territory with her. She knew that they could both be fired for having a romantic relationship within their agency, so she kept busy and ignored his subtle advances.

Finally, the second weekend after her return, Matt confronted her with the obvious. Clearly their relationship was suffering. He didn't venture to guess why, though deep down, she believed he knew exactly what had caused the change. He was willing to move out if that was her desire, at least until they could go to counseling.

In truth, her heart was not in it. Her recent time with Daniel, despite the years of their working partnership, had been love life-altering. Ironically, he was not her type. Proudly conservative, admittedly chauvinistic and entirely too spoiled, Daniel would have been the last man that she'd ever expected to sweep her off her feet. Yet there was something strangely enchanting about the Latino. His warm smile and sparkling eyes drew everyone in, but she knew more about him than those who assumed he was just a friendly, easy-going guy. He was smart, funny and loyal to a fault. It was his devotion to her that had been revealed; she knew now she could never harm a man so willing to put his life on the line for her.

Breaking up with Matt was difficult. He'd moved in; they'd made a nice life. Her heart knew that there was no going back. Opening the door, Christian smiled. The brooding face of winter had given way to glorious buds, apple green grass and luminous skies. Bear's tail slapped her leg in excitement as she waved to Doug. "Just one minute. Daniel's calling." Locking the door, she walked to Doug's car and climbed in. "Hello?"

"Christian, they got him."

"Mel?" Her heart rate sped up entirely too fast.

"Yep. His latent prints were found on the shucking hammer, as well as tissue from Whitney's forehead."

"So are they going to charge him with Whitney's murder?"

"Oh yeah! There's more. Stephanie Patterson stole his phone. There's a ton of incriminating evidence on that thing. She said she'd testify to the fact that she overhead

Mel talking to Brandon about killing Whitney as well. All of that, along with Thomas Witherspoon's admission that he kept a tab on Whitney until Mel could nab her has done it. They've also found and talked to Lobos. He has identified Mel as well. Now that bastard had been placed at the scene, we've found the murder weapon and as far as motive goes... well, we might never find out what Whitney had on Clist, but Brandon has spilled plenty of beans, too..."

Her friend paused to catch his breath. "Go on," she said yearningly. Daniel's voice felt like salve to her achy uncertainty. He was, as always, friendly and full of life.

"Well, you did it, sweetheart. You stopped that fiend. He's facing two murder charges, kidnapping... the list goes on."

"And how are you?" Christian implored.

"Missing you like crazy, confused as hell. With you and Matt, is it over?" His voice had become tender with longing.

"Yes. We'll talk tonight. Come here." There was a long pause before she could steady her voice again. "Daniel?"

"Yeah, Chrissie."

"Thanks...for everything."

She turned off the phone and leaned back in the seat with a heavy sigh.

"That man loves you, Christian. Don't waste it. He's worth his weight in gold."

She nodded, keeping her eyes closed tightly to prevent erupting tears. As they headed down the road, Doug handed her a letter. "I think you might want to read this. Stella dropped it off to me this morning at the shop."

Dear Joslyn,

I know that's not your real name, but that is how I know you now. When you first came to the ranch, I didn't like you. I thought you were just one more bitch (sorry) for me to have to deal with. Then you gave me that letter from Serena. I couldn't understand how you knew her, but today, after I was picked up by her and my Dad, I found out exactly how and why.

I didn't know that probation officers did things like you did- I mean, coming to find me and all. I have been mixed up for a long time, thinking that Brandon was the right guy for me, going to the Saints for support, and finally letting Mel have me any time. He is a bad man. I know some things he has done and I am going to tell the cops everything.

Brandon doesn't really want the baby. I know that now. But my sister, Serena, is really excited and so is my Dad. I'm going back to my Dad's. There is a school for teen mothers and my Dad is so happy he is going to be a grandfather.

I think I'm okay now. I didn't expect an angel to come in the form of a P.O., but I guess you never know when God is going to show up for you. I will send you pictures of the baby after she is born. I'm going to name her Christina, kind of after you. (sorry, but your real name, Christian, is too weird for me. It sounds like a church or something).

Your boyfriend, Daniel, said that you are going to be okay. He loves you very much. He seems like a good man for you.

Good luck and thanks again for finding me and giving me Serena's letter. It changed everything.

Your friend for life,
Stephanie Patterson

Christian was weeping quietly. She didn't expect the girl's gratitude or an outpouring of truth. Perhaps she had actually done the right thing this time, despite her obsessive desire for taking risks in the name of justice. In the process, she had learned some hard lessons about her own heart. Like Mel, she, too, had the capacity for cruelty. The new relationship road upon which she stood would be fraught with its own difficulties. While Mel's punishment would be life behind bars, her obsessive leanings presented a prison of their own. In the end, she had mostly prevailed. Yet there were more questions in her future and always, answers to be sought.

EPILOGUE
November 13, 2007

The young man looked down at the newspaper. The headlines read: *Polygamist clan leader gets life in prison.* A cunning smile crossed his face as he turned leisurely off the highway and headed down the narrow road toward Seaside, Oregon. He was in no hurry to get to his destination. Release from jail was like being on vacation. His mom and dad had been kind, allowing him to move back to the beach house. He was hoping to find a part-time job at the little shop down the street.

Already he could smell the tangy scent of ocean. He envisioned his uncle, sitting in isolation, preparing for a future of hell. He had been able to manipulate his way out, giving testimony that had cleared him of any wrong-doing. But that was the sweet part of it. He had told authorities about the older man's satanic rituals, murderous aspirations, and the way in which he had masterminded the murder of his sister. However, the true mastermind was free. The clan was no longer functioning. The women and children had eventually been removed and given to some kind of safe house. The rest of the men were all facing time for various crimes. Yet Brandon had escaped without incident, if you didn't count the six months in jail.

His parents thought him the hero, though a few others thought differently. Joe and Miasma were keeping their mouths shut, Stephanie had agreed to a no-contact order and Lobos... he considered the little punk who had banged his sister and gave testimony implicating him. Fortunately the prosecutor didn't buy it, but Brandon knew that the gangbanger was an enemy now. Soon or later, he would have to be dealt with. Until then, he had plenty of other things to do.

The Capricorn Kidnapping

By
Torena O'Rorke

Prologue
March 18, 2008

The dark-skinned man sat back in his Ford truck, watching the sexy teenager do her stretching exercises in the yard across the street. The day was bright and clear and a perfect sixty-five degrees. Every day at four, the girl went out for a run. Her skin was the color of mocha and her long hair was a bounty of curls. She wore very tight spandex shorts and a revealing sports bra. Looking at her round little butt was enough to arouse him every time, especially because he knew she knew he was watching. She preened and pranced, bending over in his direction several times before she bounced down the street toward the Creekstone running trails. He had considered asking her out, but never got around to it. Perhaps now was as good a time as ever.

Gonzalez stroked himself for a few minutes, but was interrupted by his employee who came around from the back of the house, obviously done for the day. With a frustrated sigh, he pulled a coat across his lap to hide his erection and then thought better of it. What the hell. He'd like to add another notch to his proverbial belt. He reached back and grabbed his gym bag.

"Hey, I'm going for a run. You can call Alec to pick you up." His employee grunted an affirmative as he jogged past him and into the house. The man called Stic was a strange little fellow, but he seemed willing to work hard, harder than his older brother who was born with a silver spoon in his mouth. Still, the three of them made a good team and Gonzalez's older brother was pleased with their progress so far. With the help of Alec, three kids had been placed in private adoptions. Two had been sold willingly to them by their parents and the other, by her illegal grandparents. Those first two adoptions had paid for a new house for him in the hills outside of town. The two acre plot accommodated his horse, which was all that really mattered to him. His girlfriend was more excited about decorating the new place, but he had made sure that she'd paid for the furniture out of her own salary.

As he raced to change his clothes, he fantasized about banging that cute little babe. Maybe that was the way to get more babies. Find a few lookers on the side and get them pregnant. He would have to consider that idea. It would be very pleasurable and profitable at the same time. The guy knew he was handsome and though he was from southern Mexico, he spoke with an alluring Argentine accent. He had gone to college there. Girls seemed to go crazy for him once he got them into bed. Charm and looks aside, he knew it was because he was very well endowed. It was a lucky thing to be born with, along with brains. He'd get in a run and some real fun before the day was over. Maybe Julio was as smart as his brother after all.

CHAPTER 1
April 2007

Christian Vargas crouched on the damp sand, her indigo eyes scanning the muddy riverbank for clues of the missing toddler. Brackish water pooled near her feet and a stiff breeze whipped angrily, knotting her long chestnut hair. Black and blue clouds hung like theater drapes over the White Bluffs. Another downpour was just minutes away.

Bear sniffed anxiously along the water's edge. His shiny black snout pushed at the ground as he began to dig. She stood and followed her enormous, three-legged dog, her gut churning at the thought of what they might find that morning. The two-year-old female had vanished from the steps of her adoptive parents' front porch the night before. Six deputies had been searching since dawn before they'd called out her amateur search and rescue team. The county's trained canine was apparently at the vet.

The juvenile probation officer knew something that the cops didn't know, not yet anyway. Two other little ones from the Tri-Cities were missing as well. Christian, who was just twenty-nine-years old, had spent over five years at the juvenile justice agency and had worked in nearly every department. Recently, she'd heard from Jenny Tuttlehouse, a big-mouthed staff assistant in the dependency court that two foster kids had gone missing as well. Par for the course, neither child had been mentioned on the news. From her strange dream the night before, the prescient young widow sensed that there was a link to every disappearance. Now she just had to convince the smug prosecutor and the team of inept sheriff deputies of that fact.

The first child, a girl just passed her second birthday and the second child, a female infant of fifteen months, had also disappeared from Pasco, the most rural of the three small cities. According to Jenny, the first case had happened two days prior and was written off as a parental abduction. The toddler had been left with a neighbor while the foster mother went to run an errand. A tall blonde man resembling the baby's father had convinced the neighbor that it was his visitation time and took the child. By the time, the mother had returned home and reported the abduction to the police, the Amber Alert had been issued, but five hours from the time of the kidnapping greatly lowered the chances of finding the child.

The second case was also attributed to a parent kidnapping, however this time it was the Mexican relative-placement foster family who had fled with the child after abuse allegations had been made, prompting a CPS investigation. Five days had passed since the last CPS visit. There was no doubt they had made it to Mexico and would therefore never been seen again. Yet the third disappearance was the most suspicious of the three. The victim's family lived nearly twenty miles out of town on a thirty-five hundred acre farm. A random kidnapping was an unlikely scenario. The parents were able to account for the time and were completely inconsolable. Lost babies brought back terrifying memories for the young Irish-American probation officer as well.

She glanced back at Oz Rellim. The tall, handsome Benton County prosecutor stood a head above a group of uniformed men, comparing notes and occasionally glancing in her direction. The parents stood off near a grouping of cars, crying hysterically. Their baby was the youngest of eight in the large Catholic family and their first adopted child.

From the north, bruised clouds marched over the sky's sullen face. The late winter storm was still brewing. The river's edge was murky, laced in milfoil, the insidious fresh water seaweed that plagued the three local waterways of the

Columbia, Snake and Yakima rivers. A pair of paper white cranes flew overhead, on their way to several of the Hanford Reach islands that provided a protective habitat. Snoqualmie Pass, two and half hours west in the Cascade Mountains, had been buried in another six feet of snow. It was early spring and the ski resorts were celebrating.

When the authorities had requested Christian Vargas's voluntary services on that day in early April, she'd been on her way to a day on the ski slopes. Instead she'd headed directly north of town to farm country. The Broten Ranch was a combination of orchards, potato fields, irrigation canals and residences on a block of land bordering the Franklin county side of the Columbia River. Her dog knew the area well after successfully finding an injured hunter in October the year before. Bear, a rambunctious, but keen St. Bernard mix, was used by local law enforcement on missing person cases from time to time. Most of the cases were easily solved. A child wandering away from their yard or an Alzheimer's patient determined to find their way home.

Bear began to dig deeper, his highly-sensitive nose covered in mud and debris. Christian gave a short whistle and signaled to Rellim to join her. "I think he might have found something here."

The ambitious prosecutor famous for a ninety-seven percent conviction rate jogged over to where the dog was working, but Christian had beaten him to the spot. He gazed down into her eyes. "By the way, it's nice to see you again. It's been a while."

She blushed. "You, too. I thought you were going to have my neck the last time we met."

"True, you did a number to my department, but hey, you solved the case." He gave her a warm smile and knelt down to look at something in the sand. Why was he here anyway? This was a Franklin County matter. When he stood up, she saw a thread of fear in his otherwise boyish face. She couldn't forgive him for what he'd done to her on the witness stand; the way he'd been the master of the inquisition into her personal life during the trial that had convicted a four-time killer the year before. "I'm sure you're wondering why I'm here. Tom is out of town on vacation and his deputies are, frankly, a bunch of novices."

She shrugged, gazing out at the turbulent water. "How long have you been doing this?" he asked, watching as her dog moved to another part of the beach.

"Doing what? Solving crimes or spending my Sunday mornings in the freezing cold with a bunch of irritating cops?" She tried to sound lighthearted, but the man who was indirectly her boss made her nervous.

He chuckled. "Well, I was hoping they were one and the same today."

Giving up her line of defense, she finally grinned. "If there's anything down there, my dog will find it." Her anxiety spiked. Was there was something sticking out of the sand?

"Are you okay?" He leaned into her, protecting her from the wind.

"Fine." She kept her eye on the burrowing dog.

"All the trouble you've gone through and knowing you, the trouble you could get into." His tone was now playful.

"I took quite a fall from grace, you know." She swallowed hard, remembering her manager's tongue-lashing and subsequent warning letter in her personnel file as a result of the notorious case.

As the dog gave a little yelp, the storm broke. The sharp crack of thunder echoed down the plateau to the muddy riverbank. A purple bone of clouds, like a drunk's face after a bar fight, crept menacingly towards them. A deluge followed a few seconds later. Christian pulled up her hood and ducked under the spindly limb of a Russian olive tree, watching the raindrops dance on the slick face of the river. Rellim scurried over next to her. He was close to her now. His hot breath smelled like peppermint and something sweet, maybe chewing tobacco, as he spoke. "Jeez, and I thought I might get a real run in today." His tanned face lifted away. "Hey looks like your hero might have found something." She called the dog over. In his mouth was a dirty piece of fabric.

"Let me." Rellim donned a pair of synthetic gloves and bagged the item. Then he looked at it closely through the plastic. Still the rain fell. She gave Bear a treat for his find. The intimate contact to the prosecutor was intense. She rarely found herself this close to a man. He nodded. "Look, here. There are initials on this."

The rest of the team had raced away, up the bank to where their various cars were lined up along the orchard border. They were completely alone. She gazed up at his soft pillowed lips as he scrutinized the evidence. He was ignoring her on purpose. The sensation of attraction between them was palatable.

The cloud burst stopped as suddenly as it had begun. She moved away before his men could return and see them together. Bear followed her, snorting with excitement. She crouched down to her only true companion, praising him lavishly. The moist sand beneath her feet was slippery. She began to fall forward, but Oz's hand was on her shoulder, steadying her. She stood up and gazed into his solemn brown eyes. Their corners crinkled with surprise. "Caught ya!" he cried.

Christian hesitated now as Bear trotted over to an outcropping at the water's edge. From where she stood, she could tell he'd found some more evidence. She crept over the rocks to the animal. "I have a bad feeling," she yelled over her shoulder. "I think the baby was kidnapped."

Rellim was right behind her, his face registering shock. "Why would you say that?"

"Someone brought her down here. "Look here, this looks like fresh paint." She led him down towards the shoreline. On the edge of a jagged rock, there was a line of blue paint, as though the bottom of a boat had been pushed away hastily.

He seemed unconvinced, though he knelt down, studied the mark and whistled at some of the men to come down. She could see the doubt in his eyes. After several recent gang killings, a stolen child was the last thing that their community needed. She was instantly furious. Denial was the source of so many mistakes. Furthermore, no one ever took her intuitive feelings seriously. The world was full of Doubting Thomases, her partner, Daniel, often reminded her. She was gifted and cursed at the same time. Without some form of proof, she was just another self-proclaimed prophet.

"We need to issue an Amber Alert." Her voice was sharp with fear.

"It's probably too late." Rellim rubbed his chin, now covered with a day's stubble. He stared out at the river, deep in thought.

"What do you mean?"

"The call came too late. The parents said she was in her crib last night, but neither remembered to check her room before they went to bed."

"What's with these big families anyway?" She choked as though strangled by anger.

Rellim sighed heavily. "You have to wonder. It's been over eight hours since anyone in the family last laid eyes on her. The parents didn't call us until three this morning. They tried to find her on their own. That is half the problem with using the Alert. People don't report soon enough."

"You think this is a drowning." Christian wasn't asking a question.

He neatly captured her unspoken assumptions. "Kidnapping investigations take time and money." His tone was cool. "But there is more than that. Investigations like those inevitably take a long-term toll on our emotional and physical resources. At this point in time, I'm assuming that the baby drowned. However, if you're so sure you can 'sleuth a different truth', as the pros say…" he paused for impact. "Then, knowing you the little that I do, I'd say you're probably going to go for it." Rellim laughed softly. She wanted to slug him.

Information about the author

Torena O'Rorke M.Ed. spent nearly twenty years working as a mental health therapist and juvenile probation officer. Her work sent her to visit many crimes scenes and her skills were utilized to treat juvenile murderers, rape victims, gang members and sexual offenders. She has worked with the families of crime victims and managed a program designed to prevent domestic violence between juvenile offenders and their families. Her Girl Power! curriculum for high-risk teen girls has been well-received in probation departments and other social service providers as well as being a keynote speaker for *Beyond Pink*, a Washington state conference to prevent violence against girls.

Torena has published three historical fiction novels. Her new police procedural mystery series, The Astrology Mysteries, currently has four books completed. Her Sassy Pants Mysteries has one book completed.

Married to a wonderful guy with two grown children, Torena enjoys hiking, tennis, volunteering with high risk teens and reading when she's not plotting another story for her readers. Visit her on Facebook.

> Review Requested:
> If you loved this book, would you please provide a review at Amazon.com?

Made in the USA
Middletown, DE
17 March 2024

51656300R00158